"Drew? Honey? You love me, don't you?" Gabrielle asked.

"'Course I do," he said, a little rougher than he'd intended.

"When you proposed to me, you said you wanted us to have a family. A big one. You meant it, didn't you?" she persisted.

Drew had nothing to go on now but blind faith, because she'd already left him, and if not for the concussion, Gabrielle wouldn't be here now, in his arms, asking him to help her make a baby.

Blind faith.

Lord he prayed silently, *You've got to help me out here, 'cause I'm skatin' on thin ice.*

Books by Loree Lough

Love Inspired

Suddenly Daddy #28
Suddenly Mommy #34
Suddenly Married #52
Suddenly Reunited #107

*Suddenly!

LOREE LOUGH

In thirteen years as a writer, Loree Lough has published over thirty inspirational novels for adults and kids, nonfiction books for juveniles, more than two thousand articles and dozens of short stories. She teaches writing and, even off duty, rarely stops talking about it. Loree lives in Maryland with her husband, Larry (who wears earplugs), and a twelve-year-old cat named Mouser (who can't tell a mouse from a kibble).

Suddenly Reunited
Loree Lough

Love Inspired®

Published by Steeple Hill Books™

STEEPLE HILL BOOKS

Steeple
Hill™

ISBN 0-373-87113-9

SUDDENLY REUNITED

Printed in U.S.A.

And be ye kind one to another, tenderhearted, forgiving one another even as God, for Christ's sake, hath forgiven you.

—*Ephesians* 4:32

To Elice and Valerie:
beloved daughters, dear friends.

Chapter One

Gabrielle leaned in close to the horse's neck, her hair rippling behind her like a cinnamony cape. "C'mon, Triumph," she said, snapping the reins, "give me all you've got." The animal's response told her he'd missed their morning runs every bit as much as she had.

Since leaving Drew just over nine months ago, her visits to the Walking C had been rare. If not for love of Triumph—and riding—Gabrielle didn't think she'd have come back to the ranch.

Ever.

Pounding hooves drummed in harmony to her fast-beating heart. It reminded her of the perfectly syncopated rhythm of parade drums, and she relished each rib-thumping pulsation. The more rigorous and rapid the ride, the more free she felt. If only she could find this kind of freedom on her *own* two feet.

True to his nature, Drew had not used Triumph to punish her for filing the separation papers. "You're welcome to come back and ride him any time," he'd said in his quiet, controlled way. "I promise to make myself scarce when you do."

Thankfully, he'd usually kept his word. Whether the dust cloud raised when her compact car chugged up the drive was his signal to disappear, or whether one of the hired hands had warned him of her arrival, Gabrielle didn't know.

But he'd received no such notice of her approach today; if he had, they both would have been spared that awkward, cheek-reddening scene in the barn.

Gabrielle tightened her hold on the reins. "You'd think he would've adjusted to the separation by now," she said into the wind. Triumph's caramel-colored ears swiveled back at the sound of her voice, but she barely noticed. Gabrielle was far too busy remembering the expressions that flitted across her soon-to-be ex-husband's face when he looked up from his work and saw her standing in the doorway, bit in one hand, bridle in the other. His whole face lit up with a smile, exactly the way it used to when she carried a glass of lemonade or a sandwich into the barn and insisted he take a much-deserved break. "You'd work straight through from dawn 'til dark if I didn't insist you stop now and then." If she had a dollar for every time she'd said *that*…

That bewildered, little-boy-lost expression had replaced his happy-to-see-her smile. *Who's seeing to it he gets enough rest now that you're gone?* she wondered.

Guilt coursed through her. Without her, it was a sure bet no one was making sure that Drew ate well, that his shirts were pressed, that he rested enough. And even if someone tried, Gabrielle acknowledged, it wasn't likely that mule-headed man would listen. If he worked himself into an early grave, it was none of her concern. But…who was going to stop him from doing just that, now that she was gone? She'd felt partly to blame for that, just as she felt responsible for the dark stare that replaced his bright smile once his memory kicked in and he realized she was there to ride his horse—not to see him.

Sensing his mistress's tension, Triumph snorted.

"Sorry, boy. It's okay." As though he understood her soft, soothing words, the horse ran a bit faster over the tattered trail, ran at a pace that reminded Gabrielle of the way things had started up between her and Drew....

A year ago May—three short months after meeting him—she'd agreed to become his wife. He'd seemed so sure of himself, saying he'd prayed on it, saying he felt the Lord wanted the two of them together, forever. Gabrielle hadn't even thought to ask God's opinion on the subject of marriage; she'd never asked His counsel before.

Gabrielle exhaled a sigh of agitation, and the horse's ears rotated toward her again. "Don't pay any attention to me, sweetie."

"Attention," she repeated, frowning. She'd studied dozens of women's magazine articles that listed ways wives could encourage more attention from their husbands. Not one of those articles contained the advice Gabrielle sought: how to *dissuade* attention. Like when she'd make lasagna, and he'd sweeten the sauce with a teaspoon of sugar.

Life as Drew's wife hadn't been perfect, even before that dreadful night, but Gabrielle had never been a quitter. And though she'd never been a dyed-in-the-wool Christian, like Drew, she believed wholeheartedly in the "'til death us do part" vow they'd made at the altar. But *since* that awful night, whenever sleep eluded her, she'd gone to the window and stared up at the stars, wishing for a way to turn back the clock. Maybe if she could do everything over again, she'd anticipate that he'd go off half-cocked. Maybe then she could act faster...do *something* to keep Drew from—

Biting back bitter tears of regret, Gabrielle shook her

head. There was no point in dwelling on it now. *What's done is done, and there's no undoing it.*

Triumph, reading her turbulent mood, increased his speed. She'd ridden the horse hundreds of times during her marriage to Drew, and had learned to read the animal's moods well. Riding him was exhilarating, exciting, but he definitely was not a horse for beginners.

Mere days before she left the Walking C Ranch for good, Drew had said, "He's as stubborn and single-minded as they come. I reckon that's why you get on so well with him—you're two of a kind."

He'd been grinning when he said it, but the smile never quite made it to his eyes. He saw *her* as stubborn and single-minded, because she didn't always agree with him. Jaws clamped with determination, she felt her heartbeat accelerate—in response to the wild ride, or because of the testy *Wish I'd said this or that* retorts pinging in her mind?

The wind whistled past her ears and the rocky trail whizzed by beneath Triumph's galloping feet. Stubborn? Single-minded? *You're a fine one to talk, Drew Cunningham.*

Her father used to call her stubborn, too, every time she disagreed with him. Which happened whenever he got it into his head to move to a new place.

"Can't we stay here, at least long enough for me to finish the school year?" By the time Gabrielle graduated high school, she'd asked the question a dozen times. Without fail, her words fell on deaf ears, and no matter how sincere—or pathetic—her plea, her dad went ahead and loaded their suitcases into his cramped station wagon with a promise that one day they'd settle down. Then he would pull out his battered road atlas and, eyes shut, he'd choose a page, his forefinger pinpointing their next "home."

Sulking alone in the back seat, she'd wondered why her

mother never complained about the frequent moves. If *she* ever got married, Gabrielle had told herself—all twelve times—it would be to a man who'd stay in one place, forever.

Triumph's head bobbed just as an age-old adage came to mind: Be careful what you wish for, you might just get it. Well, Gabrielle thought, laughing bitterly to herself, she had to admit, she got what she asked for. Drew was as rooted as a man could get. Rooted, and rigid, and controlling. A sob replaced the laughter. *You promised me things, Drew. If only you'd kept your word—*

She blamed the sharp scent of pine in the air for the tears stinging her eyes. She swiped them away with the back of a leather-gloved hand, then jammed her wide-brimmed black hat lower on her forehead. Few things riled Gabrielle more than her own tears. She saw them as a sign of weakness, proof that she was every bit the needy female her husband seemed so determined to protect and shelter. But shelter from what? In a few weeks, she'd be twenty-eight years old. Twenty-eight, married barely more than a year, and already about to be divorced.

Anger—at herself, for giving in to the tears; at Drew for not being the man she'd thought he was—prodded her to give the stallion yet another command: "Run, Triumph!"

He seemed only too happy to oblige, and raced over ditches carved by creeks feeding from the Great Fishtail River, around boulders that had rolled down from Granite Peak, through stands of spruce, to a barren plateau at the river's edge.

Immediately, Gabrielle recognized the place, and her heart did a little flip.

It had been a glorious fall day, much like this one, when the crisp scent of pine filled the air. Now, however, dozens of trees lay flat, their broken stumps reaching like jagged fingertips toward the blue Montana sky. The thunderstorm that had blown through the county last week was responsible for this devastation, but in time, Gabrielle knew, nature would repair the storm's destruction.

If only time could fix what Drew did to their marriage that terrible night.

Suddenly she realized that exasperation over her marital situation had made her careless, irresponsible, reckless. At this speed, one misstep could cause Triumph to break a leg, or worse.

"Easy, boy," she called, yanking hard on the reins, "you're not a racehorse, y'know." She strained to slow him down, but as Drew had so astutely pointed out, Triumph had a mind of his own.

Miraculously, he thundered through the woods unscathed, and as they rounded the river's bend, sunlight bleached the grassy knoll ahead, making the willowy weeds appear to have been dusted with snow. Anxiously, she guided the steed around gnarled trees that sprouted from the stony soil, providing patches of shade for livestock, and over clumps of wildflowers that brightened the land with surprising splashes of color. Finally, the beast slowed, came to a halt, and Gabrielle breathed a ragged gasp of relief—

Until she spotted the sidewinder, lazily sunning itself on a flat rock a few yards ahead. In an eyeblink, the snake reacted to the vibration of hammering hooves, and drew itself into a tight coil. Head raised and tongue flicking menacingly, it prepared to strike.

Gabrielle jerked at the reins—too late, for Triumph had seen the rattler at almost the same moment.

He reared up, front hooves alternately pawing the air and stomping the ground, back legs thrashing left, right, left. He threw his head back far enough for Gabrielle to see his flattened ears, curled lips, and panicky, wild-rolling eyes.

He cut loose with a high-pitched trumpet, gave one mighty buck...and sent Gabrielle soaring.

Shielding her eyes from the harsh sunlight, Gabrielle sat up and groaned softly. Every part of her, it seemed, had an ache of its own. Instinctively, she touched her throbbing temple. "Yee-ouch!" she whispered, wincing in response to the stinging pain. The lump was the size of a hen's egg. "What in the world...?" The sight of blood on the fingertips of her leather glove silenced her, and Gabrielle's frown deepened.

Dazed, she tried to get a fix what had happened, on where she *was*.

She recognized the river and the rocky terrain surrounding it, but couldn't remember heading for the plateau. And how had she gotten all twisted up in the underbrush? she wondered, carefully peeling herself from the thorny shrubbery alongside the trail.

The last thing Gabrielle recalled was saddling Triumph for their morning run, and Drew waving goodbye. "I love you," he'd called after her, raising his steaming mug of coffee in the air in a farewell salute, "so mind your *P*s and *Q*s out there, y'hear?" She smiled now, and her heartbeat quickened as she pictured the handsome face of her brand-new husband.

But where was Triumph? Through narrowed eyes, she scanned the skyline, expecting to catch a glimpse of him grazing nearby. Instead, she spied the trampled remains of a rattlesnake. Wrinkling her nose, she gasped. "There's *one* sidewinder that learned what happens when a snake spooks a horse," she muttered, putting two and two together.

She'd fallen off a horse enough times to know that occasionally the landings could be rough. *Real* rough. On her sixteenth birthday, for example, afraid that she might hurt her father's boss's beautiful new mare, she hadn't cinched the saddle tightly enough. Gabrielle's "kindness" had cost her, and she'd zigzagged around the corral at a forty-five-degree tilt—until she hit the ground. That time, it was hours before the buzzing in her brain went away.

Now, brushing dirt and grit from the seat of her jeans and the elbows of her suede jacket, she told herself this had been one of those falls, nothing more. Unfortunately, she thought, grimacing as she peeked through one squinting eye at the horizon, without Triumph, it would be a long hike back to the Walking C.

A wave of dizziness nearly knocked her down again. Easing up to the riverbank, she belly-crawled toward the water, mindful to keep a careful distance from the dead rattler. She stripped off her gloves. It felt good, pressing a cold palm against the bump on her head. Filling cupped hands with icy, mountain-fed water, she drank her fill.

Gradually, as the jitters subsided, she perched on the boulder, arms hugging her jeans-clad legs, and surveyed the territory. It had been a while since she'd taken the time to enjoy the view this way, what with keeping the ranch house clean and the ranch hands fed. The vista was like no other place on earth—and Gabrielle had seen her share of places, thanks to her dad's nomadic spirit. Here was an explosion of color and scent, from the sunlit mountain peaks to the twisting river below, from the pale azure sky to the pillowy green of faraway treetops.

An eagle screeched overhead as a fuzzy white mountain goat skittered down a rocky slope, a kid close on its heels. Cottony clouds sailed silently by, so close, it seemed to Gabrielle that she could reach up and touch them. She stared with pride at the pink snow that dappled the mountaintop, knowing Montana was just one of a handful of places in the world where it existed.

Sapphires, garnets and smoky quartz hid deep beneath the rich soil. And down the road, abandoned mining towns. No matter which way she looked, Gabrielle felt *life* pulsing in this land.

Moose and bear, bison and pronghorn shared this place with geese and ptarmigan and saw-whet owls. In the springtime, nodding yellowbells and shooting stars made way for summer's daisies. Now, fall's wild mums were in full bloom.

Gabrielle remembered the first time she'd been here— when Drew had led the way. There had been snow in the foothills of Beartooth Plateau that day—not so remarkable for a Montana autumn. But he'd packed a picnic lunch, and that *had* been memorable. After spreading a red-checkered tablecloth on this very rock, he'd set out the food and utensils, then pulled her onto his lap. "There's something in my shirt pocket for you," he'd told her, brown eyes twinkling with mischief.

It turned out "something" was a half-carat solitaire set in a plain gold band. She'd always been mesmerized by his deep, grating baritone, but never more than on that afternoon, when he cradled her chin in a work-calloused hand and said, "Will you marry me, Gabby, and change your last name from Lafayette to Cunningham?"

Had it been the love blazing in his dark eyes, or the whispery growl in his voice that prevented her from telling him how much she'd always hated that nickname? "Yes," she'd said instead, kissing him so soundly that she knocked the Stetson from his head. "Yes, I'll marry you."

The sweet memory induced a deep sigh and a fond smile, and gave her the final resolve to get to her feet and head home.

Home, where her husband waited.

There wasn't a minute to waste when she fell, she'd broken her wristwatch. Behind the cracked crystal, the unmoving hands said 11:35. She'd been a rancher's wife long enough to know a thing or two about life on the range; the position of the sun, high in the sky, told her it was past noon. She tried not to think about the fact that she'd been unconscious for nearly thirty minutes, or the fact that she wasn't exactly sure how far Triumph had carried her from the highway.

Better get a move-on, girl, 'cause you have a lot of ground to cover before sundown, and you promised to make Drew lasagna, to celebrate your two-month anniversary.

As she headed toward the highway, Gabrielle recited her favorite Robert Frost poems, memorized as an English assignment in junior high. She sang "The Star Spangled Banner" and hummed a few bars of "Swanee." She picked a handful of the wildflowers growing along the trail, made a lei of them by linking stems. But nothing, not even recounting those wonderful moments at the altar when she'd become Mrs. Drew Cunningham, could distract her from the throbbing in her head.

A battered blue pickup truck rolled to a stop beside her, tires crunching on the gravel, brakes squealing in protest.

"Hey, Troy," she said, sending him a halfhearted grin.

"What you doin' all the way out here in the middle of nowhere?"

She opened her mouth to respond, then snapped it shut. Strange, she thought, heart pounding as she struggled to remember, but she didn't know what she was doing out here.

"You okay, Gabby?" Troy pressed. "You're lookin' a mite peaked."

Shaking her head, Gabrielle frowned. "Pee-kid?"

He got out of the truck and walked around to her side.

"Lemme have a look at you, girl." Hands on her shoulders, he tilted his head up and peered down his long narrow nose to study her face. Bushy gray brows drew together in the center of his tanned forehead. "Got yourself a nice li'l goose egg there on your temple," he observed. His blue-eyed gaze took in her attire, focused for a moment on the rip in the knee of her jeans. "How'd that happen?" he asked.

Blinking and frowning, Gabrielle could only muster the energy to shake her head.

Troy grabbed her elbow, steered her toward his pickup. "Nice boots," he said.

She looked at her feet. Funny, she didn't remember having purchased new riding boots. Wrinkling her nose in puzzlement, she removed her hat and ran a hand through her hair. "Um, thanks."

"Been ridin' that ornery beast of Drew's again, ain't ya?"

"Triumph?" She smiled. "Why, he isn't the least bit—"

"Don't give me that," he interrupted. "Been 'round horses long enough to know a mean'un when I see it. And that's a mean'un. Belongs in a rodeo, not on a ranch, if you ask me."

Gabrielle nodded and took a deep breath, hoping the extra oxygen would nudge her memory.

"Looks to me like that critter threw you, li'l lady." The passenger door groaned when he jerked it open. "Get on in there, missy. Drew would have my hide if I was to leave you out here all by your lonesome. Besides, the buzzards are likely to mistake you for a—"

Gabrielle stumbled. Had it not been for the grizzled cowboy's quick response, she would have ended up a puddle of denim and leather, right there on the highway.

"Good grief, Gabby," he sputtered, steadying her, "you're white as a bedsheet."

Troy helped her into the truck, stuffing her hat in after her. Peering down his long nose again, he gently tucked her hair behind her ear and inspected the bump on her head. "That bag o' bones really *did* throw you a good one, didn't he?"

Grimacing, Gabrielle swallowed. "Troy," she whimpered, holding her stomach, "I think I'm going to be—"

In an instant, he helped her to the roadside, then held her steady until the spasms subsided. When the gut-wrenching spell ended, he casually blotted the corners of her mouth with a faded blue bandanna.

"Happens sometimes when you crack your crown," Troy said matter-of-factly. "Why I remember once when..."

She couldn't hear him above the ringing in her ears, couldn't see much past the white fog that dimmed her vision. But somehow, thankfully, Troy managed to get her into the truck. Gabrielle sat stock-still, nodding and smiling politely, pretending to take in his every word as the beat-up old truck rattled down the road.

Leaning limply against the headrest, she took a peek at her wristwatch and groaned in frustration. Still 11:35...exactly what it had said the last hundred times she'd checked the time. The broken crystal could probably be repaired, but she wasn't so sure about the buttery leather band.

Her mother had given this watch to her father. Aside from her own wedding band, it was Gabrielle's single most treasured possession.

Closing her eyes, Gabrielle sighed, conjuring the image of the photograph of her mother, Leah. No matter where they'd lived, it had been on Gabrielle's bedside table—full color, eight inches by ten.

When she was a little girl, Gabrielle had often made her father tell the story of the day he'd taken that picture. Her parents had been on their honeymoon, traveling the west coast highways, when Leah spotted a rainbow.

"She nearly gave me a black eye, pointing at the thing," Jared had said, laughing softly at the memory. "So I parked our car there on that country road, and stood her beside the fence."

It was waist high and made of gray rocks and stones. Jared told his daughter how he'd picked Leah up and perched her on that wall and said, "Smile pretty for me now...."

Gabrielle could almost touch the photo, the memory was so clear: her mother, knees bent and legs hugged to her chest, head tilted ever so slightly, love for her new husband radiating from her smile, from her pale gray eyes, her image haloed by a wide-arched, six-color rainbow that touched the ground at both ends.

The pounding in Gabrielle's head made her forget the picture and the watch. She'd fallen before, but she'd never experienced pain like this, and it was beginning to frighten her.

"...and that's how I got this scar alongside my jaw," Troy was saying. "Horse with a temperament just like that Triumph's. Belongs in a rodeo, not on a ranch," he said again.

Gabrielle smiled weakly, grateful that Troy had happened along. She'd never minded being alone in the wilderness during the daytime, because Drew had drummed into her head how to survive, should she ever be stranded out here. She'd been a good student and had learned how to build a roaring fire even from damp wood, how to tell edible berries from the poisonous kind, how to construct a lean-to of sorts from the branches of blue spruce as protection from the elements. In the bright light of day, she was as brave as any man.

But when the sun slid behind Granite Peak like a giant gold coin disappearing into a slot, Gabrielle's bravado faded, and she quaked with terror of the unseen...and the unknown.

"There's nothing in the dark that isn't in the light," Drew had said time and again. He'd intended his words to comfort and console her, to eradicate her fears—and she loved him for that. But as the old folks liked to say, her daddy didn't raise a fool. She knew full well what lurked deep in the brush: creatures of every sort and size, some predators, others prey—each with its own instinctive need to survive. And Gabrielle had no desire to be the meal that quenched a hungry appetite.

As if in answer to a prayer she hadn't even said, her mother's sweet face appeared in her mind's eye, and Gabrielle couldn't help but smile.

She was now the proud owner of the few pieces of jewelry that had belonged to her mother. Costume stuff, mostly, that Leah had collected in the cities and towns the little family visited. But the watch...the watch had been special.

According to her father, her mother had cut out coupons and saved every extra penny from her grocery money to buy it. She'd wrapped it in blue tissue, tied it up with a white satin bow, and given it to Jared on the night Gabrielle was born. *To count every precious minute with our firstborn,* said the inscription on the back. Her father's stories described character traits, habits, even minor flaws that defined Leah Lafayette, the woman he'd chosen as his wife. But the watch told Gabrielle something about the woman who had been her *mother,* the woman who'd suffered silently to satisfy the whims of the man she loved. A man with wanderlust.

How many times had Leah said that the braided leather watchband was every bit as sturdy and strong as her marriage to Jared? Too many to count, Gabrielle thought. Glancing at that band, now wrapped loosely around her own slender wrist, she understood better than ever how lucky she'd been to find a man like Drew, a man who wrested strength from the land, who loved having roots in one place for all time.

A sob ached in her throat as she looked again at the shattered glass that had protected the watch face, at the torn plaits of the braided brown band. First thing tomorrow, she'd take it to town and have it repaired.

She tried her best to remember the fall that had broken her treasure, straining her aching brain for a scrap of memory...*anything* that would help her understand why she hadn't recognized the danger ahead. She had ridden the river's edge before, had encountered rattlesnakes plenty of times. But she'd always managed to keep control of Molly, or Triumph, or whatever horse she'd been riding.

Why not this time?

She was achy and tired, and more than a little afraid. All Gabrielle wanted right now was to get home and fall into Drew's arms, where she'd always found such comfort.

"Well, missy, here you are," Troy announced, interrupting her thoughts. "Drew's in the barn. Want me to fetch him?"

The truck ground to a halt as she struggled to remember what Drew had told her earlier that morning. "No, no," she began haltingly, "I think he said something about fixing the back fences today."

The cowboy frowned. "Back fences? What about the rest of the hands?"

"Drew gave them the day off, so they could go into Livingston for Oktoberfest."

"Oktoberfest? But that was two weeks ago——"

She didn't understand why the usually talkative cowboy suddenly clamped his jaws together, seemingly feigning interest in his pocket watch.

"You reckon it's such a good idea, you bein' here alone in the shape you're in? Maybe I oughta sit with you, just 'til Drew gets in from——" his frown deepened as he looked toward the barn "——from, ah, mendin' fences?"

Forcing a smile, Gabrielle said, "That isn't necessary, but I appreciate the offer, just the same." She opened the passenger door. "I'm fine. Really." She patted his hand as if that were proof of some kind, then climbed out of the truck.

"Don't forget your hat," he said, one gray eyebrow high on his lined forehead.

She seemed to be making a habit of forgetting things. "Oh. Right," she said, taking it from him. "Thanks again for the ride, Troy." Aiming another smile in his direction, Gabrielle slammed the heavy, creaking door. Waving with the hat, she stepped back. "You're an angel," she added, "and I'm gonna bake you a cherry pie to show my appreciation."

His face wrinkled in confusion. "No thanks necessary," he called through the open passenger window. "Now, git on inside and sit down before you fall down. I'll call you later, make sure you're all right."

She snapped off a smart salute, then headed up the walk.

The kitchen clock said one-twenty. A glance around the room only added to her bewilderment. She'd never gone off and left the breakfast dishes, at least not without putting them in a wash pan to soak. Whatever was wrong—and there was plenty wrong—it had started before she took that fall from Triumph's back.

She rummaged in the cupboard for an aspirin. Where tidy rows of tumblers and coffee mugs had once stood, Gabrielle found a mismatched mess of glasses and cups. What had possessed her to put the dishes away like that?

After downing the pills, she slumped onto a ladder-back chair and held her head in her hands. This wasn't like the other times she'd fallen. She yearned for the solace of Drew's embrace.

Hurry home, honey, she thought, biting her lower lip as the tears welled in her eyes, *because I need you.*

Chapter Two

The moment he reached the end of the winding drive, he noticed Triumph, still saddled and grazing beside the barn. The beast seemed content enough, as though the dirt on his forelegs and withers didn't bother him at all. But Drew knew better. This was a persnickety horse that appreciated a thorough grooming after a hard ride.

What was Gabrielle thinking? he demanded silently. Frowning, he followed up with an equally regretful thought: she hadn't been thinking of anything or anyone but herself lately.

Dismounting, Drew strode over to where Triumph stood, ran an ungloved hand over the horse's behind. The horse had been sweating hard—that much was evident by the thin crust of grit stuck to his coat—but he'd been home long enough to cool down.

Doesn't make a lick of sense, Drew thought, shaking his head. Gabrielle did have a tendency to get sidetracked, especially in conversations and menial tasks, but he knew better than most how she felt about animals. For her to have left Triumph in this condition could only mean one thing.

Something had happened to her.

The image of her, unconscious, cold and alone, unprotected in the wilderness, flashed through his mind. It was autumn, a dangerous time of year. Cougars were on the prowl, as were grizzlies and black bears looking to fatten themselves up for winter's long hibernation. And contrary to city-folk myth, the hairy beasts much preferred fresh meat to wild berries and tree roots.

Heart pounding, he raced toward the house, making plans as he went: call the sheriff, and while the man rounded up a search party, Drew would get down on his knees and pray like he'd never prayed before. Because he loved her. Loved her like crazy. Had from the moment he first set eyes on her, would 'til he drew his last breath. Legal separation papers couldn't change that fact.

He exploded into the kitchen, not noticing or caring that he'd slammed the door against the wall.

"Drew Cunningham," she said in a loving, wifely voice, "how many times have I told you that *isn't* the way a gentleman enters a room?"

His relief was so great, he couldn't move, couldn't speak. He wanted to throw his arms around her. But they were legally separated, and she might resent an action like that.

He stood there for what seemed like a full minute, one hand on the brass knob, blinking, swallowing, thanking God.

And then he started noticing little things.

Things like the fact that her hair was still damp from a recent shower, and Gabrielle *hated* wet hair, especially when it was cool outside—and the temperature hadn't gotten above forty so far today.

And she was wearing the outfit he liked so well, the one he'd bought her in Bozeman last July, when they'd gone into town for dinner. She hadn't taken it with her when she left. Hadn't taken anything he'd given her when she left. Tiny as she was, Gabrielle caught a chill quicker than anyone he could name. So why would she be wearing a sleeveless summer dress and strappy little sandals on a day like this?

She turned back to the stove, lifted the lid of the saucepan in one hand, picked up a giant stirring spoon with the other. She looked so good, so *right* standing there, as if she'd never left. A sob ached in his throat.

Drew bit his lower lip to still its trembling, took off his hat and scrubbed a leather-gloved hand over his face. "Thank You, Jesus," he whispered. "Praise God."

"What's that, honey?" she asked distractedly.

His head snapped up in response to the endearment. *Honey?* She hadn't called him that in…

In more than nine months.

Was this some sort of trick? Some stunt her big-city lawyer had dreamed up to get her a bigger piece of Walking C pie? He felt the heat rising in him, and clamped his teeth together. His own attorney had advised him not to say anything he might be sorry for later. It should have enraged him, that she'd waltzed in here as though nothing had happened, expecting him to like it. But all he could feel was gratitude. If she was toying with him, he didn't care.

She'd almost gotten the better of him.

Almost, he thought, but not quite.

"What're you doing here?"

She shot him an *Are you kidding?* grin. "I'm polishing my toenails," she teased. After enjoying a girlish giggle at her own joke, Gabrielle added, "So, did you get the back fences repaired?"

The back fences? He tucked in his chin. He'd fixed those *last* fall.

She faced him then, and when she did, her long, luxurious auburn hair swung around her shoulders, wide gray eyes sparkling with…with *love,* just the way they had before she'd called it quits.

But wait just a minute here…what's she up to, anyway? "Triumph is out behind the barn," he began, taking care to keep a civil tone in his voice, "still saddled. Looks like he had himself one wild ride this morning."

Her pale eyes darkened, reminding him of the storm clouds he'd seen over Beartooth earlier that morning.

"What! Someone rode him, then just left him standing there, saddle and all?" Gabrielle narrowed her eyes. "What kind of cretin would mistreat an animal that way?"

She rested both fists on her hips—on her shapely, womanly hips. Get hold of yourself, Cunningham, Drew warned himself.

Gabrielle was still frowning when she said, "If I get hold of the guy who—"

She seemed genuinely angry, which made no sense. No sense at all. "Gabby," he interrupted, frowning, *"you're* the guy, er, gal who had Triumph out this morning."

She rolled her eyes and grinned. "Oh, Drew," she said lightly, "you're such a big tease! You know I'd never leave him saddled and ungroomed. I love that big bully!"

Tilting her head, she blinked flirtatiously. "Do you know what day this is?" she asked on a soft sigh.

"'Course I do." He switched the hat from his left hand to his right. "It's Saturday."

"No, silly," she said, sauntering nearer. "The *date.*"

Something warned him to take a step back, to keep his distance from this beautiful, sexy woman who, until nine months ago, had been his lawfully wedded wife. Instead, Drew planted his boots on the wide-planked kitchen floor, determined to stand his ground. This was *his* house, after all.

Until she left him, he'd considered everything that had been his just as much hers. But all that changed the morning she had the sheriff deliver the documents that said otherwise. This whole divorce thing was as ridiculous as it was unnecessary, because if she'd listened to his explanation about that night—

Smiling happily, she gave him a playful shove. "It's our two-month anniversary, you insensitive boob. Don't worry, I don't expect you to ply me with greeting cards and gifts for every month we're together." She took another step toward him, grabbed the lapels of his jacket. "But I do expect you to enjoy the supper I've made to celebrate this one."

Two months? Drew had never considered himself the sensitive type who wrote poems and counted the weeks since their marriage, but they'd been married only slightly over nine months when she left, and she'd been gone a little longer than that. Drew knew, because he'd been counting *those* days.

If she hadn't run off like a spoiled brat, they'd be celebrating a *year* of marriage soon instead of a couple of months! *What is she trying to pull, pretending that she thinks—*

It took him completely by surprise, the way she stepped right up and slipped her arms around him the way she would have before that awful night. It felt so good, having her this close, that Drew ignored the warning voice in his head, and buried his face in her mass of damp, chestnut curls. Eyes closed, he inhaled deeply. She even smelled wonderful.

"So, did you miss me while you were off riding the range?"

He heard the smile in her voice, felt the heat of her breath against his shirt. Did he miss her! Does Santa Claus have a weight problem? "Yeah," he heard himself saying, "I missed you." I've missed you like crazy, he added silently. For the time being, it didn't matter what game she was playing—if, indeed, she was playing a game.

Maybe, just maybe, she'd changed her mind. True, she'd always been impulsive, but could she really be coming back to take up right where she left off, as if nothing had ever happened? One of her greatest assets was also her biggest flaw: she was a proud woman, intent on saving face at any cost, especially if she believed she was in the wrong.

Dear God in heaven, Drew prayed, closing his eyes, let that be what's going on here, let her have come back home to stay. If that's the case, I promise to make it up to her for what I did.

Gabrielle took a half step back, but without releasing him from her hug. "Are you hungry?"

He couldn't tear his gaze from her face. The Lord had outdone Himself when He made this one. Drew thought she was the most beautiful thing he'd ever seen. He swallowed, licked his lips. "Guess I could pack away a helping or two," he said instead.

"It's lasagna." She kissed his chin. "Just the way you like it. Easy on the mozzarella, extra ricotta cheese." She stood on tiptoes to press a longer kiss to his cheek before settling back onto her heels. "I'm afraid I didn't get you a present, though," she said, running a hand through her thick curls. "Which is strange, because I could have sworn I had bought you a shirt—"

She *had* given him a shirt to celebrate their two-month anniversary. He'd worn it so often since she'd left that it was getting threadbare at the elbows and cuffs.

He grabbed her wrist and, frowning at her forehead, said, "Grandma's gravy, Gabrielle! What have you gone and done to yourself?"

Shrugging, she put her fingertips to the bump on her temple. "Oh, that." A slight flush colored her cheeks. "It's nothing. Really. I clunked my head when I fell."

She stopped talking so suddenly, Drew wondered if maybe something had stuck in her throat. "When you fell?"

Her smile faded and she stepped out of the embrace, leaving a cold, empty space where her warmth had been. "Wait a minute," she began pensively, a forefinger in the air, "I think you're right, Drew." Brow furrowed, she began to pace. "I think...I think it *was* me who took Triumph out. I seem to remember—"

She slumped, trembling, onto a kitchen chair. Her lower lip began to quiver, the way it always did when she fought tears.

Drew got down onto one knee, turned her to face him. "Shh," he soothed, "it's okay." He pulled her close. "You're okay, and Triumph is a big strong critter. He's no worse for the wear. I'll go out in a bit and give him a good brushing."

Tears were swimming in her eyes when she looked into his. "But...but it's my responsibility. How could I have forgotten something as important as that?" She bit her bottom lip, then glanced toward the window, shaking her head. "I—I don't know what's wrong with me, Drew."

She grabbed his shoulders. "How long do you think he's been out there like that?"

He shrugged, torn between comforting her and protecting himself from whatever her lawyer had put her up to. "Couple of hours, from the looks of things."

She sighed heavily. "Poor thing, standing around in that heavy saddle all this time, all dirty and sweaty. He must think I don't give a hoot about him!"

Drew tugged off his gloves, tossed them onto the table

and moved her hair aside to get a better look at the injury. "Shoo-ee. That's some goose egg you've got there."

"That's what Troy said."

"Troy?"

She nodded. "He picked me up on Highway 2-12, although I honestly don't remember how I got there."

Drew decided to give her the benefit of the doubt. She deserved that much. It had hurt like crazy when she'd given him that tongue-lashing the night she walked out. It wasn't the angry words; nothing she said could ever be as painful as the plain fact that she'd left.

Comforting Gabrielle won out in the battle between protecting her or protecting himself. "Shh," he said again. "You had a bad fall. That's the beginning and the end of it."

As though she hadn't heard him, Gabrielle said, "Never stopped me from doing my job before."

"Why are you always so hard on yourself? It wasn't your fault Triumph threw you." Lovingly, he tucked her hair behind her ears. "What made him buck?"

She rolled her eyes in frustration. "I've tried and tried to remember. Near as I can tell, a snake spooked him. When I came to, there was a dead—"

"Gabby!" Drew interrupted, giving her a gentle shake. "A rattlesnake?" He made a move as if to begin inspecting her, starting with her fingers.

"Relax, Drew," she said, smiling sweetly. "From the looks of things, Triumph pounded that snake into the dust long before he had a chance to do either of us any harm." A little giggle popped from her lips. Cuddling both of his hands beside her cheeks, she tilted her head to add, "My hero!"

"Joke all you want," Drew said, standing. "I'm just relieved you're all right."

Sighing, Gabrielle got to her feet, too.

"What're you doing?" he asked, as she headed for the stove.

"Turning down the oven so I'll have time to take care of Triumph before supper," she said. As if to punctuate the statement, Gabrielle staggered, and reached out for something to steady herself.

Drew let himself be that "something." And once she'd regained her balance, he took her hand in his. "Come over here where the light is better," he said, leading her to the window.

"Yes, Doctor," she said lightly.

But Gabrielle followed, he noted, and stood quietly as he examined the lump, peered into her eyes. "Your pupils are so dilated I can barely tell what color your eyes are." He headed for the door. "Get your coat. We're going to the emergency room."

She emitted a little gasp that made him want to wrap her in a reassuring hug.

"Don't be silly," she said with a wave of her hand. "I'm fine."

You're good, honey, he thought, *real good.* And if he didn't know her better, he might just swallow that bowl of bravado she'd just dished out. But her usually rosy cheeks were pale, and there was a blue cast to her otherwise pink lips. He didn't like the way she was weaving and bobbing around the kitchen like a boxer who'd given his all in the ring, either.

"I'm fine. Really."

"How 'bout we let a doctor be the judge of that?"

"But Drew," she protested, hanging back as he opened the door, "our romantic anniversary supper is almost ready. All I have to do is light the candles." She glanced out the window. "And Triumph, he's—"

He took a quick look around. Why hadn't he noticed before that she'd set the dining room table with the good dishes and flatware? Why hadn't he seen that she'd put the silver candlesticks in the middle of his grandma's linen tablecloth? His heart swelled, knowing she'd gone to so much trouble for him—for *them*—in her condition.

But how had she accomplished it, swooning like a drunken sailor as she must have been? *Stubbornness,* he decided, doing his best to hide a grin.

"Besides," she persisted, "the nearest hospital is an hour away, in Bozeman, and you gave the hands the day off, remember? So they could go to Oktoberfest? We can't leave the Walking C unattended that long."

Oktoberfest? But that was—

"We can," he said, turning off the oven, "and we will." He jammed the Stetson onto his head. "And I don't want to hear another word about it." He grabbed her fringed jacket from the peg behind the door and shook it a time or two, like a matador tempting a bull.

"How about a compromise?" she asked, as he helped her into it.

Drew held the door open, as she stepped onto the porch. The night she'd left, his inflexibility was just one of the things she'd claimed was driving her away. He remembered his prayer: if the Almighty would see to it that Gabrielle was home to stay, he'd do whatever it took to make everything up to her.

"What sort of compromise?"

"Take me to Livingston, instead, to see Doc Parker."

"Okay," he agreed, nodding. "That makes sense." He touched a scolding finger to her nose. "But if he sees anything suspicious, anything at all, we're heading straight to Bozeman." Narrowing his eyes, he added, "Got it?"

She sent him a flirty half grin and kissed the tip of that finger. "Got it."

Habit made him head for the pickup. And then he saw the car he'd bought the week before Gabrielle left him. He'd seen it on the lot weeks before the breakup and had thought how cute she'd look behind the wheel, how much easier it would be for her to get into and out of, especially when she got all gussied up in one of her short skirts and high heels....

Much to his surprise—and dismay—she'd taken one look at the vehicle and stomped into the house without saying a word. One week later, to the day, she left him...in that car.

More than likely, the doc would confirm Drew's suspicion that Gabrielle had suffered a concussion. How mild or severe was yet to be seen, but getting into and out of his high-riding pickup wouldn't be easy for her.

Sighing, Drew helped her into the passenger seat of the car. As he revved the motor, he tried to ignore the fact that both Triumph *and* Chum still stood outside the barn, saddled and bridled and ungroomed. First things first, he told himself, and Gabby would always be the most important earthly being in his life.

He tried even harder not to react when she slid across the front seat and rested her head on his shoulder. Without giving it a second thought, his right arm went around her. What had made her snuggle up the way she used to? Instinct? A need for protection? *Love?*

But another question rang even louder in his mind. And if curiosity had killed the cat, Drew figured, he was as good as gone. As much as he wanted to know what had brought Gabby home, he was even more curious to know if she planned to stay.

* * *

Kent Parker was an old-fashioned country doctor who didn't believe in sugarcoating things—for patients *or* their families. So it worried Drew more than a little when the doctor said, "Step into my office. I want to have a word with you in private while Gabrielle gets herself dressed."

Parker peeled off his latex gloves and tossed them unceremoniously into the nearest trash can. "Your wife will be fine, just fine. She's suffered a pretty serious concussion, but after a few days of R and R, Gabby will be her ornery old self again."

"That's a relief—"

"Bu-u-ut," the doctor added.

Drew ran a hand through his hair. For all its wide open spaces, Montana may as well have been Mayberry, U.S.A. Because there weren't a whole passel of folks around, those that *were* around knew just about everything there was to know about one another. Except for Doc Parker: he knew *more* than most. And right now, he knew there was a lot on Drew's mind.

"But," Drew began, "it only solves one of my problems." Absently, he stroked his chin. "Frankly, I'm not sure I know what 'her old self' is anymore." Besides, he'd been given a second chance here, and didn't want to blow it.

The older man dropped a fatherly hand on Drew's shoulder. "When I heard you two had split up, it nearly broke my heart." He gave the shoulder an affectionate squeeze. "But she's back now, and that's all that matters."

Drew met the doctor's clear blue eyes. "Not if she doesn't remember leaving me."

Drew had filled the doctor in on the conversation he'd had with Gabrielle in the kitchen earlier. Parker nodded understandingly and sat behind his battered wood desk. "Take a load off, son," he instructed, gesturing toward a

well-worn maroon leather wingback. Once Drew was settled, the doctor leaned back in his own big black chair and
clasped his hands behind his gray-haired head. "Living in
horse country, I've seen this kind of head injury before, too
many times to count—and so have you. We both know it
isn't out of the ordinary for someone to temporarily lose a
slice of memory when they've taken a good hard bump on
the bean."

Placing his Stetson on the seat of the empty chair beside
him, Drew leaned forward, rested his elbows on his knees
and clasped his hands. "That doesn't answer my question,"
he said to the floor. He met the doctor's eyes and waited
for an answer.

Shrugging one shoulder, Parker said, "Couple of hours,
a few days, never…" He shook his head. "Wish I had a
straight answer for you, Drew, but these things are iffy at
best." He lifted his white-bearded chin to ask, "Why is it
so important to know when she'll come around?"

Because, Drew answered silently, *when she gets her
memory back, she's likely to leave again.*

And he didn't want that. Not now that he'd had another
taste of what it felt like, being close to her, having her arms
around him and her lips pressed to his.

"I brought you into this world thirty-two years ago,
Drew Cunningham, so I know you better'n just about anybody in these parts. Now, out with it! What's eating you?"

Gritting his teeth, Drew closed his eyes. "I don't want
to lose her again." He felt like a man who'd been on death
row for nearly a year, and had just gotten a call from the
governor's office.

Parker sat forward, linked his fingers on the green felt
desk blotter. "What makes you think that'll happen?"

He looked around the room and focused on Parker's

medical degrees, framed in black, hanging on the wall behind the desk. "Just—things…"

"The subconscious mind is a strange and miraculous
thing, Drew, m'boy. Gabby didn't go back to her apartment
in Livingston after that knock on the noodle. She came
straight back to the Walking C. What does that tell you?"

He grunted and scowled. "That she's lost her ever-lovin'
mind?"

Chuckling, Parker aimed a stubby forefinger at Drew.
"No need to act all brave and bad for the likes of me. I'm
the man who stitched up your knobby knees when you were
knee-high to a gopher, set your broken arm before you were
ten. Gabrielle went to the Walking C 'cause, in her heart,
that ranch is her *home*."

A man can hope, Drew thought. Gabrielle had considered
it home, until—

What had happened that night snaked through his mind,
making him grimace. Right now, he'd give anything to
undo what he'd done, or, at the very least, find a way to
do it differently.

Gabrielle breezed into the room before Drew had a
chance to verbalize his fears to Parker. "Why the long
faces?" she asked. Grinning and wiggling her eyebrows,
she added, "I'm not dying or anything, am I?"

Dying! The very thought made Drew's heart beat double-
time. He got to his feet. "Honestly, Gabby," he complained, scowling, "sometimes your sense of humor leaves
a lot to be desired."

Her gray eyes widened and her smile dimmed. "Saw-
ree," she said emphatically. One hand beside her mouth,
she aimed a loud whisper at Parker. "I take it you just gave
him the bill?"

"No, he didn't," Drew answered in the doctor's stead.

Then added, "Why do you always tie everything to money?"

Lips narrowed, she raised her left eyebrow. "Maybe," she began, hands on her hips, "because money is always on your mind!"

Now there's the Gabrielle who left months ago, Drew said to himself.

"Now, now," the doctor interrupted, hands raised in mock surrender. "Bickering isn't going to do any of us any good, me in particular, since I'm such a sensitive soul and all."

Drew shot him a *Who do you think you're kidding?* look and said, "If there's nothing else, I guess we'll be on our way." He thought of the fully saddled horses and groaned inwardly. "I have things to tend to when I get home."

Gabrielle hung all eight fingertips from her bottom teeth. "Oh my goodness," she gasped, "Triumph and Chum!"

Her anguish immediately diminished Drew's ire. "Like I said before, they're big 'n' strong—spoiled rotten, for the most part. It won't kill them to wear their saddles a while longer, just this once."

It did his heart good to see that his words eased her distress some. Maybe, if she were home to stay, he'd get a chance to find out what in blue blazes made her so all-fired hard on herself all the time.

Drew pressed a palm against the small of Gabrielle's back to lead her out of Doc Parker's office. The action reminded him of their wedding night, when he'd guided her in the very same way into their penthouse suite at that fancy hotel in Helena. Gritting his teeth, he touched a forefinger to the brim of his Stetson and snapped off a cowboy salute.

"Thanks, Doc."

"Glad to be of service," the older gent said as he walked

them to the door. "Now, remember what I told you in the examining room, Gabby—take it easy for the next few days. And Drew, don't forget to—"

"I put fresh batteries in the flashlight just this morning," he assured. "And I'll set the alarm for the checkups."

He wondered how long it would be before she asked him to explain that last part of his conversation with Parker, and counted the seconds as they crossed the parking lot: *five, four*—as he opened the passenger door—*three, two*—as he helped her inside—*one*—

"Checkups?" she asked. "What kind of checkups?"

She was so intent on the question, and its answer, that she didn't seem to notice that he'd fastened the seat belt for her. "You're welcome," he teased, grinning.

A glance at her furrowed brow told him Gabrielle hadn't a clue what he was talking about. He slid in behind the steering wheel and poked the key into the ignition. "Doc says that for the next day and a half, I have to check your eyes every hour on the hour. If your pupils don't constrict when the flashlight beam hits them, or if they're not the same size, it'll mean trouble, and I'm to get you to the hospital, *stat.*" He didn't tell her the part about CAT scans and MRIs. No sense worrying her.

"Hospital? T-trouble?" she repeated, long lashes fluttering. "You mean—you mean as in…*brain damage?*"

Drew shook his head. The likelihood of that, Doc Parker had assured him, was slim to none. Drew's main objective was to keep her calm. "I'm a little concerned about something—"

"Concerned?" She turned on the seat to face him. "Concerned about what?"

"Well…" he drawled.

She held her face in her hands. "Arghh, you can be so exasperating sometimes!"

"Doc never said how I'm supposed to tell the difference."

"Difference? *What* difference? Drew, honestly, you're giving me a headache."

"Sorry," he said, meaning it. Drew gave her hand a pat, then pulled into traffic.

"The difference?" she encouraged, as he merged into the fast lane.

"Between the crazy way you used to act and the way you've been behaving since you thumped your head."

Her steely eyed glare was softened by a playful smile. "You'd better watch it, Drew Cunningham, or you're going to be spending your two-month anniversary night on the couch!"

Drew stared straight ahead. *Again with the two months,* he thought.

If that was the case, the Almighty had answered his prayers. He'd given Drew a second chance, an opportunity to make it up to Gabrielle for the dreadful thing he'd done.

Thank You, Lord, he prayed, *and I promise not to blow it this time.*

Gabrielle insisted that Drew let her light the candles; he insisted she let him carry the lasagna-filled ironstone pan to the table. He served it up, as she held out the plates. And as the delicious aroma of the steaming pasta wafted into their nostrils, he wrapped her hand in his and uttered a short but heartfelt grace.

"Dear Lord, thank you for all our blessings, for this food, for the beautiful woman who prepared it." He gave her hand a gentle squeeze. "Thank you for watching over my—my *wife,* for bringing her home to me, safe." He cleared his throat, then said a gravelly "Amen."

When he opened his eyes, he found Gabrielle staring at him.

"That was short and sweet," she said, grinning as she flapped a napkin across her lap. "You'd think *you* were the one who bumped his head." She leaned forward to give him a quick kiss on the lips. "I hope you didn't forget how to say a proper blessing because you're worried about *me*. Because I'm fine. Honest."

She hadn't been raised in a church-going household. He'd known that when he married her. It had been just one of the things he figured he could teach her...and one of the things that had caused conflict between them.

He focused on his plate so she wouldn't read the concern in his eyes. "I'm not worried about you," he said, knowing even as the words exited his lips that they weren't true. "I'm starved, is all. Haven't had a bite all day."

"What! There wasn't a scrap of bacon or a streak of egg yoke left on your plate when you left here this morning!"

The last time she'd made him a big country breakfast had been on the morning of the day she'd left him. But Doc Parker had warned Drew not to let Gabrielle get upset, and to remind her of that fact was sure to do just that. "Well," he began, choosing his words carefully, "I haven't had a bite *lately*."

All through the rest of the meal, Gabrielle told him about how she'd heard a wolf howling that morning, even before the cock crowed. The candle glow shimmered on her ivory skin, made her bright gray eyes glitter like polished silver.

Oh, how he loved this vital, animated woman, and oh, how he'd missed her! Her zest for life was contagious. Before he'd met her, thanking the Good Lord for every sunrise was more a habit than anything else. But since meeting Gabrielle... Well, waking to find his beautiful, lively little wife cuddled up beside him had given him a whole new and glorious reason to thank God for each new day.

He looked into her eyes—eyes afire with the love of life. Did Gabrielle realize what she was doing? Did she understand that her sweet smiles, the love-light in her eyes, the way she rested her hand on his arm now and then, was awakening memories? Did she know that this candlelit dinner—prepared and served to celebrate the day they were wed—made him yearn for that blessed day, and that wonderful night?

Being with her again was, for Drew, like feeling the sunshine on his face after a winter of cold, dreary Montana weather. She was his rainbow after a thunderstorm, his home and his hearth and the love of his life. He was grateful to have her back, so grateful that he would make any promise, swear any oath, to ensure Gabrielle would never leave him again.

Was it an accident of fate, some curious coincidence, that her soft voice and gentle touch seemed to him a signal that meant she'd come home to stay? That she expected him always to be part of her life—welcomed, wanted, *loved*—despite the despicable things she'd accused him of?

She deserved a strong man. A *good* man.

God had blessed him with a good, strong body, and in gratitude, Drew had used it to its fullest potential. Not that there was any honor in it; lately, hard work seemed to be the only thing that took his mind off missing her. But had he paid so much attention to exercising his body that he'd neglected to exercise his spirit? Was *that* the reason he'd sobbed like an orphan after she'd left him? Was that why a sob threatened to escape his throat even now?

Drew knew something about how time could sharpen the keen edge of yearning. He'd brooded and sulked for years after his mother left home. And done the same when Gabby ran off—for months.

And now she was back, more beautiful than ever.

"I'm going to take a hike, first thing tomorrow—see if I can't find that wol—"

"I don't think that's a good idea." He knew only too well her love of wolves. Knew, too, about the one she'd heard nearly a year ago. It would break her heart to know he'd found a scraggly wolf a few months back. Living out here, he'd seen it before. Lone wolves, starving for affection as much as food, usually ended up like that one.

Her smile dimmed in response to the edginess in his voice. "Why not?"

"Doc Parker said you should take it easy for the next few days, remember?" Drew made a concerted effort to lighten his tone. "Hiking through the foothills isn't exactly following doctor's orders, now is it?"

She tucked in one corner of her mouth, shoved a wide, ruffle-edged noodle around on her plate. "No," she sighed, "I suppose not." Gabrielle sat back in her chair, lay her fork beside her plate. "But the wolf was close, Drew, real close." Leaning forward, she rested both hands on his forearm. "You're gonna think I'm nuts, but I want to see it, up close."

He'd refused to let her track wolves before, citing the danger involved—another piece of evidence in *her* mind that he didn't consider her feelings the least bit important. "Tell you what," he began, "when Doc gives you a clean bill of health, we'll look for the wolf…together."

Drew focused on her ringless fingers, which were pressing gently into his skin. Until now, he'd hoped that she'd rented that little apartment in town just to cool off. That she'd pull herself together and realize what had happened between them didn't have to put an end to their marriage.

But if that were true, would she have taken off her wedding band *and* her engagement ring? Drew didn't think so.

He swallowed, hard.

Drew had never known anyone like Gabrielle. When she set her mind on something, she was like a puppy to the root. He didn't see any point in telling her they'd had a similar conversation, before she left.

He'd try to move Granite Peak, lasso the sun, change the course of the Fishtail River if she asked it of him. Disappointing her was the last thing Drew wanted to do.

It hadn't been the rage that gave her melodious voice a ragged edge, the memory of which, even as recently as last night, kept him awake for hours. It hadn't been the heat of the angry words themselves that made him feel more ashamed than he'd ever felt to date. No, it had been the disappointment in her eyes that haunted him, wouldn't give him a moment's peace. If the Good Lord would see fit to give him a chance to make it up to her, Drew had vowed night after lonely night, he'd never make the same mistakes again.

"We can go tomorrow, Drew. It'd be safe—if you were with me."

Gabrielle waited for his response, a sweet smile curving her lovely lips.

She had come back to him. What more proof did he need that God had answered his plea?

"I dunno, Gabby. Doc said—"

"I'm not a baby, Drew," she snapped, snatching back her hands. "I don't need to be coddled."

The truth came spilling out, like the rapids spilling over timeworn rocks in the bend of a river. "Gabby, sweetie," he said, reaching for her, "I'm sorry if it sounds like that. I don't mean it to, honest. It's just that I love you and I'm worried about you. I know how you push yourself. I've had a concussion, myself, so I know you can feel terrific one minute, dizzy as a drunkard the next.''

She gave him a halfhearted grin. "Do I smell a compromise in the air?''

Drew hung his head and chuckled softly. Leave it to Gabby to put her own spin on it. "Okay. Okay. I know when I'm licked,'' he admitted, grinning. And crouching beside her chair, he wrapped her in a hearty hug. "But honest, Gabby, if anything ever happened to you,'' he whispered against her freckled cheek, "I don't know what I'd do.''

Gabrielle turned to face him, putting her lips no more than an inch from his. And bracketing his face in her warm hands, she gazed lovingly into his eyes. "Nothing is going to happen to me,'' she stated matter-of-factly. "You're forgetting that I'm a Lafayette!''

"You *were* a Lafayette,'' he corrected, praying his words wouldn't jog her memory.

She kissed him then, not the way friend kisses friend, or parent kisses child, but the way a woman kisses the man she loves. "You're absolutely right,'' she said on a sigh. "I'm a Cunningham now, and mighty proud of it.''

Her mouth was soft and searching, her breath whispersweet. Drew's heart pounded as she leaned back and combed her fingers through his hair, and he was shocked at his eager response to her scrutiny.

"You know what I've been thinking?''

He cleared his throat. *The more things change,* he quoted silently, *the more they stay the same.* Why did she always pick times like these to get chatty? But God help him, he loved her with everything in him. If talking's what she wanted, then talking's what she'd get. Despite himself, he smiled. "What've you been thinking?''

Her delicate forefinger traced the contour of his upper

lip, the angle of his jaw, the slope of his nose. Raising one well-arched brow and grinning mischievously, she began in a breathy voice, "That it'd be awfully nice to hear the pitter-patter of little feet around this big, old, empty ranch house."

Drew blinked, stunned into openmouthed silence at her suggestion. Was she kidding? Was this part of some cruel, vengeful joke? Or had he misunderstood her entirely?

"Y-you...you want to—"

Gabrielle tilted her head, her smile broadening slightly as she looked over his left shoulder and focused on some spot near the ceiling. "I've been experiencing some very strange sensations the last couple of days..." She snuggled closer, rested her cheek against his chest.

He held his breath for a moment before saying, "It's the concussion." Nodding, Drew added, "Normal. Very normal. Dizziness and—" He cleared his throat. "Is your stomach queasy?"

She tilted her head back, sending that gleaming, luxurious hair cascading over one shoulder like a fiery waterfall. "Well, no-o," she singsonged, "but it co-o-ould be, if you'll just cooperate a little."

Much as he wanted to take her upstairs—and he wanted that a lot—Drew couldn't let himself give in to the temptation. Wouldn't be fair to Gabby, he told himself. It'd be like using her. And as he stared into her loving eyes, he admitted it wouldn't be *like* using her, it would *be* using her. She was vulnerable right now, weakened physically and psychologically by the concussion, and certainly in no emotional condition to be making decisions as life-altering as having a baby!

He remembered the times she'd asked that question, on their wedding night, and weeks after the honeymoon, and every other day, it seemed. "Not yet," he'd said each time, citing their small savings account and everything that needed doing around the ranch as reasons to wait.

Besides, if her "strange sensations" managed to produce the results she seemed to want them to, it wouldn't be fair to the child, wouldn't be fair to *Drew,* because if she got her memory back and changed her mind again after they were sure a baby was on the way—

"Drew? Honey?" she crooned, fingers playing in his hair.

He cleared his throat again.

"You love me, don't you?"

"'Course I do," he said, a little rougher than he'd intended. "You know I do," he added more gently.

"When you proposed to me, you said you wanted us to have a family. A big one. You meant it, didn't you?"

The idea of Gabrielle bearing his children, of having little Gabby and Drew look-alikes running around the house, appealed to him more than he cared to admit. But he wanted to be sure. Sure of a lot of things before they started having kids. For one thing, he wanted to know there'd always be enough money in the bank to keep a tight roof over their heads, plenty of food in the pantry. But more than that, he wanted—*needed*—proof that Gabrielle wouldn't up and leave when some good-looking musician came to town, the way his mother had.

He had nothing to go on now but blind faith, because she'd already left him. And if not for the concussion, Gabrielle wouldn't be here now, in his arms, asking him to help her make a baby.

Blind faith.

Lord, he prayed silently, You've got to help me out here, 'cause I'm skatin' on thin ice.

"Yes, Gabrielle. I want to have a family with you. I want that more than you'll ever know," he answered at last.

Gabrielle stood, held out her hand to him and smiled sweetly. Drew didn't know what possessed him to put his hand into hers, or why he so willingly let her lead him down the long, narrow hall into the foyer, or why he followed her up the curved mahogany staircase.

But he did.

He wanted nothing but good things for her—happiness, fulfillment, robust health. It was only because he believed with everything in him that *he* was good for her that Drew prayed, *Lord, if it means she'll leave me again, don't ever let Gabby get her memory back.*

Even as the words formed in his mind, he admitted the selfishness of them. But he needed her every bit as much as he loved her; he'd make it up to her in a thousand ways, for the rest of his days.

"I hope I won't be sorry in the morning," she whispered, her voice husky and trembly as she back-stepped into their room.

Sorry?

His heart thundered against his ribs. Sorry about what?

"For letting the dishes wait. Mozzarella cheese gets like concrete when it sits."

His earlier concerns that this might be a mistake—a big one—were blotted out by velvet sighs and fluttering hands that caressed his face, his shoulders, his back. Pulse pounding and heart hammering, he gave in to the moment, but not so completely that he didn't hear those words ringing in his ears: *"I hope I won't be sorry in the morning."*

Chapter Three

Sleep—what there had been of it—came that night in fits and starts, for Drew didn't want to take the chance that while he dozed, she might remember the months she'd forgotten.

Almost from the moment she'd fallen asleep, Gabrielle had snuggled close, the way she used to in the early weeks of their marriage. In this position—nose tucked into the crook of his neck, one arm across his chest, a leg flung over his thigh—he couldn't see her face, despite the bright swath of moonlight slicing into their room.

But he didn't need to look at her to see her, for he'd watched her sleep countless times before she'd left him. After she was gone, he'd seen her with his mind's eye, night after lonely night: thick lashes that dusted lightly freckled, sleep-flushed cheeks; lush, velvety curls against porcelain skin; the hint of a smile that turned up the corners of her mouth. Too many nights to count, Drew had listened to the slow, steady breaths that sighed softly past her luscious, slightly parted lips.

Her breathing was so shallow, so faint that he often

found it necessary to hold his own breath to hear hers. Some mornings he'd tease her, pointing out how odd it was that a gal who bubbled with energy and chattered like a chipmunk during the daylight could grow so still and silent while she slept. On those mornings, Gabrielle would yawn and shrug daintily and, voice still morning-hoarse, grin and whisper, "Guess that's just one of my womanly mysteries."

Smiling now, Drew nodded as he admitted just how right she'd been. Everything about her had been a mystery to him, from the way she seemed to fall boots-over-bonnet in love with him right from the get-go, to the way she made him feel like a smitten schoolboy every time she aimed that innocent-yet-womanly gaze of hers in his direction.

Gabrielle stirred in his arms as a sigh rustled from her, reminding Drew of the musical murmurings she'd hummed into his ears hours earlier. "'Oh, let me hear thy voice, for sweet is thy voice, and thy countenance is lovely,'" he quoted from *Song of Songs*. "'Thou art fair, my love, thou art fair.... My beloved is mine, and I am hers....'"

But *was* she his?

And if she was, for how long?

He'd known from the instant her car disappeared from view that fateful night that he would miss everything about her, from her generous nature to her drive toward perfection.

Was the heat of their marital love a result of her determination to be the best? Or was it exactly what she'd called it at the conclusion of every interlude: physical proof of the love in her heart?

They'd been apart a long time, but not so long that he'd forgotten she liked having the window open, even on cold nights, so she could feel the breath of the cool wind on her face. She liked the sheets folded neatly over the comforter, too, and hated for the covers to be tucked too tightly over her feet.

Drew glanced at the window, where a crisp autumn breeze had set the sheer white curtains to billowing gently, like a sail that's been filled by an obliging sea breeze. But the blankets, unencumbered by hospital corners, had gotten twisted, and he tidied them now, straightening the top sheet until it lay smooth.

His efforts roused her briefly, causing her to cuddle closer still. "I love you, Drew," she murmured, kissing his neck before drifting off again.

He didn't know its cause or source, but a sob swelled in his throat. Blinking back stinging tears, he managed to croak out a quiet "Ah, Gabby, I love you, too."

He'd told her he loved her before, hundreds of times, and had meant it each time. But never more than now.

He'd have hugged her tighter, but she needed her rest, and he couldn't chance waking her. He'd be nudging her in a few minutes, anyway, as Doc Parker had instructed. Every hour on the hour, he'd given her a gentle shake, just enough so he could pry open one eye at a time and study her pupils under the flashlight beam. Once he'd returned the light to the nightstand, he reset the alarm. But he hadn't needed to: he hadn't slept a wink all night.

He'd lain awake to do what the doctor had ordered—that much was true. But it was only part of the truth. The main reason for his sleeplessness was terror—cold and grim and hard as steel. Because what if, as he slumbered peacefully, Gabrielle woke up and got her memory back? She'd hate him, that's what, and she'd leave again.

He never would have admitted it—not even to Gabrielle—but being abandoned by his mother twenty years earlier had left its mark. There hadn't been one visit, one phone call or one note in all that time, so Drew and his only brother had had no choice but to take his father's word that her leaving was proof she'd never cared a whit about any of them.

He'd been twelve at the time, young enough to hope and dream that she'd come back someday, old enough that it cut like a knife when "someday" never came.

When Gabrielle stormed out, all those feelings he'd repressed—fear and hurt, anger and confusion, and a powerful mistrust of women—came rushing back with the force of a mile-wide tornado. The biggest difference was that his mother had left without so much as a "See you later." At least Gabrielle had shouted out a list of explanations for her decision to end their life together. Even with those reasons echoing in his mind, Drew still didn't understand why she'd gone away any more than he'd understood his mother's sudden departure.

What Gabrielle had said as she quietly closed the front door behind her confused him most of all. *"I love you, Drew Cunningham, and I probably always will, but I can't live with a man who thinks so little of me."*

That made no sense to him at all, because he thought the world of her. Didn't she know that? Why, he loved her with everything in him, and would gladly have done anything to protect her, to give her the feelings of security and stability she'd never known as a girl.

What's a man to do, he wondered, when the things he's done to provide his wife with what he believes she needs are the very reasons she walks out on him?

Exhaling a ragged sigh, he ran a hand through his hair, as Gabrielle mumbled something in her sleep. He hoped it wouldn't be just a matter of time before who he was drove her away again. *God,* he prayed, *let me change. Don't let me botch it this time.* His concern was forgotten the moment she nestled against him, tangling her limbs with his.

For the moment, at least, it didn't matter that her absence had sent him into a black despair for three-quarters of a year, because it felt so good holding her close, so good that the only thing he really gave a hoot about right now was making her happy, any way he could.

She'd lived a hard life, and he had no right making it harder still by being thick-headed and narrow-minded. With a little luck and a whole lot of prayer, maybe he'd have the puzzle figured out by the time she got her memory back, and those things that drove her away would become the reasons she'd want to stay. Heart throbbing with hope, he touched his lips to her temple, as if sealing the prayer with a kiss.

The first rays of daylight now spilled over the windowsill, flooding the room with a deep purple hue. By the time he woke her for the next examination of her eyes, the sun would have crested the horizon. And because she'd always been an early riser, there'd be no more shushing her, no kissing her closed eyes to convince her to go back to sleep once she saw the bright light of day, as he'd done after every other time he'd checked her out.

Drew hoped his heart, thumping hard against his spine and onto the mattress, wouldn't wake her before the daylight had a chance to. He willed it to stop pounding, but it was no use. Much as he wanted to see her open those big beautiful eyes of hers, he wished she would stay this way forever—peaceful and quiet and wrapped in the arms of his love.

Because when she woke up, would she have her memory back? Would she realize he'd taken advantage of her vulnerability?

"Good morning, handsome." Gabrielle ran her fingers through his hair. "Did you sleep well?"

Relief coursed through him; for the time being, it seemed, she hadn't remembered.

Drew gave a shaky nod. "I slept fine."

Grinning, she gave his chest a playful slap. "Fibber. You didn't sleep a wink, I'll bet, what with your insistence on subjecting me to hourly torture sessions." She snickered. "Now I know why detectives in all the movies use that bare lightbulb when they're interrogating bad guys."

Chuckling, he shook his head. "It was for your own good."

She combed her fingernails through his chest hair. "So what's the diagnosis, Doc? Did I pass muster?"

He tried to ignore the hunger her delicate touch aroused. "You're mixing your variables, but yes, you seem okay to me."

"Metaphors," she said, kissing his throat, "not variables."

His brow crinkled. How did she expect him to think, let alone talk sense, when her fingertips continued drawing little circles on his chest? "Meta—"

She kissed him full on the lips, then said, "If I have to choose between a guy who knows the difference between variables and metaphors..." Gabrielle pressed as close as her satiny nightgown would allow and, with her lips lightly touching his, said on the heels of a raspy sigh, "Let's just say I choose you, hands down."

If she didn't quit it, she'd get another dose of last night, right now.

No, he couldn't let that happen. It wasn't fair to Gabrielle—not in her condition, not under these tenuous circumstances.

"Do you have any baby names in mind?"

He swallowed. "Baby names?" Drew took a deep breath, because if anyone had asked him to describe what a woman's voice might sound like when she asked a question like that, he'd have said it would come off as cheery, lighthearted—a little giggly, even. But seductive? Sultry? He'd never have guessed *that* in a million years, and yet passionate was precisely the way his wife's voice sounded now.

What's a man to do with a li'l gal like this? he asked himself. *Dear God, tell me, what's a man to do?*

The answer came sandwiched between her lingering, breathy sigh and the kiss she placed—of all places—on the tip of his nose. *Love her,* said a voice from deep inside his heart. *Just love her.*

And so he did exactly that.

"Drew, do we have company?"

He finished buttoning his shirt as he walked toward the window. Standing beside her, he followed her gaze to the driveway below. "No. Why?"

Gabrielle pointed. "Whose little red sports car is that?"

Both brows drew together as he studied her profile. And then it dawned on him: he hadn't bought her the car until a week before she'd left, and if she didn't remember leaving, then she didn't remember how all-fired mad she'd been about that car.

Should he tell her the truth? No, Doc Parker had made it perfectly clear: *"Keep her as quiet and calm as possible. Don't let her do anything that might cause another blow to the temple. Don't even let her rattle her brain by jostling her head."*

Drew didn't want to talk about that car. Fact was, he'd come to hate the sight of it, crunching up the gravel drive every Saturday morning as she headed in for her weekly ride with Triumph. In his mind, the vehicle was the beginning of the end of them. If he told her it was *her* car down there, the knowledge might jog her memory, start a whole domino series of memories toppling—if remembering now made her half as upset as she'd been on the night she'd left.

"Lie, steal and cheat if you have to," the old doctor had insisted. *"Do whatever it takes to keep that girl calm."*

The possibility of causing further damage to his delicate, defenseless wife made Drew's heart ache. She looked so beautiful, standing there with the morning light gleaming in her hair, her narrow shoulders wrapped in a pink robe that matched her satiny nightgown. He was about to tell her so, when she faced him and smiled the way she had as they stood at the altar, hand in hand, ready to exchange wedding vows.

"Well?"

Without thinking, he reached out and wrapped a lock of her hair around his forefinger. "Well…what?"

Giggling, Gabrielle gave him a good-natured poke in the ribs. "The car, silly. Whose is it?"

Drew's cheeks felt hot, because he took pride in the fact that he could count on one hand the number of times he'd deliberately lied in his lifetime. But what choice did he have? If a lie would keep her calm…

"It's, uh, it belongs to a guy."

"A guy? What guy?"

"Somebody, uh, someone in town. He, um, he asked if I'd take a look under the hood and—"

She threw herself into his arms, gave him a good long squeeze. "It's your own fault, you know."

With his chin resting atop her head, he prayed, *Don't let her remember, Lord.* Because if she remembered, she'd leave him. And this time, it might be for good. It hadn't been easy, going on after she slammed out of his life. But he'd plodded along, hoping that God would answer his only prayer: *Bring her home. Just bring her home.*

After last night, after this morning, he didn't think he could pretend the past hadn't happened. Didn't know if he had the strength to try.

Reminded again of the selfishness of his prayer, Drew closed his eyes in shame and revised his heavenly plea. *Don't let her remember...at least not yet.*

He was as afraid of the answer as he was of the question, but Drew asked it anyway. "What's my fault?"

With a tilt of her head and a saucy grin, she said, "If you hadn't developed this—this reputation for being so good with motors, people wouldn't always be asking you to fix their tractors and their cars and their lawn mowers." She squeezed him again. "But your helpful nature is just one of the reasons I love you."

She'd likely said "I love you" a hundred times since he found her standing at the stove yesterday afternoon. How many more times would she say it before everything came back to her?

"Has he been here before?"

"No. Why?"

She shrugged. "Because that car looks...familiar."

Drew swallowed, hard.

"When will he be picking it up?"

Lost in the depths of crystal-gray, long-lashed eyes, Drew's mind swam with memories of his own. Gabrielle had told him all about her gypsy-like past, how painful it had been, trying to fit in every time her father plunked her down in a new town; how, just when she'd started feeling like a place could be home, he'd up and move the little family again.

Drew's childhood was anything but nomadic. "Stability" might as well have been his middle name. His great-grandfather had bought the parcel of land that eventually became the Walking C, and Cunninghams had worked that land ever since. Drew remembered the accusations she'd hurled at him that night. If only she had let him explain, she'd have seen that—

A light tapping on his chest roused him from his thoughts. He looked down to find her pinching the bridge of her nose. "Earth to Drew, Earth to Drew..."

Chuckling, he shook his head. "Sorry. I was—"

"Thinking about last night?" She sighed dreamily and nestled closer. "Another one for the memory book, wasn't it."

Memory book? he repeated silently. The mere mention of the words jarred Drew as if she'd broadsided him with a two-by-four.

He chose to concentrate on what she'd implied, rather than the fear her question evoked. "That's putting it mildly," he said, forcing a grin. Fact was, he hadn't realized how precious a gift they'd shared, all those nights before she'd left. If he'd known then what a treasure she was, how priceless and irreplaceable her love would be—

"So when...is...the... man...coming...for...his...car?" She enunciated each word individually.

Another blast of heat warmed his cheeks, his ears, his neck. "He—I, ah, I told him I'd drive it to town today."

She wrinkled her nose. "But Drew, how will you get home?"

He had to think about that for a minute. Lying wasn't something he'd gotten much practice at over the years, and he'd told her two in as many minutes.

Grinning, Gabrielle ran her thumbs over his whiskered cheeks. "I'll just bet you're about to ask me to follow you into town in the pickup and wait while you make your Little Red Car delivery."

Too many chances she'd have a memory jog. "No."

"But why?"

"Because I said so, that's why."

He saw the flash of hurt in her eyes and was immediately reminded what she'd said that night, about how he thought he knew the answer to every question. No wonder she left, he admitted silently, regretfully.

Drew shook his head, knowing how ridiculous, how bull-headed he'd sounded. "It's just, I hadn't thought that far ahead." That, at least, was the truth. "I'll get Troy to follow me."

She wiggled her eyebrows and snuggled closer still. "But if I drive you, we could have lunch at the diner. I haven't had one of those soft ice-cream treats they serve in days."

Dread pounded in his heart. Those first days after leaving him—before she'd hired on as a loan officer at the bank—Gabrielle had taken a job as a waitress at the diner. What if going in there, being surrounded by all that black-and-white tile and chrome, brought everything racing back?

He took a deep breath and shook his head. "Absolutely not. You suffered a concussion, don't forget, and I don't want you driving the truck yet." Another truth to add to the good side of his lies-v.-honesty ledger.

But there was something dark in her eyes. Anger? Resentment? Was it any wonder, when seconds ago he'd admitted how bullheaded he'd sounded, and here he was doing it again?

He quickly added, "That old jalopy doesn't have power steering or power brakes. I want you to rest today." Almost as an afterthought, he tacked on, "Okay?"

She frowned. "Honestly, Drew. Why do you always treat me like I'm made of spun glass?" Doubling a fist, she shook it under his nose. "I'm tougher than I look, mister. So I got a little bump on the head."

"Gabrielle," he began, one brow high on his forehead and a finger to the tip of her nose, "Doc said you weren't to exert yourself in any way." He drew her nearer to add, "I've already broken that rule by allowing you to talk me into, um, exerting yourself, twice in twelve hours. You want him to take a poke at me?"

Hiding a grin behind one hand, she shook her head. "And he'd do it, too, wouldn't he."

She must have remembered the story he'd told her, about the time when he was six or seven, and Doc Parker whacked his behind for climbing to the top of his TV antenna. "You do anything like that again," the man had warned, "and I'll paddle your bottom."

"Yep," Drew agreed, "he would."

Her laughter was like cooling salve on a raw burn. She seemed to be enjoying his company, the way she had back in the early days of their marriage, before she started thinking of him as—what had she called him that night?—a control freak, a bossy know-it-all, a rigid and uncompromising jerk.

Drew placed both hands on her shoulders, grateful as all get-out for the love-light radiating from her eyes. He decided, standing there in the warm glow of it, that he'd be a fool to mess this up. How many chances did he think the Good Lord was going to give him? It was in His capable hands now, whether she got her memory back, started hating him again, left for good.

If she left again, Drew thought grimly.

On the other hand, maybe by the grace of God, he'd be able to use this time wisely, show her that he knew how to be the kind of husband she'd said she wanted, the kind of husband she deserved.

"So tell me, Mrs. Cunningham, what can I fix you for breakfast?"

She frowned again, but a smile gentled it considerably. "I'll have you know that I spent the better part of yesterday afternoon putting my pantry and cupboards back in order. Seems you must have offered to empty the dishwasher, and in a weak moment, I foolishly said yes." Wrapping her arms around him, she kissed his Adam's apple. "After the mess you made, you don't honestly think I ever intend to let you into my kitchen again, do you?"

He remembered how she'd always lined up the cups and glasses in the cabinets, how every spoon and fork in the silverware drawer ended up in a neat stack, how she kept the canned goods in straight rows in the pantry, how she organized their closets with military precision. For a while after she left, he'd tried to keep things that way, but before long her "way" of doing things only served to remind him how very much he missed everything about her.

"I'll get Troy to follow me into town," he said suddenly. "Soon as we get some eggs and ham into your—"

She grabbed his hand, lay it flat against her stomach. "By Jove," she said, imitating a thick British accent, "oy think we did it."

"Did it? Did what?"

Pressing his hand more tightly to her, she rolled her eyes. "Made a baby, of course!"

It took every ounce of self-control for him to keep his mouth shut. Because, as he had watched her sleep last night, he'd more or less hoped the same thing. On the one hand, God couldn't grace them with a better gift. On the other, if a baby *was* a result of their loving night, and she got her memory back.

Drew preferred not to think about that right now. Right

now, she needed his strength, his stability, his protection—not his self-centered doubts and fears.

"Are you as happy as I am, Drew?"

Looking into those wide, sparkling eyes, staring at that angelic, naive face, how could he say anything but "I've never been happier, Gabby." Three lies, three truths. At least there's some balance to this miserable mess, he told himself.

His answer seemed to satisfy her, and she walked into the closet, lifted a pair of jeans from a shelf and took a T-shirt from its hanger. "Drew?"

He followed her into the closet, wrapped his arms around her from behind. "Hmm?"

Pointer finger aimed at the wall, she said, "Where did all these shelves come from?"

He'd built them in the weeks after she left, hoping that when she came to her senses, when she came *home,* she'd see this small alteration in his otherwise well-regulated life as proof that he was willing to compromise, for her.

But admitting that would only upset her, and Doc Parker had made it clear what could happen if she got riled.

"I wanted to surprise you," he began his next lie, "so while you were—while you were out riding Triumph, I, ah, I built them."

Gabrielle turned partway around. "But Drew, you said once that you didn't want to change anything in this house, in case your mother ever came home."

If he hadn't had his arms wrapped around her, he'd have slapped himself in the forehead. She'd called him a jerk that night. And she'd been right, he admitted. Because who else but a jerk—a mama's boy—would say a thing like that to his new bride, to the woman he's supposed to love?

Drew gave her a gentle squeeze. "I guess after twenty years, it's fair to say she won't be coming back. *You're* the most important woman in my life, Gabby. Have been from the minute I laid eyes on you, will be 'til I draw my last breath.''

Facing him, she dropped the clothes onto the floor and threw her arms around his neck. "What a wonderful, thoughtful thing to do." Standing on tiptoe, she pressed a kiss to his chin. "I love you so much!"

He shrugged as a blush darkened his weathered cheeks, because as usual she was overreacting. He'd built a few lousy, lopsided shelves in a hundred-year-old ranch house, when she deserved a mansion on a hill. "It's a few boards and a couple of nails. Let's not get all mushy about it, okay?''

"Okay, Macho Man," she teased, stepping away from him. "I'm going to take a shower." There was a twinkle in her eye when she added, "And if you're still serious about that breakfast…"

He could only nod.

Bending to retrieve her jeans and T-shirt, she tossed them over her shoulder. "I'll have two eggs, over easy, with buttered toast and plenty of crispy bacon." Breezing by him on her way to the bathroom, she added, "Oh, and a big glass of tomato juice to go with my coffee." She patted her stomach. "Decaf, of course, 'cause caffeine isn't good for unborn babies, y'know.''

He heard the shower doors roll open, then close. It wasn't until the steady *hiss* of water began beating on the glass that he realized he was still standing where she'd left him, in the middle of their walk-in closet. Because all he could concentrate on were her words: *"Caffeine isn't good for unborn babies.''*

His boot heels seemed to be filled with lead as he headed for the kitchen. Halfway down the stairs, he heard her off-key rendition of "I love you so much it hurts me."

"I hope not," he muttered as he descended the stairs. "I surely hope not."

She came into the kitchen, eyes wide and filled with tears. He was beside her in a heartbeat, wrapping her in a warm embrace.

"Oh, Drew," she cried into his shoulder, "I've misplaced my wedding rings. I've looked everywhere and—"

Of course she hadn't misplaced them. He'd noticed immediately that first Saturday all those months ago, when she came back to ride Triumph, that she'd removed them. But he couldn't tell her that.

"Shh, sweetie," he said, giving her back an affectionate pat-pat-pat. "Remember what Doc Parker said."

Sniffing, she stepped out of his hug and snatched a napkin from the basket on the table. In the time it took to blow her nose, she'd all but regained her composure.

She's some kinda woman, he told himself as she dabbed at her eyes. Some kinda woman. Faced yet again with the choice of telling her the truth—that her rings were probably somewhere in the apartment she'd rented in town—or a lie, Drew repeated the old doctor's advice in his mind. "They'll turn up," he said, nodding reassuringly as she took a seat. "But even if they don't, we can always get you a new—"

She stood so quickly that the chair nearly toppled over behind her. "I don't want new rings!" Eyes filling with fresh tears, she pouted prettily. "I want the diamond you gave me that day on the mountain trail, and the gold band you put on my finger on our wedding day."

Her words touched him, right on down to the marrow of his bones, because it looked to him as though she meant every word. Sitting there, wringing that paper napkin in her tiny hands, she made him feel like a heel. He could end her torment right here and now, by telling her where she could find the rings.

But if he did, his own agony would begin again, because the news would likely start her memory ball rolling, and when it got to the bottom of the hill, she'd be long gone—and he'd be alone again.

His own self-pity was quickly forgotten when Drew noticed her flushed cheeks, when he heard her quick, shallow breaths. It told him she'd gotten upset enough at the thought of losing her rings that her blood pressure had increased. *Lord,* he prayed, *help me cheer her up, or calm her down, or whatever it takes to keep her safe.* "You're not supposed to get worked up. Doc Parker said—"

"Easy for him to say." She folded her arms across her chest. "I'd like to see how he'd react if he lost *his* wedding ring."

Stepping up behind her, Drew put his hands on her shoulders. "Doc has been a widower for more than a decade," he said, massaging her neck. "I doubt he even wears a wedding ring."

Gabrielle turned in the chair and shot him a heated glance. "It's gold with little leaf etchings on it—not that I'd expect *you* to notice a thing like that."

The heat of her words stunned him into silence, and his hands froze.

Gabrielle didn't understand what had inspired her angry outburst. No, it was more rage than anger, white-hot and prickly, which confused her all the more. She blamed it on a night with practically no sleep, since Doc Parker had ordered Drew to wake her every hour on the hour. She blamed the pounding headache that hadn't let up since she'd refused to take the pills the doctor prescribed. Because what if she and Drew *had* made a baby last night?

Surely the powerful painkillers wouldn't be good for the child.

Good for the child. Gabrielle sighed. *Careful what you ask for,* she thought again, *because you might just get it.*

"You okay?" he asked, voice laced with uncertainty.

Nodding, Gabrielle patted his hand. "I'll be fine when I find my rings," she said dully.

He turned up the fire under the frying pan, while she rearranged the silverware he'd set out beside her plate. Would she be fine? Somehow, she didn't think so. Because from the moment she came to yesterday, she'd sensed something was wrong. Dreadfully wrong. Something that had nothing whatever to do with the blow to her head.

Maybe it was just the decision to insist on starting a family, right now, despite everything Drew had said. She'd been badgering him about having children almost from the minute he proposed. To give him his due, whenever the subject came up, he'd listed common-sense reasons why the timing wasn't right. So for the life of her, she couldn't help but wonder why he'd consented so quickly, so easily last night.

The memory of him kneeling near her chair hovered in her mind. If she didn't know better, she'd have said he looked guilty about something. And shouldn't it have been Gabrielle who looked guilty, seeing as she was the one trying to talk him into doing something he wasn't ready to do?

"We'll hunt for your rings after you have a healthy breakfast," he was saying.

Nodding, she smiled absently and stared at her reflection rippling darkly on the surface of her coffee. Now that it seemed possible that a baby was on the way, Gabrielle didn't know if she wanted to be—if she was *ready* to be— a mommy.

Would she have the patience, the strength, the never-ending love to give a child everything it deserved? Was she made of sturdy enough stuff to be there, round the clock— changing diapers and nursing, wiping noses and sticky fingers—without complaint?

Maybe she should have listened when Drew suggested they wait a year or two. Perhaps it was a good idea to pad their bank account with a little more cash before bringing a needy infant into the world.

"How do you want your eggs?" Drew asked over his shoulder.

"Not eggs," she answered. "Just one, over easy."

"But you said you wanted two. With toast and bacon and—"

"Not as hungry as I thought," she interrupted.

Drew gave her a look that said her behavior since yesterday had confused him every bit as much as it confused her.

Payback time, she told herself.

She'd always been one of those people who acted first and lived with the consequences later. Everyone said so— her father, her mother, Drew. Gabrielle had a sneaking suspicion that this time living with the consequences of her impulsive actions wasn't going to be easy. What else could explain this grim and gloomy doubt prickling in her heart and mind?

The answer was right there, she thought again, grimacing as she struggled to grasp it. If only she could reach it—

Drew's quiet humming broke into her thoughts, and she turned slightly so she could watch him. He didn't cook often, but he seemed to enjoy it, and the proof was the merry tune he always sang under his breath while he worked.

What would Drew do if uncertainty attacked him? she

wondered. Sighing, Gabrielle rolled her eyes. He'd say a prayer of some sort, as usual, and hand the whole matter over to "the Good Lord."

Well, God certainly hadn't been there for *her* family.

Every time her father lost a job, he'd say, "Where's God when we need Him?" And when her mother died, he'd kicked the dirt beside her coffin and snarled, "We're like a bunch of sparrows down here, and when He gets bored, He plucks one of us out of the sky, just for sport." She'd mimicked his attitude when they lowered his own coffin into the ground, because what kind of god allowed a girl of eighteen to go through the rest of her life with no grandparents, no siblings, no mom or dad?

Until her wedding day, Gabrielle had never set foot in a church. And since they'd exchanged "I do's," she'd gone to Sunday services only to quiet Drew's unrelenting pleas that she accompany him. God had never been a part of her life; why in the world would she turn to Him now?

Nagging apprehension refused to turn her loose. Head still throbbing and heart aching with fear of the unknown, she closed her eyes and held her breath. Maybe it wouldn't hurt to shoot a word or two toward God's ear.

The sound of Drew's butter knife, scraping across a slice of rye toast, captured her attention, and she watched as he sliced the bread in half. *And he teases* me *about being precise,* she thought, grinning a bit.

He was a good man. A decent man. And if she could talk him into seeing that she didn't need his constant protection, if she could convince him that compromise and negotiation were but two of the many important components of a healthy marriage, he'd be a good husband, too.

Good husband?

Where had that thought come from? she asked herself. Shaking her head, Gabrielle frowned and took a sip of black coffee. *God,* she began hesitantly, *if You've decided it's time for me to become a mother, then maybe it's a good idea to let me in on the dark secret that's niggling at the back of my brain.*

She waited, breathless, for some kind of heavenly response. Every sound seemed amplified, from the *tick-tock* of the kitchen clock, to the bubbling of tomato juice Drew poured into a stubby tumbler, to her gulp as she swallowed her coffee. She listened carefully, but heard no answer.

She should have known prayer was a useless exercise.

Just then, she sat up straight in the chair. A memory was forming somewhere in a corner of her mind: a chestnut mare with white mane and tail, and her name was Molly. Something horrible had happened to the horse, but *what?*

"Drew," she began tentatively, "do we own a horse named Molly?"

His brows dipped low in the center of his forehead, telling her more than that they owned a horse called Molly, telling her that Molly had indeed suffered a dreadful fate.

Gabrielle couldn't explain the wild beating of her heart or the clamminess of her palms. Couldn't explain the guilty, mortified expression on Drew's face, either.

"Eat your eggs before they get cold," he said, sliding them from the skillet onto her plate.

Gabrielle stared at the dish in front of her. She'd asked for one egg, over easy, and he'd made two, sunny-side up. Wasn't that just like him, she fumed, doing it whichever way he thought was best, no matter what.

A tremor began in the pit of her stomach and quaked to her fingertips as she shoved the plate away. There was no reasonable explanation for the rage roiling inside her. Drew had lovingly doted on her from the moment he'd first spotted the bump on her temple. What kind of ingrate was she? There were husbands out there who wouldn't lift a finger for their wives, injured or not, and some who'd make it clear they didn't appreciate being made to bother if they did lift a finger.

Gabrielle pushed back from the table and slowly stood. "I think maybe you're right, Drew. Maybe I've overdone it a bit."

The guilt that had darkened his face disappeared, and in its place was loving concern. She would have reached out, smoothed that stubborn, wayward lock of dark hair back into place, if he hadn't whisked her off her feet.

"You're getting right back into bed, missy," he scolded, taking the stairs two at a time, "and you're gonna stay there 'til I say otherwise. You got that?"

Nodding weakly, she leaned her head on his shoulder, thinking maybe he was right. Maybe all she needed was a good long nap.

And maybe when she woke up, she'd find her wedding rings.

Maybe she'd understand the source of her incredible concern for a little filly named Molly, and the gloom that had darkened Drew's eyes at the mention of it.

And maybe she'd even awaken with answers to all these questions floating around in her head.

Gabrielle hoped so. Because nothing terrified her more or made her angrier than being kept in the dark.

Chapter Four

How did he expect her to relax enough to sleep, with a virtual stranger in the house? "But I barely know Emily," Gabrielle pointed out.

Drew hesitated, as if preparing to disagree. Which was ridiculous, since she'd only spoken to the woman once since their wedding reception, and that brief conversation had taken place on the telephone.

"Sweetie," he said in his usual unruffled way, "you aren't strong enough yet to come to town with me, and you can't stay way out here all by yourself."

Well, the Walking C *was* miles from the nearest neighbor, and even farther from the closest town. Gabrielle supposed it did make sense to have someone on hand, just in case.

"I won't be long."

Wrapping her in his arms, he pressed his lips to her forehead, the way her father used to when she agreed to try, at least, and make the best of a new town.

"And if you're up to it when I get home, maybe we'll take that hike, look for your mystery wolf."

A reward for your "good little girl"? was her silent question.

Almost immediately, Gabrielle regretted her sarcasm. She was puzzled by it, too, because it seemed too well-rehearsed, as though she'd said and done all these things before. And why would she have done that—married to a man whose nature was to be loving, patient and kind, the way he'd been since learning about the concussion? Since even before Doc Parker confirmed it, she admitted, remembering the worry that had lined Drew's brow when he inspected her temple.

And running the ranch kept Drew on call nearly twenty-four hours a day; he'd already shifted many of his duties to Troy and the other hands in order to follow the doctor's orders. Besides, if she was going to behave like a spoiled brat, she shouldn't be surprised if he treated her like one.

"Sorry," she said on a sigh. "I know you've been neglecting things to take care of me." Forcing a cheerful tone into her voice that she didn't feel, Gabrielle looked into his eyes. "I might just take you up on that offer."

Relief shone in his eyes as a smile brightened his face. "The hike, you mean?" He chuckled. "Can't think of a thing I'd rather do."

She stood in the open doorway, waving as he climbed into his friend's little red car, waving as Troy started up Drew's battered old pickup. Gabrielle might have stayed there, watching until their vehicles disappeared down the long, winding drive, if the pot-clanging sounds filtering in from the kitchen hadn't distracted her.

Had Troy's wife taken it upon herself to rearrange the kitchen? Prepare a meal? Clean up the breakfast dishes? Annoyance propelled Gabrielle toward that end of the house. When she rounded the corner, she found Emily on her hands and knees, half in, half out of the oven.

"I thought you were supposed to be *napping*."

Her singsong, grumpy comment made it clear that under similar circumstances, Emily wouldn't be pampering herself.

Under *different* circumstances, Gabrielle might have been able to come up with a stinging retort. But what she saw as she stepped up to the stove stunned her into silence.

As a kid, one of her household chores had been to keep the blue-speckled interior of her mother's stove clean. Since marrying Drew, it became a special challenge to make the neglected, decades-old oven as shiny as new. And she'd succeeded, too. So why was this yellow-gloved outsider scouring away at what appeared to be months of cooked-on grease and grime?

"I appreciate what you're doing, Emily, but—"

"Ain't doin' it for you, missy," she snapped. "Doin' it for Drew."

Gabrielle strained to hear the rest of Emily's angry muttering.

"...young gal leavin' her man...no good reason...gone all this time...back, expectin' royal treatment, just like before."

"What 'gal'?" Gabrielle asked. "Who left her husband for no good reason?"

That brought the older woman out into the open. She knelt there, steel wool pad in one hand, and gripping the oven door with the other. "Well, now," she said, shaking her head, "don't you just take the cake."

If she didn't know better, Gabrielle would have to say Emily had been talking about *her*. But how could that be? She'd never leave Drew. She loved him!

"I'm afraid this blow to the head has left me a bit addle-brained, Emily," she started, keeping things friendly, "because I'm not following you at all." Drew had told her the woman had been like a mother to him. It was reason enough to be polite.

Emily frowned and harumphed and rolled her eyes, then went back to work on the oven. "No need to follow me, missy. Just go on up to your room, why don't you, and take your little *nap*."

Gabrielle's jaw dropped in response to the muttered phrase that punctuated Emily's terse remark. Surely she hadn't said, "I'll give this house a woman's touch...since you won't."

She could think of no reason why Emily would be so angry with her. Why she seemed to feel perfectly within her rights to show that anger in Gabrielle's home!

Bristling, she shoved trembling hands into her jeans pockets. If the woman wasn't Troy's wife... Over the years, Drew's foreman had become more a cross between a best friend and father than an employee. Out of respect for that, Gabrielle bit her tongue and started upstairs.

Her head was pounding, and the solution sat within arm's reach, there on the nightstand. The contents of the small brown vials containing the painkillers Doc had prescribed would probably stop the pain. But what damage would they do to the baby? she wondered.

In the bathroom, Gabrielle dampened a washcloth with cold water, then brought it with her to the bed. Stretching out on the mattress, she draped the cool compress over closed eyes and took a deep, cleansing breath. It wasn't likely she'd sleep, what with Emily's comments swirling amid all the other questions and concerns in her mind, but a short rest surely wouldn't hurt.

Hurry home, Drew, she thought. *Please hurry home.*

An hour later, Gabrielle woke with a start, unable for a moment to get her bearings. Why had she expected to look across the room and see a colorful Van Gogh print hanging on a bright yellow wall? And why did the big burled-wood chifforobe look so out of place?

Sitting up, she held her head in her hands. She glanced at the clock, trying to determine how long she'd slept. Fat lot of good that would do when she didn't know what time she'd gone upstairs in the first place.

The argument with Emily echoed in her mind. Considering the woman's attitude about naps, Gabrielle felt a twinge of guilt for having fallen asleep at all.

She explained it away, telling herself Emily had been born at a time when a woman believed her primary duty was seeing to the needs of her man. That Emily was a hard worker hadn't been lost on Gabrielle; weathered skin and gnarled knuckles were proof of a life spent toiling for love of her family.

How many times had her girlfriends scolded her for getting up at the crack of dawn to fix Drew's breakfast, for packing him a healthy lunch on the days he'd be too far from the house to eat at home? How many times had they advised her to "get that man trained and corralled now, before it's too late!"? And how many times had they told her to teach him to run the vacuum and cook a few meals, because "Honestly, Gabrielle, it's *his* house, too."

A lot of what they said made sense, and she'd listened to it all with an open mind. So when their lectures ended, and it was her turn to talk, why couldn't they see that she didn't pamper Drew because he demanded or expected it? She did it because she loved him, because she *enjoyed* taking care of him.

Too many times in her life, Gabrielle had thought she'd been born during the wrong century. If she'd come into womanhood when the pioneers first began traveling west, there wouldn't have been a need to explain why she liked "doing" for her man.

As things were, she felt out of step with today's women. Felt like a traitor, on one hand, for doting on her husband. Felt like a shrew, on the other, when she put her friends' advice to the test and asked for Drew's help around the house.

Maybe all these restless thoughts were the natural result of the fitful nap she'd just taken, a nap that had been interrupted by strange, unsettling dreams.

Dreams of a chestnut mare put down in her prime, and a heated argument between her and Drew. Were the two connected? Gabrielle didn't know.

Before marrying Drew, she'd lived in Bozeman, in an apartment that was one of six in a plain brown building. The name on her mailbox said, simply, Lafayette. But in her dream, her home had been a two-room apartment above Tildy's Dress Shop in Livingston, Montana. The number 513 was on the red brick mailbox beside her name: Gabrielle L. Cunningham.

But her middle name was Marie...

Red had never been one of her favorite colors, yet in another dream, she'd seen herself driving a little red car. The same kind of red as the one in the driveway this morning.

Lying on her side, Gabrielle stroked Drew's pillowcase. He'd only been gone a few hours, but oh, how she missed his calm, reassuring presence.

Once last night, she'd opened her eyes to find him staring at her. It had been startling to read immeasurable love—and undeniable fear—in his dark orbs. She understood the love; he was her husband, after all. But the fear? The fear troubled her deeply, because he'd always been the strong one. What reason did he have to be afraid?

Rolling onto her back, Gabrielle blinked up at the ceiling, glowing white-gold in the mid-morning sun. A tiny black spider had spun a web in the corner, and did a trampoline dance now in its center. She could have sworn she'd taken a broom to that the other day...

Rising, she went to the window and looked down at the front yard and the long gravel drive ribboning from the garage to Highway 540. There, in the raised flower beds flanking the front porch, her black-eyed Susans should have been in full bloom; instead, the bright pink blossoms of chrysanthemums bounced in the cool morning breeze.

Nothing that had happened since yesterday made a lick of sense. If she hadn't already had a wicked headache, the acknowledgment would surely have caused one.

One palm to her queasy stomach, Gabrielle walked woodenly to the bathroom and, without switching on the light, twisted the sink's cold-water knob. The steady trickle threading from the faucet made a hollow, gurgling sound deep in the old copper pipes as she filled her cupped hands with cool water.

A glance in the mirror told her the swelling of her temple had gone down some, but the bump was quickly becoming a blotchy, purple-blue bruise. Thing is, it was her only reminder of that nasty fall.

Suddenly, she got a picture of Triumph, fully saddled and ungroomed, grazing beside the barn. Annoyance-turned-frustration became contrition, despite the fact that Drew, after they'd returned from Doc Parker's office, had settled her in the family room with a mug of herbal tea and the TV's remote before heading out to see to the horses.

He'd grown up here on the Walking C, she reminded herself. Ranching was in his blood and had been for generations. Still, resisting the urge to check on the horses took more than a little effort. He'd never have let concern for her cause him to do less than his best. And his concern had been visible; he'd been as taut as the clothesline out back where she hung fresh-washed bedsheets to dry when the thermometer read forty degrees or more. If only there had been some way to comfort *him.*

After running a comb through her tangled curls, Gabrielle went back into the bedroom. As she perched on the edge of the mattress, her big toe traced the cream-colored swirls of leaves and petals on the blood-red Persian rug beside the bed.

She couldn't explain the low-burning anger that surged through her, but there it was, nonetheless. She gave the rug a kick, sending it scuttling across the hardwood planks like a hockey puck on skate-dinged ice. It landed with a quiet *thunk* against the intricately carved leg of the mahogany chifforobe. "Goal!" she said into her hand.

There was no humor in the muffled shout, because something told her she hadn't scored a point. Gabrielle had the sense she'd never be lady of the manor.

Eyes narrowed and teeth clamped tightly together, she got to her feet and put the rug back where it had been before her mini-tantrum. Where it *belonged,* was the sarcastic retort in her mind. Like everything else in the house, the rug had been put there—not a foot to the left or six inches up or down, but *right there*—by Drew's mother. And nothing had been moved—not the pewter candlesticks on the mantel or the hideous wrought-iron sconces on the foyer wall, since the day that woman walked out on her family.

The place reminded her of a murder scene, where the cops drew white chalk borders around everything. There was a purpose for these invisible lines, too: they ensured that nothing would change...ever.

The echo of an argument between her and Drew pinged

at the fringes of her memory, and it seemed to Gabrielle she'd once said pretty much exactly that. Had she dreamed it? Or had it been real? As she opened the window and inhaled the crisp, sun-kissed air, the fog began to lift.

"While you're in town today," she'd told him over breakfast that day, "I'm going to rearrange the living room. It needs a good, thorough cleaning, anyway, so why not—"

He'd shot her a dark expression that was a mixture of shock and warning. "Oh, no, you're not."

Giggling, she'd rolled her eyes, waved his comment away. "What? You think I'll pull a muscle or break a nail or something?"

She'd straightened in her chair upon realizing he hadn't taken her comment as a joke. "I declare, Drew, I love your old-fashioned cowboy ways. I mean, it's very flattering to know my man wants to protect me from all the evils of the world, but really, you have to stop treating me as if—"

The metal brads capping the feet of his chair squealed across the floor as he shoved away from the table. "Just leave things be, all right?" he'd said through clenched teeth. And in response to her wide-eyed surprise at the heat of his words, he'd blinked those big brown eyes of his and, standing, added, "The parlor is fine just the way it is."

"*Parlor,*" she'd mocked, half smiling, half frowning. "Nobody calls it a parlor anym—"

"Gabrielle," Drew interrupted, pointing a finger in her direction, "don't start with me."

She didn't understand his attitude, and said so. Said this was more a museum than a house. Said he'd turned it into a shrine to his mother. Said that was wrong and unfair and…

Midway through her angry discourse, she'd stopped talking. She might as well have been venting to that leftover piece of cold toast, because he'd tuned her out. He'd reached the back steps already, before realizing he'd forgotten his hat. Half in, half out of the house, he reached around the door and grabbed his Stetson from the peg on the wall. "I'll be back by lunchtime," he said to the floor. "You need anything in town?"

"No," she'd snapped, "unless they sell Get With It juice down at the Pantry Pride. You could buy about a gallon of the stuff, and drink it on the way home."

He jammed the hat onto his head. "See you at noon," he all but snarled before closing the door with a deliberate *click*.

He'd been angry enough to slam that door—narrowed eyes and a muscle bulging in his jaw told her that—so why hadn't he? Gabrielle wondered. *She* would have slammed it, good and hard.

Gabrielle concluded that he held his temper in check to keep others from knowing what he was really thinking; self-control was Drew's way of protecting himself from exposing his emotions.

But he hadn't hidden his feelings last night. Hadn't hidden them this morning, either. Why, there had been tears in his eyes when she caught him staring at her.

Just then, Gabrielle noticed a book on Drew's nightstand. Funny, she thought, flopping onto her stomach to reach for it, she didn't remember seeing it before.

The title was *Don't Blame God: Making Sense Out of Tragedy and Suffering,* an odd book for a rough-and-tumble cowboy to be reading, especially one who professed to believe in the Lord's might and power, the way Drew did.

Sitting cross-legged in the middle of the mattress, she held the book in her lap, where it automatically fell open to a section entitled "Losses in our Lives." One of two dog-eared pages, this one had been read dozens of times; she could tell by the way the ink had faded ever so slightly from having Drew's fingertip pass over the text again and again. A tiny smile brightened her mood slightly as she pictured the way he often used his forefinger to help keep his place while reading. "Helps me fix the words in my mind," he'd told her once.

He'd highlighted one sentence on this page: "No matter how desperate our need for help, 'my God shall supply all your need....'" She turned to the second bookmarked page and read through the bright yellow marker: "We are overcomers...."

She thought it odd that a man like Drew—strong, stoic, steady as the mighty Rockies—believed he had need for a self-help book. Something else seemed even more out of place than that. Her husband had a problem—a big one, if this book was any indicator—and he hadn't shared it with *her*.

Holding the open book against her chest, Gabrielle closed her eyes. The headache had dimmed considerably, and a whole new pain had taken its place, as she admitted the obvious.

He believed her too weak, too inexperienced, too flighty to help him cope with whatever trouble he was facing. And how was he to know that she *could* handle life's quandaries, when he'd never allowed her to show him what she was made of?

"It's your own fault," she muttered, because she'd thought it was "cute" before they were married, when, in addition to opening doors and pulling out chairs and helping her into her coat, he'd insisted on fighting all her battles, from reprimanding a mechanic for double-billing her to insisting on changing her oil *himself* from then on. She'd called him her knight in shining armor, her guardian, and Drew had lapped it up the way a pup slurps milk.

Didn't he understand that she felt supportive and protective toward him, too?

No. Probably not. Because of Drew's self-imposed resolve to buffer her from all the ills of the world, they'd never discussed *her* feelings.

None of that mattered now, she admitted sullenly, because she'd gone and hit her head, awakening his hero urges. If she brought the book to his attention now and demanded to know why he found it necessary to study it so thoroughly, he'd only repeat what Doc Parker had said about rest and calm.

This book in her hands confirmed what she'd begun to suspect while still on their honeymoon: his need to act as her human haven was so great that he'd likely never notice how much Gabrielle wanted—sometimes, at least—to do the same for him.

She'd hit her head before. Had had a concussion, too. But for the life of her, she didn't remember ''short-temperedness'' and ''frustration'' being on the list of symptoms.

Grinding her molars together, she considered throwing the paperback against the door. No sooner had the thought formed in her mind than a soft knocking sounded from the hall.

''Gabby?'' came a grating voice. ''You awake in there?''

She put the book back where she'd found it, just as Emily opened the door.

Smiling, Gabrielle said, ''I was just lying here debating whether to come downstairs and make myself some coffee or a cup of tea.''

Troy's wife patted a lock of cottony hair back into place. ''Nonsense. Ain't that why I'm here?''

She met the woman's eyes head-on. ''To be honest, I don't know why you're here.''

A flicker of heat glinted in the steely blue eyes, making Gabrielle wonder what cause the woman would have to be angry with her. But Emily was a tough old bird, and recovered quickly. Too quickly, as evidenced by the gruff tone to her voice. "'Course you know why I'm here." Pausing, she forced a stiff smile. "Drew didn't think y'oughta be by yourself, what with the concussion and all."

"Yes," came Gabrielle's dry reply, "my husband, the hero."

Either she hadn't heard Gabrielle's comment, or chose to ignore it. Emily started down the stairs. "What say I brew us up a pot of coffee?" she tossed over her shoulder.

If she didn't know better, Gabrielle would have said Emily had given birth to Drew, because they seemed to share the same tenacious attitudes toward hard work, the same conviction that theirs was the only way to get it done. If she'd already made up her mind to put on a pot of coffee, nothing Gabrielle could say would stop her, and so she didn't try.

The older woman reminded Gabrielle of a cyclone, blowing through life with the energy of two women half her age. Her quick wit and sharp tongue held others at bay, but these were traits Gabrielle respected and admired— traits that told her Emily considered her smart enough, hardy enough to be dealt with as an equal.

It dawned on her, as she had the thought, that under the right circumstances, Emily might be able to provide some answers.

"Set yourself down." Emily held one finger aloft to forestall any disagreement, and gave a satisfied smile when Gabrielle complied. "By the way, Doc Parker called while you were asleep," Emily announced as she grabbed the glass pot from the coffeemaker.

"He did?" Now *that* was perplexing, because the extension telephone was on her side of the bed, a mere six inches from her ear. "I didn't hear the phone ring."

Emily seemed to pretend to busy herself, filling the container with water, but not before Gabrielle noticed the way her hands froze for an instant as she held the pot under the faucet, and the guilty look that skittered across her face.

"I guess Drew must've turned the bell off," Emily suggested, "on account of he didn't want to take a chance it'd wake you."

Nodding, Gabrielle said, "Sounds like something Drew would do."

After spooning grounds into the coffeemaker's basket, Emily turned on the machine and joined Gabrielle at the kitchen table. "Save the pretense for Drew," she advised. "I don't much appreciate bein' involved in somebody else's marital disputes, either."

If she was making any effort to hide her annoyance, it didn't show. Emily's icy tone, underscored by her frosty stare, made it clear Gabrielle wasn't her favorite person.

"I like Drew. Always have. He's been more'n fair with my Troy, letting him keep working when other bosses would've made him retire years ago." She scraped a thumbnail over a nub in the tablecloth. "Ain't never been one to air my dirty laundry in public." When she met Gabrielle's eyes, it was to add, "It's old advice, but good advice." She aimed a hard blue-eyed stare in Gabrielle's direction. "You'd do well to take somethin' from it."

Any hopes she had of getting information out of Emily died before the old woman's veined hand punctuated her statement with a hard slap to the tabletop.

The coffeepot gurgled and sputtered—a fitting backdrop, Gabrielle thought, for the scolding she'd just taken. But if she thought Emily had said her piece, she was wrong.

"Loyalty ain't somethin' to be taken lightly. Somebody

does me a kindness, or does one to someone I care about, I stand by him, through thick or thin.'' Bushy white brows knitted in a frown. ''More'n I can say for *some* folks 'round here,'' she said, more to herself than to Gabrielle.

What loyalty had to do with anything, Gabrielle didn't know. But something told her she didn't want to ask Emily to explain herself. At least not while she was in *this* frame of mind. Smiling to herself, she remembered hearing something about the way menopause affected a woman's moods, making her short-fused and argumentative. If she didn't know better, she'd say that was Emily's problem. But Emily had likely gone through that phase of life decades ago.

''Well, ain't it just like a spoiled-rotten big-city gal,'' Emily muttered, getting to her feet, ''to take a bit of well-intended advice and turn it into a private joke.''

Gabrielle was about to admit she had no idea what Emily was rambling about when the woman put a mug on the table in front of her—and none too gently.

''Makes no sense,'' Emily grumbled, filling the mug with fresh-brewed coffee. ''No sense a'tall.'' She replaced the pot on its burner with a loud *clunk* and marched toward the living room, mumbling under her breath, ''I'll stay 'til Drew gets back, but I'd rather be whooped than set here passin' the time of day with the gal who walked out on that boy, left him to fend for himself for nearly a year.''

Heart racing and pulse pounding, Gabrielle started after her. *Walked out?* On Drew? she repeated mentally. *Left him to fend for himself for nearly a year?*

Bravado died the instant she admitted that if she asked Emily to explain, the woman would do it, gladly.

She headed back upstairs and quietly closed herself in their room—or, more accurately, Drew's *mother's* room—to come up with a plan.

She sat at the rolltop desk where Drew kept his checkbook and the calendar where he scribbled the ranch hands' schedules. It wasn't as pretty as the one she'd hung on the inside of the pantry door—the one that followed the life cycle of one wolf from birth to adulthood—but it was better than going back into the kitchen and risking Emily's wrath again.

Whose house was this, anyway? she grumbled silently. She remembered Drew's mother. Not Dora Cunningham's, certainly, but not Emily's, either.

The world seemed to come to a grinding, screeching halt as she noticed the year at the top of the calendar's first page. The digits would have been hard to ignore—big and bold and black as they were.

Instinct made her touch her temple, and the act reminded her that she'd hit her head only yesterday. *Hard enough to knock a year from your memory?* she wondered. Maybe it hadn't been such a good idea to talk Drew out of taking her to the emergency room, after all.

Flipping through the calendar, she read some of Drew's entries. An appointment with his banker. A church social. Chuck Carter's wedding. Ordinary, everyday things that shouldn't be a source of concern or alarm, except that she hadn't known about a single one.

It appeared that Drew had a whole secret life going on, behind her back. Her girlfriends' well-intended advice echoed in her head: *"Keep that man on a short leash, Gabrielle, or he'll get totally out of control in no time at all."*

Gabrielle grabbed the checkbook next, and paged through the ledger. She hadn't heard of half the companies he'd written checks to, and the other half, well, why should *they* make any sense when nothing else did? Who were these companies Drew had been doing business with?

She noticed, then, the fanciful script that spelled out Bozeman Savings and Loan. When she'd taken care of their bills last month, they'd been paid on checks from The Livingston Bank. Did Drew have two accounts? And if he did, why hadn't he bothered to mention it to her?

She could excuse the self-pity she'd allowed herself in those first frightening moments after waking up beside a dead rattlesnake out there on the wilderness trail. She could pardon the tears shed over her broken watch, and not knowing where Triumph had gone.

Maybe it had been acceptable, feeling sorry for herself when this lousy headache refused to go away. Might even have been permissible to aim some sympathy in her own direction when her mind started buzzing with more unanswered questions than a hive has bees.

But no more.

Headache or not, she aimed to get to the bottom of this mess. Before nightfall, she'd have some answers, or her name wasn't Gabrielle Marie Lafayette!

Cunningham, she corrected, as a renewed sense of self enveloped her.

Stacking the calendar and the checkbook one atop the other, she headed for the kitchen, where she poured every drop of the coffee Emily had made down the drain, telling herself that caffeine wasn't good for her unborn baby. Immediately, Gabrielle started a pot of decaf. When it finished brewing, she decided, she'd sit at the table with a big mug of it, waiting for Drew to come home.

You have a lot of explaining to do when you get here, she told him mentally. *A lot of explaining to do.*

Chapter Five

Drew guessed that the woman frowning past the chain lock was ninety, perhaps a hundred years old. She stood, bent at the shoulders and waist, trembling from the energy it took to wrap the arthritic fingers of one hand around the tarnished brass doorknob. How like Gabby to settle in with someone she believed needed to be looked after, he told himself.

"I'm sorry, Mr. Cunningham, but I make it a policy never to admit anyone to a tenant's apartment except in the case of an emergency."

She appeared to be so frail that a healthy breeze might blow her over. Still, despite the appearance, her voice was startlingly strong and self-assured, and he unconsciously subtracted a decade or so from his guess at her age.

He didn't want to upset the old gal, but he'd come here to gain entrance to Gabrielle's apartment. If her landlady wouldn't let him in the easy way, well, he'd do it the hard way if he had to. Because he wasn't leaving here without Gabrielle's wedding rings.

He'd try the easy way first. "This *is* an emergency of sorts, ma'am. There's been an accident, and Gabby——"

She slammed the door, startling him. He was considering stalking off, then kicking in the door to Gabrielle's apartment, when the sound of the chain lock sliding out of its track grabbed his attention. This time, the landlady opened the door wide.

One gnarled hand gripped the curve of her cane as she extended the other. "Blake is the name," she said, "Tildy Blake."

Gently, Drew grasped the frail fingertips.

But like her voice, Mrs. Blake's handshake was surprisingly firm. She withdrew her hand to fiddle with the necklace of keys dangling around her neck. "Gabrielle's all right? It's nothing serious, I hope."

Warmed by the genuine concern he read on her face, he smiled—in part to reassure the landlady, in part because he wasn't surprised that yet another person had grown fond of Gabrielle. "She was thrown from a horse, ended up with one mean concussion."

Mrs. Blake gasped. "Oh, how dreadful." Then she added, "Where *are* my manners?" Stepping aside, she gestured for Drew to enter her apartment. "Come in. I'll pour us some tea, and you'll tell me all about it."

Drew raised his chin a notch. "Thank you kindly, ma'am, but I don't have time for tea." He looked down the hall toward Gabrielle's apartment. "I promised not to be gone long. I've asked a friend to stay with her until I get back."

Smile fading slightly, he wondered how much more about Gabrielle's condition he'd be required to share before the woman handed over Gabrielle's key. He cleared his throat. "Gabby has amnesia," he said, his voice more stern than before, "so I need to get into her apartment and——"

The old woman frowned, adding to the many lines creasing her face. "Why do you call her 'Gabby'? I realize you weren't married long, but surely you were with her long enough to discover she doesn't like it."

She had him dead to rights, and he knew it.

Drew remembered the day after meeting Gabrielle, when he'd leaned over the table at that steak house in Bozeman and said, "Gabby, you're about the prettiest thing I've ever seen." Even in the dim light of the flickering candle, he'd seen her blush. Other women he'd dated would have giggled at his flattery or would have denied it, waved it away, forcing him to slather still more praise upon them.

Not Gabrielle! She'd ignored the compliment entirely, saying instead, "I realize that 'Gabby' is the perfect nickname for someone who talks as much as I do—especially someone whose parents named her 'Gabrielle'." She'd wrinkled her nose and shivered, as though a blast of icy wind had just shot down her back, adding, "Maybe that's why I've always hated it."

"So what do you want to be called?"

She shrugged. "Brie?"

He grinned. "You mean like the cheese?"

And she'd giggled. "On second thought, I guess Gabby is better than that!"

Regret coiled in his gut, because yes, he'd known from the start how much she disliked the nickname. But he'd convinced himself, since she'd never corrected him and *always* chided others who used it, that she considered him…special.

"Amnesia, you say?"

The woman's pointed question reminded him why he'd come here. Straightening his back, Drew spun the Stetson in front of him like a disconnected steering wheel. "Um, yes, ma'am.'' He cleared his throat. "The doctor doesn't think it's permanent, but…''

Raised by a father whose Number One rule was "What goes on under this roof is private,'' Drew would rather wrestle a coyote than tell this stranger that, until Gabrielle regained her full memory, he was under doctor's orders to do whatever it took to keep her calm.

"Mr. Cunningham, I'm sure it doesn't surprise you that in the months Gabrielle has lived in my building, we've become friends.'' One side of her mouth lifted in a wry smile. "That hardly makes me special, mind you. Everyone around here thinks the world of her.''

He glanced impatiently at his wristwatch. He had two more stops to make before returning to the Walking C, and had no time for this idle chitchat. Of course Tildy Blake and the rest of the shopkeepers on Decatur Street loved her. Person would need a heart of stone *not* to love her. But what did that have to do with anything? Drew wondered.

"She has said very little about your impending divorce,'' Mrs. Blake began, "except that it's nearing the final stages, but I gather it was one of the most difficult moves of her young life.''

He didn't hear anything after *divorce*. The word thudded into his head like a wrecking ball, and he clamped his teeth together, afraid he might just tell this nice li'l old lady to keep her nose out of his business.

"I didn't live to be ninety-two years old by being stupid, Mr. Cunningham.''

Frowning, Drew shook his head, wondering what he'd said to made her think he saw her as anything but intelligent.

"My grandmother taught me to sew, and, if I do say so myself,'' she said with a dainty shrug, "I got pretty good at it.''

Waiting was something he wasn't very good at. Why had the Lord made him so all-fired bad at it? Exhaling a sigh of frustration, he prayed for a moment of patience.

Mrs. Blake's sewing ability was very interesting, Drew thought in place of an "Amen" to his prayer, *but he needed that key.*

"I paid my way through college by sewing dresses and skirts for friends and relatives," she continued, grinning, "and when I graduated, I became a school teacher. Took a job at the high school in Helena." A wistful expression crossed her face. "That's where I met Mr. Blake, you see."

He could see was she was engrossed in her story. A comical thought jabbed at him: she probably wouldn't even notice if he grabbed the key; he could be in and out of Gabrielle's apartment before Mrs. B finished her life story.

"…and before retiring and opening this dress shop," he heard her say, "I spent twenty-five years teaching mathematics. So I'm very good at adding two and two, Mr. Cunningham, even at my advanced age."

Again, with the insinuation that he'd called her stupid. Women, he grumped, unconsciously fiddling with his wedding band, sure seemed to be good at twistin' a man's words.

The landlady held up one gnarled finger. "Gabrielle has amnesia—" another bent digit joined the first "—and you want admittance to her apartment." A grating chuckle punctuated her words. "I presume you're here to find her wedding rings—keep her from remembering that she left you, *why* she left you."

She seemed proud to have figured it out, all by herself. A mite too proud, Drew grumbled to himself. But there was no denying that she'd hit the proverbial nail on the head. He didn't have a moment to spare. Not if he wanted to get home by lunchtime, as he'd promised Gabrielle. And he'd disappointed her too often in the past, a situation he'd vowed to remedy whether she got her memory back or not.

The mere thought that Gabrielle might well leave if that happened caught in his throat, and he swallowed, hard. "So you'll let me into the apartment, then?"

"My dear, departed Charles had a bout of amnesia many years ago," she said.

She was stretching Drew's patience to the limit. He pinched the bridge of his nose. *Lord, give me strength.* If Mrs. Blake noticed, it didn't show.

"...I remember how confused he seemed," she said. "The strangest things would frustrate him." She shook her head, then popped a key from the chain around her neck. "The headaches would intensify whenever he got upset." Staring at the key, she whispered, "I've always wondered, is that what weakened him?" She straightened slightly. "A stroke took him, you see." Sighing, she pressed the key into Drew's hand.

Was that a tear in the corner of her eye? he wondered.

"I hope she'll be all right, Mr. Cunningham," she said. "And I hope this little scheme of yours is successful, because if you ask me, you young folks don't try nearly hard enough to make a go of your marriages. And that's a shame." Turning slowly, she said in a quavering little voice, "Just leave the key under the doormat when you're finished." And with that, she softly closed the door.

Drew stood there half a second, staring at the silver key resting on his palm, thinking about what Mrs. Blake had said. Although it hadn't been his idea to dissolve the marriage, he hadn't tried very hard to keep Gabrielle from leaving. Hadn't tried very hard to convince her to come back to him, either.

Should he blame false male pride? Stubbornness? More like flat-out stupidity, he admitted. During those achingly long months that Gabrielle had been gone, he'd started admitting at least *some* of the things she'd said the night she left were true.

Closing his fingers around the key, he headed down the hall. But none of that mattered now, because Gabrielle was home again, where she belonged—he jabbed the key into its lock—and if he had anything to say about it, home is where she'd stay.

The instant he shoved open the door, sunlight washed over him, and he stepped around the navy sofa that divided the entry from the living room. Beside it, an overstuffed chair, blanketed with a multicolored afghan, sat in front of a tan ottoman. On the tables, crafted of pale wood, fan-shaped arrangements of news magazines were balanced by white candles in brass holders of every shape and size. Gabrielle had painted the walls sea green...the color she'd suggested for the living room at the ranch house.

Rather than dwell on the fact that he'd said "no" to the change, Drew reminded himself why he'd come here and walked toward one of two doors straight ahead. The first door opened to the bathroom, which she'd decorated with seashell-shaped soaps and miniature wood carvings of ocean-loving birds. She had wanted to do their master bath over this way.

Swallowing his regret, Drew opened the other door. Here, too, sunlight poured through the window, spilling across the gray-carpeted floor and onto the twin bed against the far wall. Something pulled him toward the sunny warmth puddling near the plain wooden headboard, and Drew found himself crossing the room to sit on the edge of the mattress.

Hand resting on a plump, sun-warmed pillow, he thought of how, on most nights after she'd left, he had tossed and turned alone on their queen-size mattress. Had she found herself a new man? he'd wondered. And if she had, was she sharing her bed with *him* now?

The thought was enough, he believed, to stop his heart. Running a hand through his hair, he remembered how he'd "comfort" himself by thinking she hadn't been raised in a Christian household. The do's and don'ts spelled out in the Bible meant nothing to her. Besides, he'd told himself, she'd paid the sheriff to deliver a fat envelope filled with official court papers—documents that released her from the bonds of their marriage. She was free to seek love elsewhere if she chose to.

From the moment the possibility that she'd allow another man into her world had slithered into his mind, a tight ache had coiled around his heart, like a constrictor, until he was barely able to breathe. But now, seeing that she'd spent her nights in this small, single bed, the feeling dissolved like honey in hot tea. Unaware that he was smiling, Drew took a deep breath and looked around the room.

A tall bureau stood alone against one wall. In front of the window, a wicker rocker, and beside that, a table bearing a cherry-wood box and a hobnail lamp.

He crossed the room in three long strides and stared at the box. Gabrielle's father had given it to her for her eighteenth birthday. She'd told him so on the night she'd asked permission to move his mother's silver comb and brush aside to make room for it on their dresser. His heart thudded with guilt, because it had been the only change he'd allowed her to make in the ranch house.

He sat in the wicker chair, balanced the box on his knees and slowly opened the lid. A tiny ballerina danced a dainty pirouette to a tinkling music box tune, her performance reflected in a small oval mirror behind her. Gabrielle had laughed at Drew's initial reaction to the childish look of the gift, saying, "I guess Dad always saw me as six years old."

Even then, he'd understood her father's feelings, because full-grown, Gabrielle barely measured in at five feet tall. Her petite frame called out to everything manly in him, awakening primal urges to protect and shelter and defend her against the evils of life. Was that so wrong? he wondered, poking a clumsy finger into the tangle of beads and baubles in the jewelry box. Wasn't that part of a husband's duty, to provide and care for his wife?

His digging uncovered a small, pink velvet box—the one her engagement ring had come in. He picked it up, rolled it over in his palm a time or two. Again his heart ached, because the velvet was all but worn from its edges. For this to happen, he knew, Gabrielle would have had to open and close it, possibly hundreds of times. His heart throbbed at this first real awareness that she'd regretted the end of their marriage, too.

He pried open the lid, wincing when it creaked.

It had creaked that day on the trail, too. Once she'd gotten a gander at what lay nestled in the white satin lining, she'd met his gaze, and the love he saw sparkling in her tear-filled eyes had put the glint of that diamond to shame.

Behind the diamond, she'd tucked the plain gold band he'd slipped onto her delicate finger on their wedding day. It was *that* ring more than anything else that reminded him yet again why he'd come here.

His plan was simple: put the rings in a not-too-obvious spot, so it would appear she'd taken them off to do the dishes or scrub the sink.

Drew held the box for a moment, aware of the sudden silence that descended upon the room. Running a calloused hand across the cool, smooth wood, he heaved a heavy sigh, then put the box back where he'd found it.

He hadn't realized that his eyes were brimming with tears until one tracked slowly down his cheek. Angrily, he swiped at it with the back of a hand and stood abruptly, setting the chair rocking so hard that it hit the wall with a quiet *thud-thud-thud*.

As Drew slid the rings into his pocket, he remembered that Troy had agreed to meet him at the dealership at ten o'clock. And the Good Lord willing, he'd have the car sold quickly. In the past, it wouldn't have seemed important, getting back to the ranch by noon. But he'd promised Gabrielle.

On his way back to the front door, Drew caught sight of the tiny kitchen, where black and white tiles gleamed in the bright morning sunlight. She'd softened the hard look of wrought-iron hardware on white cabinets with splashes of color—red ceramic apples here, lush green plants there—and a bright blue rug in front of the sink.

The same one she'd bought on a shopping trip to Bozeman? The one he wouldn't let her put down to replace the rag rug his mother kept in front of *her* sink?

He was about to blast himself for the mule-headed behavior that had driven her away when he noticed the blinking red light of the answering machine.

He'd had the foresight to call Gabrielle's boss at the bank. He had also given clear instructions to Emily and the ranch hands: she was not to be told about the separation or the shouting match that had led to it. She wasn't to be told about the amnesia, either. "Doctor's orders," he'd told them all. Which was only partly true. Doc Parker *had* warned him to keep Gabrielle's environment as restful as possible. But Drew wasn't taking any chances where his future with Gabrielle was concerned.

He stared hard at the blinking red light. It wasn't any of his business, really, who'd left messages in the few days she'd been gone. But what if, when she didn't respond, the callers tracked her down at the Walking C? And what if, when they did, one of them reminded her?

Heart hammering, he depressed the Play button and, arms crossed over his chest, waited for the tape to rewind. Then Drew held his breath and listened.

The print she'd ordered at a decorating party had arrived. "The balance is $49.95," said the chipper voice of the hostess. "Let me know when to deliver," she added, and left her number.

Gabrielle's dry cleaning was ready, and the photographs she'd dropped off six months ago were going to be destroyed if she didn't pick them up by end of business, today.

He thought about hitting the Save button. But if he picked up the photographs and the dry cleaning, and paid for the picture, there'd be no need to store the messages in the answering machine's memory.

No need for Gabrielle to come back here.

A glance at the cheery apple-faced clock above the stove told Drew it wasn't likely he'd make it home in time for lunch. Not unless he hotfooted it to get everything done before meeting Troy at the car dealership.

Locking the apartment door behind him, he raced down the hall so quickly that he completely forgot to stop and put the key under Mrs. Blake's doormat.

From the looks of things, she'd been sitting there, crying, for hours. Drew took one look at her red-eyed, puffy face and dropped the packages on the floor. "Gabby—Gabrielle," he sputtered, kneeling beside her at the table. "Sweetie, what's wrong?" He combed the bangs from her forehead. "Is the headache worse?"

She drummed a forefinger on the checkbook. ''I want to know what's going on, Drew.''

The only other time he'd heard her sound like that had been on the night she'd left. The harsh, angry tone cut through him like a hot knife through butter. ''Honey,'' he repeated, drawing her into a hug, ''calm down. We'll—''

''Don't 'honey' *me,* Drew Cunningham.'' She turned in the chair to face him, and, hands on his shoulders, said, ''I realized something this morning. Why it took me this long, I don't know.''

Icy fear tracked through his veins, making his heart beat double-time. Teeth clamped together, he closed his eyes and tried to concentrate on the fact that she was kneading his shoulders, that her eyes, though bloodshot from crying, blazed with love.

At least, he hoped it was love.

Drew braced himself for the inevitable. ''What did you figure out?'' he asked in a coarse whisper.

''This bump on the head gave me a whopping head-ache—''

'''Course it did.''

''And a case of temporary amnesia. I called Doc Parker while you were gone, and he confirmed it.''

He wondered if she could hear his heart knocking against his ribs, because it sure was beating hard enough for that. ''You talked to him? What did he say?''

''That it could pass in a day or two, or it could last forever,'' she said matter-of-factly. Gabrielle picked up the checkbook, thumped it against the calendar. ''So I want you to tell me what's been going on. Bring me up to speed.'' She held up one hand, traffic-cop style, to silence him. ''Don't tell me I need to stay calm. I know all about how my pulse rate can affect the head injury.'' Linking her fingers behind his neck, she smiled slightly and added,

"Don't you think it'd be a lot easier for me to relax if you help me remember the things I've forgotten?"

Drew swallowed, torn between giving her what she'd asked for and protecting her from that very thing. "Okay. All right," he began, getting to his feet. "But what say we have a bite to eat, first. I'm starving." He headed for the refrigerator, praying as he went that God would hear his plea, and let Gabrielle cooperate. It was for her own good, after all.

He was poking around in the crisper drawer when he heard her coming toward him.

Grabbing his elbow, she pulled him back and stood in his place. "I'll make us sandwiches," she said, her voice muffled slightly by the insulated interior of the refrigerator. Plate of leftover ham in one hand, jar of mustard and the bread package's twist-tie in the other, she elbowed the door shut. "Well, go on," she added, dumping her load on the counter, "start talking."

"Gab—" He'd almost said Gabby again, but caught himself. "Let me do that," he said instead, muscling his way into her spot. Since common sense wasn't working, he tried joking: "I'm a pretty smart guy, y'know. I can talk and fix sandwiches at the same time."

Hands on her hips, she shook her head. "Drew, I declare, you can be the most exasperating man. Your friend *Emily* in there," she snarled, pointing toward the living room, "has made it very clear what she thinks of the way I take care of you. If she were to come in here now and catch me sitting on my behind while you're making sandwiches..."

"What are you talking about?"

"She started going on about how I left you for no good reason, how I neglected you for nearly a year and—"

She stopped talking so suddenly that Drew turned to see why, and when he did, he saw her grimace as she pressed the heels of both palms into her temples. Then, as though in slow motion, she began crumpling to the floor.

When he reached out to catch her, the butter knife clattered to the tiles, along with the jar of mustard, which shattered and splattered its contents across his boots.

"Emily!" he bellowed, voice quaking with worry. "Emily, get in here!"

She appeared immediately, as if she'd been standing in the hall, listening. No matter. Drew would get to the bottom of what Gabrielle told him later, when things settled down. *Please God,* he prayed, *let them settle down.*

"Oh, good grief," the woman griped when she caught sight of Gabrielle, limp in Drew's arms. "What's she tryin' to pull this time?"

"Emily," he growled, ignoring her sarcastic criticism, "there's no time to call an ambulance. I'm heading for the hospital in Bozeman." He grabbed his jacket from the peg beside the door and wrapped it around Gabrielle. And, jamming his hat on his head, he flung open the door, not even noticing that the lock had put a dent in the wall. "Call Doc Parker," he ordered. "Tell him to meet me there." When she didn't immediately respond, he shouted, "Now!"

That got her moving, and Drew sent a silent prayer of thanks heavenward as he belted his unconscious wife into the pickup. The truck started on the first crank, and he sent another grateful prayer skyward. He hit the gas pedal so hard, the truck tires spewed gravel in a wide, gritty arch.

Turning on the flashers and the headlights, he sped down the drive, the speedometer soon registering 50 miles an hour. *Easy, man,* he warned himself. *You won't do her any good if you broadside a semi turning onto the highway.*

Gripping the steering wheel tightly, Drew forced himself to slow down. He could make like Mario Andretti once he hit the asphalt.

He prayed for a cop to stop him, so they'd have a police escort to the hospital.

Prayed for light traffic.

Prayed the threatening storm clouds held off, at least until he had her safe inside the emergency room, because one thing he didn't need between here and Bozeman was wet pavement.

Drew glanced at her, limp, eyes closed, head bobbing slightly, as the pickup hurtled down the road. He forced himself to look away, through the windshield, at the double yellow lines splitting the highway in half, and prayed for green lights all the way.

Tears stung his eyes, blurring his vision, and he blinked them away.

Just let her be okay, Lord, he added to his list. *Even if it means I'll lose her, let her be okay.*

Smiling stiffly, Dr. Adams snapped shut the aluminum cover on Gabrielle's chart. Tucking it into the plastic folder attached to the footboard of her bed, he nodded for Drew to follow him.

She seemed to be resting comfortably, yet Drew hesitated, not wanting to leave her.

"She'll be fine," the neurologist said, holding the door.

Drew wanted all the details about Gabrielle's condition, so he stepped into the hall.

Adams's sneakered feet squeaked across the polished linoleum as he headed for the nearest vending machine. "Coffee?" he asked, dropping coins into the slot.

The only thing Drew wanted was information about his wife's condition, and he said so.

Adams punched the Black button, and crossed both arms over his chest. "Well, Mr. Cunningham, it's like this—" Grabbing the cup, he walked toward the small waiting room across the way. "The CAT scan shows definite evidence of TBI." He blew a stream of air over the top of his coffee.

"TBI?"

"Traumatic brain injury. Your wife suffered a blow to her temporal lobe—a hemorrhagic contusion, to be exact. The bruise to her brain is noticeable, but not severe, so we're lucky on that score."

He slumped onto the seat of a bright blue plastic chair and hooked his feet around its narrow chromed legs. "She didn't suffer a skull fracture, and there is no evidence of hypoxia." He took a sip of the coffee. "Miss Rosie's posies!" he exclaimed, grimacing. "My daughter's mud pies taste better than this stuff!"

Drew sat beside him in a red plastic chair. "What's—what's hypoxia?"

"Oh. Sorry." He ran a hand through graying blond hair and said around a slanted grin, "I've been on duty going on twenty-eight hours now. If I forget to speak English again, gimme a punch on the arm, will ya?"

Maybe under other circumstances, Drew would have found the comment comical. Not today. "Happy to oblige," he said, scooting his chair around to face Adams's.

The doctor's brows rose slowly. At the same time, a good-natured smile broadened his face. "Touché, Mr. Cunningham. Touché." After another swallow of the coffee, he said, "Hypoxia is a lack of oxygen. Doesn't appear the fall caused—" He chuckled. "Let's just say your wife passed all the tests. When I asked her to state the standard 'date, time, name and address information, she answered without a moment's hesitation.

"She's fully able to follow instructions, both verbal and written, so there's no damage to any of the twelve cranial nerves. There were no abnormal movements, so that rules out muscle damage. And her reflexes and sensory functions, balance and coordination all appear normal.''

Adams sighed and, frowning, he leaned forward slightly. ''Aside from the memory loss, have you detected anything unusual?''

Drew blinked. Until the accident, he hadn't spent more than a few minutes with Gabrielle in nine long months. Would he know ''unusual'' if he saw it? ''I, ah, I don't think so.''

He remembered another thing his father always said: *''What goes on under this roof stays under this roof.''* In Drew's experience, it had been more than a sensible rule. It was good advice. He didn't like the idea of talking about the particulars of his life with Gabrielle—especially painful details—but if the information would help Gabrielle…

''Gabrielle and I were separated,'' he began, staring at the floor. ''The concussion, the amnesia…'' He heaved a sigh. ''She's forgotten that she left me.''

''I see,'' Adams said. ''How long ago?''

Still looking down, he cleared his throat. ''Just over nine months.'' Drew shrugged. ''But she came back home every Saturday to ride Triumph, the horse that threw her.''

''I see,'' the doctor repeated.

From the corner of his eye, Drew could see him, sitting there squinting at the black liquid in his cup as if he thought he could find the answer to Gabrielle's amnesia problem there in its dark-shimmering surface.

''Well,'' he said after a while, ''in addition to the CAT scan and the EEG, I ordered an MRI, just to be safe. In all likelihood, the amnesia is temporary.''

Leaning back in the chair, he drained the paper cup. ''Tell me exactly what you observed the afternoon of the fall.'' He crumpled the cup and tossed it into a trash can in the corner.

As Adams gave the "attentive doctor" nod, Drew repeated what he'd told Doc Parker about Gabrielle's condition that day. "If it hadn't been for the bump on her head and dilated pupils," he finished, "I wouldn't have noticed anything out of the ordinary...at first."

The neurologist sat up straight. "At first? What do you mean?"

"Well," Drew explained, "after standing there a while, her face got more pale, and the color of her lips seemed to fade. She couldn't walk a straight line, and complained of a headache." He paused, swallowed. "And Gabrielle was never one to complain."

Adams got to his feet. "I haven't been around as long as Doc Parker," he said, grinning, "but I think I can safely say your wife is on the mend."

Drew stood, too. "But what about the amnesia? Is there any way to tell if it's short-term? Or will she—"

The doctor pocketed both hands and stared at the yellow arrow on the floor that directed visitors to the rest rooms. "For all our sophisticated tests and years of diagnostic training," he began, meeting Drew's eyes, "we still don't know much about amnesia. We know enough to classify your wife's condition as retrograde amnesia, which doesn't really explain a blessed thing, if you want my honest opinion."

"Well, that's helpful."

Pulling a stethoscope from one deep pocket, he draped it around his neck. "I'm with Doc Parker when he says folks deserve to hear the truth, even when it isn't pretty. Trouble is, we don't know what the truth *is* in cases like your wife's."

In cases like your wife's, Drew repeated silently. It had an ominous echo to it that made his stomach churn.

"I've seen similar cases—couple dozen of them, matter

of fact. Usually, a few months down the road, we discover the accident was the vehicle that gave the patient permission to block or repress memories associated with a traumatic event."

He hesitated, as if to give Drew time to admit to himself that for Gabrielle the separation could be that traumatic event.

So it was possible that Gabrielle would never remember the year she'd lost. Easy as that would make life for *him,* Drew couldn't help but wonder what kind of an effect it would have on Gabrielle. He'd already seen what trying to figure things out had done to her. The mental image of her pained expression as she slumped to the floor, checkbook and calendar in hand, flashed through his mind.

"Let's say she never gets her memory back," Drew began. "It wouldn't be right, wouldn't be fair, to keep things from her—" he met the doctor's eyes "—would it?"

"I'm not a psychiatrist, Mr. Cunningham, but your wife seemed mentally stable to me. More than likely, she'll start putting two and two together on her own."

He adjusted the pens in his pocket protector. "Off the record, if she were my wife, I'd let her handle this as she sees fit. You're a smart guy. You'll know when to intervene and when to back off."

"If I did," Drew blurted, "we probably wouldn't be separated."

"Well, you're together now. She came back for a reason."

Drew frowned. "But—but shouldn't she be told about the things that have happened during the months she's forgotten?"

Adams shook his head. "Ever heard that old joke, the one where the little boy says, 'Dad, where did I come from?' So the dad starts stammering and stuttering and sweating bullets while he goes through this long, drawn-out explanation of reproductive biology. And afterward, the kid scratches his head, looking all confused and worried and scared, and he goes, 'B-but *Dad*, Jimmy is from Chicago. All I wanna know is...where did *I* come from?'"

Drew was in no mood for humor, and it must have been apparent in his expression, because Adams raised his shoulders and held out both hands. "If she asks a question, she's probably ready for the answer." He pointed a cautioning finger and added, "Just don't make the mistake that boy's father made, and dole out more than she asks for."

Adams turned as if to leave, then faced Drew again. He ran a hand over his stubbled chin. "Anything specific you can think of that might have traumatized your wife?"

Drew didn't have to ask *physically or psychologically?*, because he knew the answer to that one. "Other than the separation, you mean?"

Adams nodded.

The car had upset her a great deal, but Molly's death was what sent her over the edge. "Recently?"

"Not necessarily. Could be something that happened some time ago, something she hasn't been emotionally willing or able to cope with. Like the death of a loved one."

Or an impending divorce? Drew said nothing.

Shrugging again, Adams said, "Well, I'd better get back to business—" he pointed to Gabrielle's nurse "—before I'm reported to the hospital administrator." He started down the hall, then stopped in his tracks. "Cheer up. Mrs. Cunningham is young and healthy. No reason to expect anything but a good outcome."

Mrs. Cunningham. Much as he loved the sound of it, Drew couldn't help but wonder how much longer it would be her official name. "Thanks, Doc."

"Get some sleep. You'll need to be well-rested to take

care of your wife after I release her in the morning.'' Then he disappeared around a corner.

Hands still deep in his jeans pockets, Drew headed back to Gabrielle's room. Dr. Adams wanted her to stay overnight ''for observation,'' and the only available space had been a private room. Which was fine with Drew. *Because if anybody was going to do any observing,* he'd thought at the time, *it's gonna be me.*

While the x-ray technician had Gabrielle downstairs for tests, Drew had used the pay phone to bring Troy up to date on her condition. He also made it clear he'd be spending the night. The nurse had strongly advised against that, but Adams had outranked her. ''There's an extra blanket in the closet marked Staff Only,'' he'd stated, ignoring her indignation. ''Anybody gives you any lip, tell 'em to come see me.''

No one seemed to mind Drew's presence, least of all the nurse. Why would she mind, when Drew had made it clear *he* wanted to do all the little things that made Gabrielle comfortable?

The hospital had quieted considerably now that visiting hours were over. He shut Gabrielle's door, closed the curtains and, after turning down the lights, settled himself in the high-backed orange Naugahyde chair beside her bed to watch her sleep.

He'd reprimanded Adams and the nurse for not giving Gabrielle something for her headache.

''She's here for observation,'' was the doctor's straightforward response. ''What's to observe if she's drugged?''

But while Drew had been in the middle of agreeing, he had overheard Adams instruct the nurse to give Gabrielle some acetaminophen for the pain. The medication seemed to have done the job, at least well enough so that she could rest.

Drew was uncomfortable, but he didn't mind. And during the twilight hours that ticked silently by, he made a decision: the moment the doctors gave him the go-ahead, he was going to tell Gabrielle everything, including the reasons she'd listed for leaving him that night. She'd figured most of it out on her own, anyway—and look what the lack of information did to her, he acknowledged, remembering again that scene in the kitchen.

He recalled Adams's quote from Doc Parker: *"Folks have a right to hear the truth, even when it isn't pretty."*

He looked at her. *She* was pretty. The most beautiful thing that had ever happened to him. If hearing the truth drove her away again, well, his heart would break, that's what.

But this isn't about you, he admitted. *It's about Gabrielle.*

He inhaled a shuddering breath. "Lord," he whispered, "give me strength."

Chapter Six

She bristled when the nurse forced her to ride a wheelchair to the hospital's entrance, and frowned when Drew insisted on lifting her into the pickup. "Sometimes I wish I were six feet tall and two hundred pounds," Gabrielle grumbled, as he started the truck.

"Only sometimes?" Drew asked, chuckling.

Grinning, she slid across the bench seat and hugged his biceps. "Most of the time, I have to admit, I like the way I feel—all petite and protected when you wrap your big strong arms around me."

He was about to admit that she felt pretty good in his arms, too, when she patted his chest.

"What's this?" she asked, digging in his pocket.

Between the mad rush to the hospital and worrying about her condition, he'd completely forgotten about the rings. How was he going to explain *that?* "Buckle your seat belt, Gabrielle. We're coming up on the Interstate, and you know people drive like maniacs."

She opened the box. Eyes wide, hands fluttering, gasping, she all but shouted, "My rings!" Tossing the box aside, she slid them onto her finger. "Where did you find them?"

He had to think fast. "I, ah, I found them on the windowsill above the kitchen sink and—"

"When?"

She'd extended her hand—to catch a sunbeam in the diamond's facets, Drew supposed. "Um, this morning. Before I went into town."

Turning slightly, she looked into his face. "Why didn't you tell me? You knew I'd been turning the house upside down, looking for them." She frowned a bit. "You could have spared me the—"

"I noticed the diamond was loose," he interrupted. He would deal with his guilt later. His job right now was to see to it she remained calm, happy. "And since I was going to be in town, anyway, I figured I'd have the jeweler tighten it."

Brow furrowed, she sat back, the thumb of her right hand positioning the rings on her finger.

"Seat belt, Gabrielle." He hoped the reminder would distract her from whatever suspicious thoughts were whirling around in that head of hers.

After a moment's hesitation, she buckled the seat belt, then hugged his arm again. "It was a very sweet and thoughtful surprise." She kissed his cheek. "I love you, Drew."

"Love you, too," he said quietly, knowing even as he said it that she deserved more, deserved better than the likes of him. Because he knew as he sat there, staring through the windshield, feeling the warmth of her little body pressed tightly against his side, that he had neither the desire nor the courage to tempt fate. His decision to "'fess up" died right there, like the groundhog that never made it across the busy stretch of highway.

"Hungry?" he asked.

"Matter of fact," she said, resting her head on his shoulder, "I'm starved. Do you know what they brought me for breakfast? A box of corn flakes and an itty-bitty carton of warm milk." Grabbing her throat, she groaned. "I don't like milk even when it's ice cold, and—"

"And you like corn flakes even less," he finished, chuckling. "There's a truck stop just ahead. What say we stop."

"No," she said firmly. "Let's just go home, okay? We have eggs and ham in the fridge."

"All right, but only on one condition."

"That I'll let you do the cooking, *again*."

"Again?" he said, laughing now. "I can probably count on one hand the number of times I've made a meal since..." Dare he say it? Would it jog a memory? *Lord,* he prayed, *give me strength to say it.* "Since we got married."

"Wow," Gabrielle said, giggling. "You haven't dirtied the stove in a whopping two months." Counting on her fingers, she squinted. "Let's see, that's sixty days, times three meals a day."

Should he point out to her they'd been together nine months when she left him? "Don't tax your brain, sweetheart," he said. "You've just suffered a concussion. Besides," he added, forcing a grin, "I know how much you hate math."

"Everyone knows I hate math," she said distractedly. Then she added, "One hundred and eighty, minus a couple dozen lunches and dinners in town. Say," she said, squeezing his thigh, "the girls are right. You *are* spoiled!"

"The girls? What girls?"

Gabrielle gave a dainty shrug. "Carol and Donna. Suzie, too," she told him. "They think I should make you do more of the housework. That I shouldn't get up with you every day, or fix your breakfast, or—''

He feigned a tough-guy face. ''You're to stop seein' those trouble-makin' females, startin' now,'' he growled. ''You know how us cowboys keep our women chained to the stove.''

''Barefoot and pregnant, so I've heard.'' Her musical laughter filled the cab. ''Oh, Drew,'' she sighed, ''I hope it worked.''

''You hope what worked?''

''I'm not crazy about the ball-and-chain,'' she said, ''but if that'll get me the babies I've been dreaming about...''

He'd socialized his fair share before meeting her, and a few of the gals he'd dated had said they wouldn't mind giving him a child. Their professions had always sounded too rehearsed, making him assume they hadn't meant a word of it. But right from the start, he'd sensed that Gabrielle had been serious.

''Well, I guess I'll just have to learn to put up with the clanking and the rattling.''

Lord, but he loved her. ''You're a nut, do you know that?''

After kissing his cheek again, she whispered into his ear, ''Which is only one of the reasons you're madly in love with me.''

If he had the power to freeze this moment in time, Drew would do it. Because this was the way things had been before...

Before the hundred acts of stubborn selfishness that drove her away. Before the barn, the rifle, Molly. It all flashed through his mind, and he blinked to clear it from memory. In place of the hot shame of that moment, there was cold fear. Because she'd already asked about Molly.

How long before she put *all* the puzzle pieces in place, and ended up with a picture of what happened that night?

You're a coward, Cunningham.

Not an easy admission for a man who'd braved winter's fiercest storms to rescue stray cattle. Not a comfortable confession for someone who'd put himself between a rattlesnake and a newborn foal. As a rancher, he'd braved nature and myriad other events without a moment's thought. His courage had never come into question.

Until now.

But ugly as the word sounded—even in the privacy of his own mind—Drew would rather have everyone in Montana know he was a yellow-belly than risk losing Gabrielle. Because without her, nothing else mattered. Not the ranch that had been in the Cunningham family for generations. Not his prize-winning stallions. Not even his mother's return.

Gabrielle fiddled with her rings. "They just don't *feel* right," she said. "It's as if I've lost weight or something." She leaned forward and looked into his eyes. "The jeweler didn't enlarge them by mistake, did he?"

"If he did, he didn't charge me for it," Drew said, knowing as he said it that he'd better be careful, because he was getting awfully good at lying.

He had solved the problem about the rings easily enough. And the car dilemma had been simpler still. A two-thousand dollar loss was a small price to pay for keeping the vehicle out of her sight—and his.

Molly was another matter entirely. Soon, Gabrielle would remember that Molly had been *her* horse, bought and paid for with her bank teller's salary. She'd lit up like a fireworks display the day he'd backed her filly into the stall beside Triumph's.

"No more rented spaces for you, sweetie," she'd cooed,

ruffling the horse's mane, "and no more strangers taking care of you. You have a family and a real home now!"

If he had to, he'd search the whole county, scour all of Montana, to locate a horse that looked like Molly. Shouldn't be hard, he thought. The horse was a horse, after all.

But guilt drummed inside him. He admitted to himself that Molly was far more...to Gabrielle.

All the way home, she chattered as if they'd never discussed painting the interior of the ranch house, as though they hadn't talked about new living room furniture, or turning his mother's sewing room into a nursery for the babies they'd have together.

And he let her talk; he was *glad* to let her talk.

Because she'd been right when she accused him of turning the house into a memorial for his runaway mother. And while he couldn't deny that a spark of hope still glowed— maybe, someday, his mother would come back—it wasn't fair to make Gabrielle pay the price for the woman's desertion.

If and when his mother returned, Drew decided, it would be to Gabrielle's house, not hers. Because it had been Gabrielle who'd turned the place into a home, lighting up every room with her loving smile and her stubborn determination to make him happy.

He'd been blind not to have seen it before.

And with the recognition came responsibility. Responsibility *to Gabrielle*. He'd never shirked his duties before, and didn't intend to start now.

Even if it meant he'd be forever branded a coward.

Every day that he stayed away from the fields, the barn, the trails, the list of things he'd left undone grew longer. In the past, merely acknowledging such a thing would have driven Drew to distraction. And yet, he didn't mind at all, once they'd returned from the hospital, when they spent the remainder of the day talking and cuddling and watching old movies on television.

They ate popcorn instead of a sensible lunch, and washed it down with hot chocolate made from a mix. For supper, he pulled a pepperoni-and-mushroom pizza out of the freezer, and they ate it on paper plates, by candlelight.

During the commercials between evening game shows, she changed into a long cotton nightgown, and he replaced his flannel shirt and jeans with well-worn sweats. While the TV contestants vied for a grab at the wheel, Drew and Gabrielle—side by side on the couch, white-socked feet in a tangle on the coffee table—thumb-wrestled until he held up his hands and dubbed her Short-Digit Champion of Montana.

Before Gabrielle's accident, if anyone had asked him whether a grown man could change, he would've scoffed and said, "Why *should* he, if there's nothing wrong with him?" If the question were posed now, his response would be dead in the water, because there he sat, living proof that even a stubborn, know-it-all cowboy like himself could change—provided the stakes were high enough.

And right now, they were about as high as they could get.

Later, once he'd made his nightly rounds, locking windows and doors, snapping draperies shut, he scooped her into his arms and carried her upstairs.

"You're gonna pay for this," she teased, when he laid her gently on their bed.

He'd pay for a lot of things since the day before yesterday, when she had come back to him.

She scrambled from the mattress and dashed into the bathroom, giggling. "I have a surprise for you."

"Part of the payback?" he asked, tossing his sweats onto the overstuffed chaise longue across the room.

Her voice, muffled by the closed door, was barely audible. "No. Fortunately for you."

One of the reasons he'd been drawn to her in the first place had been her sense of humor. No matter what else might be going on around them, Gabrielle had the power to make him laugh, see the lighter, brighter side of things.

Like the time when a computer error caused all their checks to bounce. She'd refused to tell him why there was a pillow under one arm and a blanket under the other. But he figured it out the moment she stretched out on that fancy velvet sofa in the bank lobby. "Your mistake means there's no electricity at our house," she told the befuddled manager. Shrugging and smiling, she added, "No hard feelings, but until you straighten things out with the power company, we're going to stay right here, where it's nice and warm."

Half an hour later, the mistake was corrected.

On April Fool's Day, she'd put sugar in the saltshaker and salt in the sugar bowl. "I declare, Gabby," he'd said, rubbing a paper napkin across his tongue, "you're nothing but a juvenile delinquent."

"At my age, I guess that'd make me a *delinquent* delinquent," she'd said, handing him a mug of cold milk to wash the salt from his mouth.

On Valentine's Day, she'd used colored markers to draw a six-foot-tall tiger—with his toe caught in a mousetrap— inside a big red heart. "In my heart, you're the cat's *meow!*" said the bold black letters across the bottom.

She'd left him a few days after Valentine's Day.

Drew reminded himself that Gabrielle had a talent for making him feel like a man, too. Riding wild mustangs and roping frantic cattle proved he had the brawn for the rancher's life—but he'd seen trained chimps do all that for laughs at a rodeo. It didn't make a man of him.

He'd been running the Walking C, almost single-handedly, from the time he turned sixteen, which showed he had brains. But anyone with a calculator could add up columns in a ledger.

He'd considered sharing his days, and his nights, with other women, but not one had made him want to share *himself.* Not one had what it would take to share *her* life with cows and horses and land that stretched as far as the eye could see.

Gabrielle had what it took. And she'd proved it, from the moment he first showed her the ranch, by making suggestions and offering opinions that would make his life easier.

The time a bucking stallion's kick nearly cracked his knee, she'd chopped a wagon load of wood, and built a roaring fire in the potbellied stove in the living room.

When the length of barbed wire he'd been stretching from fence post to fence post snapped and carved up his forearm, she'd finished the job herself, using a crowbar as a makeshift come-along.

With that taut-muscled, diminutive body, Gabrielle was as strong as she was bullheaded. And was she bullheaded! Drew thought, smiling to himself. Though she'd lived a transient existence in one big city after another, she had taken to life on the ranch better than some women who'd been born to it. She'd have done more around the Walking C, plenty more, if he had let her.

Why hadn't he let her? he wondered, frowning at the ceiling. Chivalry? Protectiveness? Male pride?

He shook his head, because while he'd given the matter a lot of thought in the months since she'd left him, Drew didn't understand it any better today than he had the night she'd walked out.

"You've made it perfectly clear that you don't think of me as your partner," she'd accused.

Closing his eyes, he tried to blot out the image of her standing there at the front door—suitcases at her feet, purse slung over her shoulder, lower lip trembling—as she said, "I feel like an intruder here, Drew. If you don't want to share your life with me, just say so, and I'll be gone like that—" She'd snapped her fingers, as if that would get his attention.

But he'd never seen her this way before, and having had no sisters, no mother or grandmother to teach him what was normal womanly behavior and what was not, Drew had no way of knowing how to react, or what to say.

And so he'd stood there, staring dumbly at the floor...and she'd read his silence to mean he didn't want to share his life with her.

Nothing could have been further from the truth.

He should have gone after her.

Should have said something, before she managed to load her suitcases into the car, before she headed down the driveway—and out of his life.

Stubbornness, stupidity, fear—something had held him there, speechless, had kept him from following her that night.

If he had told her what she wanted—what she *deserved*—to hear, things might've turned out very differently. If he could have found it in himself to admit she was right, at least about some of the things she'd said...

Could've, would've, should've, he thought now, grimacing. *Fat lot of good all that does me.*

The only place he'd found any consolation since she'd

been gone was the Good Book. That, and the rumpled copy of *Don't Blame God* that the pastor had given him.

Solace was fine, but he learned only too quickly that it couldn't replace solutions. He knew what he should do, knew what he should say, and kept praying for the right time to do it.

Trouble was, it never seemed to be "the right time."

Well, she was here now, and he intended to make the most of it.

Drew folded his hands under his pillow and thanked God for this time with her. And speaking of time, he thought, glancing at the clock, she'd been in the bathroom fifteen minutes.

"What're you doing in there?"

Voice echoing in the tiled space, she answered, "Never you mind."

Chuckling, he said, "Just wanted to make sure you're all right."

Suddenly she stood beside the bed, arms akimbo, and grinning like the Cheshire cat. "I'm fine, as you can see."

Levering himself up on one elbow, he whistled.

She'd piled her long, curly hair atop her head, and a few stubborn tendrils had worked themselves loose, giving her a disheveled, rumpled look that was every bit as appealing as the thigh-length satin nightie. He'd seen her in red, in blue and purple and black. But ivory was her color, for it accented the faint pink hue of her smooth skin and made her long-lashed gray eyes stand out, like the beam of a lighthouse piercing through heavy fog.

Yearning could be likened to a fog, he decided as he reached out and took her hand in his. "No sense standing out there in the cold," he growled, "when you've got the Human Furnace to warm you."

She'd called him that nearly every night they were together. It had been one of the thousand things he'd missed in those agonizing months while she'd been gone. If she was going to remember anything, he hoped it would be the good times. Because there had been plenty of those.

"You thinking of adding some insurance?" she asked, slipping between the covers.

"Insurance?" *Don't ask me questions that make me think,* he tacked on mentally. *Not when you look like—*

Her kiss silenced him. After half a dozen more just like it, Drew ground out, "Gabrielle..."

"Drew," she sighed.

"Ah, Gabrielle..."

"Oh, Drew..."

It was a game they'd played dozens of times in the early days of their marriage. If not for her melodious giggling, he might have been able to hold the mood. Rolling onto his back, he gave in to the moment and laughed with her.

He couldn't remember the last time he'd laughed like that.

Yes, he could. It had been more than nine months ago.

It felt good, felt natural, lying there with his wife tucked close beside him. So right that suddenly, the laughter stuck in his throat, threatening to become a sob.

It wasn't until Gabrielle's gentle fingers caressed his closed lids that Drew realized there were tears in his eyes. It wasn't sadness that caused them, he admitted, but happiness. That, and contentment, and pure blessed *relief,* because she loved him, and it showed in her voice, in her touch, in her eyes.

Eyes that turned down at the corners upon seeing his distress, eyes that welled up with empathy for whatever had dampened his just now.

Shamed by his display of weakness, Drew turned slightly to keep her from seeing his tears. He wanted her to think of him as strong, as solid and dependable, as someone tough and hard-edged who could stand up to life's troubles, who could stand up for *her*.

How was he supposed to show her everything he hoped to be if he allowed her to see him blubbering like a baby?

Drew could count on one hand the number of times he'd allowed himself to cry. He'd cried the night his mother left, and when his brother died, and at his father's funeral, too. But no one had *seen* his tears. Coming from a long line of rough-and-tumble cowboys, Drew frowned on behavior that seemed acceptable to others these days, like smooching at the movie theater or airing a marital dispute at the mall. And crying was something to be done in private. Period.

"Sweetie," she soothed, kissing his moist lashes, "what's wrong?"

"Nothin'," he muttered, knuckling his eyes. "Must've gotten a speck of dust in—"

"Shh."

Gabrielle lay a finger against his lips, silencing his explanation. Then, holding that finger aloft, she added, "Listen—"

Blinking, he lifted his head from the pillow. "To what?"

"Can you hear it?"

He strained his ears. Except for the wind whistling past the window, he didn't hear a thing.

Staring boldly into his eyes, she took his hand in hers and pressed it against her chest. "Hear that?"

She looked at him the way she had when the preacher led her through the wedding vows, chastely rosy-cheeked, eager and earnest, as if she saw in his face the fulfillment of her every hope and dream. And oh, how he'd wanted to make that happen.

Grinning crookedly, he managed to croak out, "Your heart knocking against your ribs, you mean?"

She'd left a tall, fat candle burning on the dresser behind her. Its glow surrounded her mass of curls like a golden halo, so that when she smiled, Drew thought of the foot-high angel that had topped his boyhood Christmas tree.

Nodding, Gabrielle tilted her head, and when she did a lustrous lock of mink-soft hair brushed his cheek. Absent-mindedly, he wrapped it around his forefinger.

"Did you watch cowboy movies when you were a little boy?"

He'd spent nights on the open range, too many to count. Out there, alone in the shadows of Montana's Beartooth wilderness, he'd heard the wind rustling through the pines and over knee-deep field grasses. Her voice, so near his ear, was like that, husky and whispery and a little bit dangerous.

"I watched my share of shoot-'em-up reruns, I guess."

"Remember the way the Indians sent messages from the mountains to the valleys?"

"Smoke signals?"

Quiet, womanly laughter tickled his lips when she said, "Yes, sometimes smoke signals, but I'm talking about the *drums.*" She pressed his hand more tightly against her. "Every beat had a meaning of its own."

Transfixed by her steady, loving gaze, Drew licked his lips. "And what message is your heart sending me, Gabrielle?" *Please God,* he prayed, heart thumping like that of a marathoner who'd just run a hard race, *let her tell me what I want to hear.*

Eyes closed and smiling serenely, she sighed. Her lips touched his, and she said, "I'll give you three guesses, and the first two won't count."

There were calluses on his knees, from countless hours he'd spent on them, praying for her to come back home. Night before last, after they'd celebrated what she believed to be their two-month anniversary by trying to make a baby, he'd lain awake watching her sleep—and thanking God for answering that prayer at long last.

He'd done a heap of praying since that night, too—on the drive into Bozeman this morning, and while sitting in her bedroom, and while waiting at the counter as the drugstore clerk looked for her photographs.

Would she stay? Or would she leave him alone again?

Show me a sign, he'd asked the Almighty.

And because he'd wanted to, because he *had* to, Drew had read her behavior ever since to mean that through faith, all things are possible.

He was about to tell her how much she meant to him, how much he loved her, when she opened her eyes, touched the tip of her nose to his, and released his hand. Then one by one, she kissed his fingertips, kissed each callus and every blister that hard work had etched into his palm. "You never answered me," she said, her breath warm on his skin.

"Answered you?" Did she honestly expect him to know what she was talking about? "S-sorry," he admitted, shaking his head, "but I've forgotten the question."

"In-shoor-ance?"

"Insurance," he repeated, nodding, feeling witless and helpless.

A giggle spilled from her, but in Drew's heightened mood, it sounded more like a purr. Combing big fingers gently through her lush curls, he chuckled quietly. "Gabrielle, much as I love the sound of your gorgeous voice, the last thing I want to do right now is hear you talk, especially about something as boring as insurance."

Dipping her head a bit, she looked up at him through dense, dark lashes. "Not even if the insurance would increase our chances of making a baby?"

He knew of only one way to make that happen.

Drew sought the Lord's guidance. Tried to, anyway. Because the question was, should he take the chance that their coupling might actually produce a child? What *insurance* did he have that she'd stay, once she got her memory back, even if a son or daughter was one result of tonight?

He didn't need guarantees, Drew realized suddenly, happily. He had his faith. "Ask and ye shall receive," the Good Book said.

Closing his eyes, he held his breath. *Well, I'm askin', Lord, askin' like I've never asked before. Let her forgive me, make her stay, keep her loving me like she loves me now, forever.*

When he opened his eyes again, Gabrielle was looking at him. No, staring was more accurate, as if waiting for him to make some proclamation.

And so he told the truth that lived in his heart: "I love you, Gabrielle," he said, meaning it, *understanding* it more than ever. "And no matter what, I always will."

Elbow bent, she propped her head on one palm and watched him sleep. From the very first time she saw it, she'd thought he had the most magnificent, masculine profile. On their wedding night, she'd traced the contours of it, her fingertip sketching from his forehead to his nose, over his lips and chin. "If I were a sculptor," she'd told him, "I'd carve your likeness of wood and spend years rubbing away the rough edges."

She'd felt him stiffen when her palms caressed his cheeks, when her thumbs massaged his jaw. The breath he'd been holding escaped slowly, hotly, when her fingertips smoothed across his brow.

He'd had a few rough edges when they met. That much was true. For one thing, he didn't seem comfortable talking unless he had something specific to say. For another, he had a stubborn streak as wide as the Fishtail River. And if that barbed wire incident a while back didn't prove it, nothing would.

Moonlight slanted through the window, across the floor and onto the bed. In its bright white beam, Gabrielle could see the arm that had been ripped and torn by the razor-sharp fencing. He'd taken the bandages off a week or so ago, started protesting every time she ordered him to hold his arm over the basin so she could wash the wound and smear on a dab of antibiotic ointment.

Stubborn man, she thought, shaking her head as she moved in for a closer look.

Levering herself onto one elbow, she swallowed a gasp of surprise. She was a fair-to-middlin' nurse, she thought, brow furrowed with confusion as she stared at the silvery scars left by the barbs, but who'd think his arm would heal *that* quickly? If Gabrielle hadn't been there the afternoon it happened, even she wouldn't have believed the wounds were mere weeks old.

She flopped back onto her pillow and exhaled a frustrated sigh. Nothing made sense anymore. Not the dirty oven or the cobwebs in the corner of their bedroom, not the calendar year or Drew's business checkbook. And certainly not half-inch deep cuts that had healed themselves completely in so short a time.

It was the amnesia, she told herself. Dr. Adams had said it was perfectly normal for things to get jumbled up in a person's head after a fall like the one she'd taken.

But along with things that just plain didn't make sense, how many other things had she forgotten, the way she'd forgotten where she'd put her wedding rings?

What if something important had gotten "jumbled up" in her brain?

And how long would things stay this way?

Drew rolled onto his side, draped an arm across her stomach. "Can't sleep?"

"I slept, for a while."

He sat up halfway. "You have a headache? Want me to get you an aspirin?"

He looked adorable with his hair all sleep-rumpled and his eyes all puffy, she thought. "I'll be fine," she assured, patting his hand. "Just thinking, is all."

Resting his head on her pillow, Drew whispered, "'Bout what?"

He'd already worried enough about her to induce a huge guilt trip. "About you. About us," she fibbed.

"What about me...us?"

There was a tightness, a tension in his voice that she couldn't explain. But why should that make sense when nothing else did?

Rolling onto her side to face him, Gabrielle bracketed his face with her hands. "Insurance," she whispered, and kissed his forehead.

One side of his mouth lifted in a sexy, sleepy grin. "I don't know what our agent is chargin' for that policy," he said, wiggling his eyebrows, "but it's worth every dime."

She linked her fingers behind his neck, pulled him closer. "There's a payment due, you know."

Gabrielle didn't know why this baby-making idea seemed so all-fired important to her. She only knew that it did. It felt as if a child—not in a year or two, but now, *right* now—could make the difference between success or failure. As a woman, she wondered, or as a wife? She was only twenty-seven; her biological clock wasn't ticking that loudly...yet.

So why all the urgency? she asked herself.

One more question without an answer.

One more nagging suspicion that something was terribly, dreadfully wrong.

One more fear that the solutions would be more deadly than the problems.

"A payment due, eh?" he repeated, wrapping his arms around her. "When?"

She kissed him as if their lives depended on it, because that's exactly how she felt. "Tonight," Gabrielle sighed. "Now."

A manly chuckle started deep in his chest bubbled from his throat. "Well, you know what I said on our wedding night," he began, drawing her closer still.

Why did she remember *that* so clearly when so many other things seemed vague, seemed hazy and out of reach?

"On our wedding night—" Her voice sounded so timid, so weak in her own ears. She could only hope it didn't sound that way to Drew, because he'd only start worrying that her headache was back, or that something else might be wrong. And he'd worried enough since this amnesia episode began.

She cleared her throat and began again. "On our wedding night, you promised to love me until you took your last breath."

He nodded. "I meant it."

The intensity in his eyes, in his voice, made her take a sharp breath. She was about to tell him that she'd believed him then, that she believed him now, when he said, "I still mean it. I'll always mean it," he added through clenched teeth.

"Drew?"

He blinked as if waking from a deep sleep. "What?"

"Did anyone ever tell you that you talk too much?"

And smiling, he shook his head. "No. Because usually, that's my line."

Raising one brow, she tilted her head. "If the shoe fits…"

He pressed his lips against her throat. "I like you better barefoot," he whispered.

"And pregnant?" she finished, smiling.

She felt the tension drain out of him, felt the heat of his breath against her neck. "Whatever you want, Gabrielle, that's what I want, too."

"I want you to call me Gabby, like you did on our wedding night."

He held her at arm's length, and, frowning slightly, stared into her eyes. "But…but I thought you didn't—"

She kissed him, softly at first, then more insistently. "I don't like it, except when—"

Thankfully, Drew got the message, and silenced her with a sizzling kiss.

Chapter Seven

The second-to-last thing Drew said was "Don't let me sleep past five." His *last* drowsy words had been "I love you, Gabrielle."

In response, she'd brushed a wayward lock of dark hair from his forehead and whispered, "Do sleep tight, my bright light, and do not let the bedbugs bite!"

Her mother had recited those enchanting words, even on nights when the tiny family had been forced to bunk down in the car during one of her father's "move on" moods. The words had been so comforting that long after stuffed animals and baby dolls became a thing of her past, Gabrielle continued to chant the little poem before closing her eyes at the end of each day.

On their first night as husband and wife, after she was certain he'd fallen asleep, Gabrielle breathed the rhyme into Drew's ear. She'd been wrong about his sleep state, but if there had been any doubt of his love for her before that, the look of wonder and amazement glowing in his dark eyes squelched it.

Closing her into the protective circle of his embrace, he

confessed—after a lot of prodding from her—that his own mother had never tucked him or his brother into bed, never crooned lullabies, never read a bedtime story. He'd tried to mask his true feelings behind a brave chuckle and a "Who gives a hoot?" attitude. When she'd said how much it must have hurt, he'd replied, "Nah, a little girl might need coddling, but a boy doesn't need it, doesn't miss it, doesn't even want it! I got used to doin' things my way, so it made a man of me."

If it doesn't hurt, she'd thought at the time, *then why does he have that wistful look in his eyes?*

But by then, she'd known him a total of four months, more than long enough to recognize pain in his voice when she heard it. Maybe the sheltering hug wasn't for her benefit, after all, she'd thought.

"I'll bet she did those things when you were very small, when you were too young to remember it." It hadn't been easy, hiding her shock and disgust at his mother's behavior. Because if he looked this guileless and genuine now, as a full-grown man, how much more innocent had his little-boy face been?

He'd pulled her closer, saying, "You'll be a terrific mom someday."

Flushing in reaction to the intensity of his stare, she'd giggled nervously. "You've only known me a few months, not long enough to—"

His brief kiss silenced her. "I know this—you don't do anything halfway, and that includes *love*. And everything else a kid will ever need starts right there," he'd said, pressing a fingertip above her heart.

Drew couldn't have known that his heartfelt words would sear her soul, making her his. But they had.

With a background like hers, Gabrielle didn't think she'd ever want to settle in one place, with one man, for a lifetime. She'd thought all the last-minute picking-up-and-going had turned her heart as hard as iron, because there had never been time to get to know anyone well enough to make a commitment—lifelong or otherwise.

Then along came Drew, her very own six-foot, hundred eighty pound, handsome Gabrielle magnet.

The memory evoked a smile, and Gabrielle resisted the urge to kiss his cheek. *You're aptly named,* was the mental message she sent him instead. He looked so peaceful, so content lying there in the dim predawn light that Gabrielle couldn't bear to wake him, even though the clock on the nightstand said five-fifteen.

He needed the rest more than she did.

The past few days had been stressful for her, but they'd been harder still for Drew. If she hadn't learned anything else about him in their months together, she'd learned that he couldn't bear to see her suffer.

As she slipped carefully from the bed so as not to wake him, she remembered her first visit to the ranch. Drew had saved the barn for the last stop in the Walking C tour, and while he was introducing her to Triumph, a spider had dropped from the overhead beams and bitten Gabrielle on the neck.

"I feel like Little Miss Muffet," she'd laughed, rubbing the quickly swelling lump, "standing here among the curds and whey."

Concern rendered him incapable of seeing the humor in her remark. Drew half guided, half carried her to the house, where he wrapped ice cubes in a kitchen towel and sat beside her at the table, holding the make-do compress in place.

She was torn between feeling flattered at his worry, and uneasy about the level of it. "Drew, it wasn't a black widow. I'll be fine."

"All spiders are poisonous to some degree or another."

He'd said it with such seriousness that her heartbeat had doubled. Almost immediately, she'd seen the teasing glint in his eyes, and relaxed.

Sort of.

Because while his grin effectively erased the fear that she'd been bitten by a deadly spider, it hadn't eliminated the uncertainty.

For a reason she couldn't explain, Gabrielle felt the same way now, vacillating between overwhelming love and all-encompassing apprehension. In the doorway, belting her robe, she glanced back over her shoulder at him, as if one more look would be the clarifier.

Sleep had a way of softening the angles and planes of his masculine features. He could have been ten instead of thirty-two, she thought, smiling at the innocence of his face—one of many points on the list of inconsistencies and discrepancies that described this man she loved so much.

Despite his hard-calloused hands, his touch had always been tender—gentler, even, than her father's.

She'd seen that square jaw clamp in his grim determination to get a hard job done; had seen it slacken, too, as he laughed at one of her silly pranks.

His voice could be downright brackish when reprimanding a lazy ranch hand, and it could be quietly soothing, too, the way it got when he helped a terrified, wild-eyed mare through a painful breech birth.

Drew was a self-made man, physically and emotionally stronger than any she'd ever met. And yet, if she woke him and managed to coax the truth from him, he'd admit that the sting of being abandoned by his mother burned almost as hot now as it had on the day she left.

He claimed to have complete faith in God. But if that was true, why did he believe the Lord's love came with stipulations and conditions? Why did he think his heavenly Father demanded good deeds and twice-weekly appearances in church, and hours of Bible study every day? Gabrielle had spent a total of one hour in a Sunday school classroom, and even *she* knew that the Almighty loved His children equally, and without restriction or limitation.

But it was in Drew's dusky eyes that Gabrielle found the greatest contradiction of all. He'd learned to freeze his features, which enabled him to disguise anger, disappointment, guilt. Good as he'd become at masking himself, though, he hadn't taught himself how to keep his true emotions from shining from his eyes.

Her smile gone now, she remembered the way he'd looked when she asked him about Molly. Gabrielle couldn't pinpoint a specific reaction.

Fear, yes—but something else, too.

Shame?

Guilt?

Ridiculous, she told herself. He knew the Bible better than anyone she'd ever met. He was thoughtful and kind, good and decent. The type of man who, if he made a promise, kept it—even if it cost him. What would he have to feel guilty about?

Carefully pulling the bedroom door shut, Gabrielle tiptoed down the stairs, thinking of something her father used to say. *"If you make mountains out of molehills, your whole life will be an uphill battle."*

The mild scolding had never failed to stop her from whining when the kids at a new school didn't welcome her with open arms. Gabrielle hadn't liked admitting it at the time, but the advice gave her a different view of life, a perspective that relaxed her and made her more acceptable to classmates. If the mind-set worked then, when she'd been a spoiled, immature only child, surely it would have an even more positive effect now that she was a grown woman.

She could almost hear her father saying, *"The more you dwell on a negative, the bigger 'n' badder it gets."*

Gabrielle tried not to dwell on the fact that he'd only doled out that bit of advice to a teary-eyed child huddled in the back seat of a beat-up station wagon, to a little girl who'd made the mistake of wishing aloud for her own house with a real yard, and a dad with a regular job—like a *normal* kid. And it was probably better to ignore the fact that each time her father had spoken those words, he'd had been looking through the windshield as yet another Interstate whizzed beneath their mismatched tires. To do otherwise, especially now that he was gone, was to admit that her daddy, her hero and all-time favorite human being, had feet of clay.

Work, she'd learned, was an effective way to get her mind onto something other than her own petty problems. And so she decided to start with a big country breakfast for Drew. Once he'd cleaned up his plate, she'd send him on his way with a kiss and a "have a good day" wish. Then she'd grab the broom and rid the place of cobwebs; it was a big, rambling house, with dozens of corners that were sure to keep her busy for hours. When she ran out of corners, there were windowsills and closets and bookshelves galore....

He woke to the scent of fresh-perked coffee and sizzling bacon. Stretching and yawning, he squinted at the clock.

"Seven-thirty!"

Drew sat up, surprised not only at the hour, but that Gabrielle was gone—and hadn't roused him as he'd asked her to. Feet flat on the floor, he drove all his fingers through his hair. It wouldn't surprise him to find her in the barn mucking out stalls, or in the shed patching that flat tractor tire. What was a man to do with a woman like that? he wondered.

Rising, he worked the kinks from his neck and grinned, remembering her "insurance" talk from last night. He thought, *He keeps right on loving her, that's what.*

He hurried into his clothes and half ran down the stairs, buttoning his shirt as he went. "Gabrielle," he began, stepping into the kitchen, "what do you think you're doing? The doctors made it clear you—"

"Cracking eggs and buttering toast is not strenuous exercise."

She'd set the table exactly the way she always had—spoon and knife to the right of his plate, fork on the napkin to its left, glass of juice at two o'clock, coffee at ten. "Where'd the flowers come from?" he asked, grabbing the mug.

"Good thing you decided to be a cowboy instead of a cop," she teased, putting a saucer of buttered toast in the noon position above his plate.

He pulled out his chair and took a seat. He had no idea what she meant, but saw no point in admitting it. "I would've made an okay cop."

Giggling, she mussed his hair. "No way. You aren't the least bit observant."

But he noticed how gorgeous she looked in her knee-length terry-cloth robe, noticed her pink cheeks and bright eyes...

Gabrielle adjusted a golden bud in the big glass vase. "These mums have been blooming beside the front door for—"

She stopped speaking so suddenly that alarm bells went off in his head. "What?" he asked, grabbing her hand. "Is the headache back? Are you dizzy?"

Frowning, she sighed. "No. It's just…"

She sat in the chair beside his, rested her chin in an upturned palm. "It's just, I would've sworn there were black-eyed Susans growing in that flower bed last time I looked."

Drew picked up a slice of toast, bit off one corner. "I wouldn't know," he said, nodding at the bouquet. "Those things all look alike to me." Half truths seemed better than outright lies.

But she looked so sad, sitting there, confused and frustrated, that he put down the toast and caught her hands between his own. "I think you're right," he began. "There might've been different flowers growing out front a couple of weeks back." Another half truth, because he knew full well that the blooms she'd referred to had been there a year ago.

Wide-eyed, she bit her lower lip. "Black-eyed Susans."

"Daisy-like things? Yellow petals and a fuzzy brown center?"

Grinning, she nodded. "Yes."

Suddenly, her smile vanished, and in its place, there was a look of near panic. "It's the amnesia," she whispered, hiding behind her hands.

A moment later, she came out of hiding and, leaning forward imploringly, wrapped her slender fingers around his wrists. "I've been trying to pretend I haven't noticed things, Drew, like the fact that it's October, and it should *be* October." She gave his wrist a little shake. "How much time have I lost? Please don't sugarcoat it. I need to know."

Remembering what the neurologist had told him about volunteering only the information she asked for, he chose his words carefully. "Nine months, give or take a week."

Her fingers tightened around his wrists. Other than that, Gabrielle showed no outward signs of distress. Then she gave a little nod and shook her head. "Well," she sighed, "this is going to take some getting used to."

"Nah," he said, winking, "it's been a slow news year. You haven't missed much."

Tilting her head, she sent him a sad smile that made him quickly add, "But I'll help you fill in all the holes in your memory. Promise."

She stood, gave his shoulder a squeeze.

He'd gladly carry this burden for her if he could. *But since I can't,* he prayed, *give me the strength to carry her as she shoulders it.*

"Sunny-side up or over easy?" she asked.

"Surprise me."

Wiggling her eyebrows, she forced a sad little giggle. "The way I surprised you last night?"

He remembered the nightgown, the impatient kisses, the eager hugs, and every loving moment that followed. Chuckling, he said, "Give me time to recuperate. I'm older than you, don't forget."

Combing her fingers through his hair, she tidied the rumpling she'd given it earlier. "I'm thinking maybe I'll take a package of chicken out of the freezer, make some stewed chicken for supper," she said, moving toward the stove.

The freezer was as empty as the pantry, and he knew it.

Those first couple of nights after she left, he'd cooked, mostly out of spite. Kind of a "got along without you before I met you" mind-set that inspired him to prepare baked chicken and pan-fried pork chops, until everything she'd stocked away was gone. Since then, he'd pretty much been surviving on hot dogs, peanut butter and jelly sandwiches, and the occasional frozen pizza. Much as he hated to admit it, meals without her were almost as hard as nights alone, because she had put as much love and care into cooking as she had—

He shook the thought off. That was then, this is now, he told himself. Later, he'd drive into town, pick up a few staples. And in the meantime, he'd simply concentrate on the fact that she was back.

Thank you, Lord!

He wanted to turn his chair and watch her cook, the way he used to. But she might take it to mean he didn't trust her with the egg turner, or whatever. So he counted the mums she'd put into the vase on the table. *Eight.* Brushed his bread crumbs from the place mat into his palm, dusted them onto his plate.

"More toast?" she asked, putting down a plate of crisp bacon strips in front him.

Smiling, he took one.

"Coffee?"

Pointing, he said, "Got some, but thanks."

He didn't like feeling this way, fumbling around for something to say that would put an end to the awkwardness caused by his admission. He wondered if she felt it, too, now that she knew nearly a whole year had died in her mind.

Gabrielle efficiently slid two perfect fried eggs onto his plate. He took the frying pan from her and sat it atop the toast.

"But Drew," she protested, "you'll mash the—"

"I don't care," he said, pulling her onto his lap. Arms around her, he kissed her cheeks, her chin, her nose. "I hope you get your memory back, sweetie, and I hope it happens soon, because I know this whole thing has got to be mighty scary for you."

Laying a finger over her lips, he silenced what would probably have become a challenge of one kind or another that she'd decided to set for herself. "But even if you never remember, it isn't going to matter one whit to me.'' He kissed her forehead as if that would stir a memory or two.

''Why?'' she asked, grinning mischievously. ''Did you do something, uh, something naughty during the months I've forgotten?''

It felt as though his spinal cord had been replaced by a steel rod, as if every muscle in him had been cinched tight.

If he wanted to come up with a believable lie, he'd have to tear his gaze from her bright eyes. He glanced around the tabletop. ''Nah,'' he said lightly, ''it's just 'cause you make the best bacon this side of the Mississippi.''

Gently, Gabrielle grasped his earlobes, gave them a little tug. ''If you ever get tired of ranching, you can always get a job writing greeting card verses.'' Standing, she added, ''You'd better go upstairs and brush your teeth again, because all this sweet talk is sure to rot them right out of your gums.''

Unwilling to let her go just yet, he drew her close, rested his cheek against her chest. ''I love you. You know that, don't you?''

Gabrielle gave his hair another tousling. ''Who else would eat ice-cold eggs,'' she hinted, pointing at his plate, ''rather than hurt his wife's feelings?''

His wife. Ah, but he loved the sound of it. Drew was about to pull her into his lap again, when Troy rapped at the kitchen door.

'''Mornin','' he said, opening the door wide enough to poke his head into the kitchen.

'''Morning yourself, stranger.'' Gabrielle grabbed a mug from the cupboard shelf. ''Eggs and bacon?''

''No, thanks. Emily made pancakes and sausage gravy for me this morning.'' He held up a hand to prevent her from filling the mug. ''I'll take a rain check on that coffee, though.''

He met Drew's eyes. "Mind comin' with me, boss? We've sorta got a problem down at the barn."

There was no mistaking the impatient gleam in Troy's eyes. And Drew knew exactly what it meant. The search he'd begun yesterday for a Molly look-alike had obviously paid off.

Drew gobbled down a few bites of his eggs and picked up two strips of bacon on his way to the door. "Leave those dishes, understand? Because the doctors said—"

"Scat," she said, grinning and waving him on. "Go on. *Shoo.* Get out of my kitchen."

He liked the way that sounded: *her* kitchen. And if it hadn't been for Troy, restlessly shuffling from boot to boot, he would have told her so. "Back in a heartbeat," he said instead, dropping a kiss on her cheek.

Halfway between the house and the barn, he asked Troy, "So what gives?"

"Guy over in Bozeman claims to have a couple of fillies that match your description." Troy frowned. "Says they're family pets, but he might be willing to let one go…for the right price.'"

"Doesn't matter how much he's asking. We're comin' home with a horse named Molly." Drew patted his shirt pocket, where, inside the Walking C checkbook, there was a photograph of Gabrielle, sitting astride her beloved horse.

"Well, let's get crackin'," he said, feeling better, happier, more relieved than he had in months. "We're burnin' daylight!"

Dishes done, Gabrielle walked toward the refrigerator, thinking to get a head start on supper. She'd been feeling at odds with herself all morning, and reasoned it was probably because before the amnesia, she'd had a job of some sort. And if she wasn't mistaken, it had something to do with numbers. *Which is absurd,* she thought, *when I know how I feel about—*

Last time she'd looked, the freezer compartment had been full of steaks, hamburger, chicken. Now, one cheese pizza and a carton of fish sticks sat among half-empty ice cube trays and a frosted-over container of Neapolitan ice cream.

It might have staggered her, if Drew hadn't told her that the head injury was responsible for nine missing months. Closing the door, she leaned her forehead on the cool white enamel, hands gripping the wood-grain handle so tightly that her fingers began to ache.

For a moment, she was tempted to thump her head against the smooth surface. Maybe her damaged brain cells were like those last peanuts in the jar: jostle them just right, and they all settled neatly where they belonged.

Doc Parker and Dr. Adams couldn't have been more different, but they'd both made it clear what could happen if she reinjured her head before the bruise on her brain had a chance to heal. Permanent memory loss, or worse.

Grabbing a kitchen towel, she polished the chrome faucet. The already clean shining stovetop. The counters and the table. If she could remember where she had worked—if, indeed, she had a job at all—she'd go there right now, put in a few hours. Maybe work would distract her from wondering if things would ever get back to normal.

Normal. A bitter laugh escaped her lips as Gabrielle remembered when, pouting in the back seat of the station wagon, she'd wished for a normal life, a normal family. What she wouldn't give to have that so-called abnormal life back again, she thought, slamming the towel into the sink.

Drew had accidentally brushed toast crumbs from the table and onto the floor, and Gabrielle reached into the pantry for the broom. As she swished the straw bristles over the wood planks, her eyes filled with tears.

When had she turned into such a blubbering idiot? she demanded of herself. As far back as she could remember, she'd always done her level best not to give in to the urge to cry. Because self-pity, she believed, was one of the least attractive character traits of the species.

Jerking back on the broom handle, she knocked Drew's leather jacket from the peg behind the door, and it hit the floor with an odd-sounding *splat*. Leaning the cleaning tool against the wall, she bent to retrieve the coat, and when she did, glossy color photographs spilled from its inside pocket.

She hung up the jacket and stacked the pictures in one hand. And seated at the table with a fresh cup of coffee, she began going through them, one by one.

There was a shot of her sitting on a snow-covered picnic table, and one of Drew building a snowman. As self-appointed family photographer, he'd taken a picture of the overstuffed picnic basket, and later, captured their meal on film.

According to the faint blue stamp on the back of each snapshot, they'd been taken a year ago, January…

Like a tiny crystal bell, the memory of that day chimed in her mind. Gabrielle forced herself to remain calm, afraid that expressing her excitement, her joy at *remembering* might just blot everything from her brain.

Slowly, as she sipped the coffee, another memory came into focus. She'd gotten up even earlier than usual that morning to fry up the chicken and make potato salad and corn bread for their lunch. Next, she stuffed cold-weather gear for each of them into a canvas duffel, and hid it beside the picnic basket behind the bench seat in Drew's pickup truck.

After church services, she'd suggested a Sunday drive. "Where to?" he'd asked.

"The pine grove up on Beartooth."

And he'd nodded. "Oh, *now* I get it. My little 'remember the anniversary of everything' wife wants to celebrate the first time I said 'I love you.'"

It had surprised her that he remembered, and she said so.

"Sweetie," Drew said with a wink and a grin, "it'd be awful hard to forget, since it was the first time I'd ever said it to a woman." With that, he parked behind a grove of pines, while she pulled out the duffel. In no time, the pickup's windows were fogged from the exertion of their trying to change clothes in the cramped cab.

Smiling with fond remembrance of the day—and relief that she'd assembled so much of it in her mind without his help—Gabrielle continued to look through the stack.

Not all the pictures had been taken in the pine grove. There was a picture of Triumph, Drew's pride and joy, and of Chum, the trusty work horse that helped him accomplish everyday ranch tasks. Drew had taken one of Troy, grinning sheepishly as he forked hay into the horses' stalls, and one of Gabrielle, peeking from behind laundry that flapped on the lines out back. And Molly, prancing around the—

Molly!

Gabrielle's hands began to shake and her mouth went dry. *Molly, the horse she'd bought and paid for with her bank teller's wages.*

She *had* worked at a job involving numbers, she realized. And—and she'd been a loan manager, too, until...

The memory was there, balancing precariously on the rim of her mind.

And then, with the electrifying power of a lightning bolt, it happened, and the memories started falling like dominos.

They'd bickered for weeks after Drew moved the money

she'd added to their savings account into a certificate of deposit—twelve thousand dollars she'd inherited when her father died. It was money she intended to use for a car that would get her back and forth to work. "It'll earn more interest in a CD than it will in savings," Drew defended. If she hadn't had plans for the money, she might have invested it just that way. It wasn't *what* he'd done that infuriated her; it was *how* he'd done it, without so much as discussing with her.

If that argument hadn't been heaped on top of others that were the result of her suggestions to make small, wifely changes around the house, it might not have festered like an open wound. It might not have made other things seem as big as the Montana horizon.

Things like the way he stubbornly refused to so much as consider allowing Gabrielle to move a stick of furniture, or hang new curtains, or replace a worn-out rug. "If you're so much in love with your mother," she'd shouted once, "why not hire someone to find her, so you can marry *her!*"

It had been an immature, mean-spirited thing to say, and she'd admitted it to herself even then—partly because of the hurt it painted on his face, partly because Drew had told her about the detective whose hundreds of hours and thousands of dollars yielded only dead ends and hopeless disappointment.

Gabrielle defended her bad behavior by telling herself *Drew's* behavior had been unreasonable and selfish. Because, while she had gladly given up everything to move into a house in the middle of nowhere, she couldn't believe he really expected she'd keep it organized and clean but not want to make it a little bit *her* home, too.

By the time he came home driving a small, four-door, red compact, she'd had it up to *here* with his bossy, "Do it my way" thinking. Her friends' husbands treated them like equals, why couldn't hers at least *try?*

He'd looked so pleased with himself, so proud when he handed over the keys to the car. All she could think of at the time was that her twelve thousand dollars was supposed to get her the used sports utility vehicle she'd been drooling over.

"You don't appreciate a generous gift when you see one," he'd said, all snarly and disgruntled.

"No, *you* don't appreciate how good it would have felt, plunking down my own cash to pay for the kind of car *I* wanted!"

There had been myriad similar situations, things that from Drew's point of view would have remained inconsequential, if she hadn't turned them into issues. "Making mountains out of molehills...*again,*" he'd accuse. According to him, if she wasn't "obsessing" over one thing, then she was in another of her "black moods" over another.

So the little things had added up, until one day frustration drove her to the barn, where she saddled Molly and took a wild ride through the woods. If she hadn't been so all-fired angry, would she have seen the rotting tree trunk there in the creek bed? If she hadn't worked up that hot head of steam, would she have been able to react in time to guide the horse around it?

Gabrielle would never know, because the filly she'd rescued from a gap-toothed old carnival man stepped right into that hole and squealed with pain. Panicked, Gabrielle had tied Molly to a tree and run full-out all the way back to the ranch, where she insisted that Billy hitch the horse trailer to Drew's pickup. When she and the ranch hand reached that tree, Molly was trembling, whimpering, unable to stand.

"Gonna hafta put her down," Billy said, as they drove toward the Walking C.

"Maybe not," she'd said hopefully. "Maybe Doc Ivers will have a liniment or something. No one knows horses like he does."

Shrugging, Billy drawled, "Well, Miz C, I hope so, 'cause I'd hate to see a purty li'l horse like Molly go down."

Home again, Gabrielle made Molly as comfortable as possible, then contacted the veterinarian. And though he pretty much agreed with the young ranch hand, Doc Ivers suggested two remedies that Gabrielle might try.

She'd never know if one method or the other might have worked, either, because while she was inside, mixing up the concoction according to the vet's instructions, Drew shot Molly.

"It had to be done," he'd said. "She was in pain."

"There were other things we could've tried first."

"I've been a rancher all my life. Never liked having to do things like this, but it's kinder than letting an animal suffer."

Despite all the sense it made, she'd packed her things and left him.

Now, reeling from feelings of betrayal and loss, Gabrielle stood on shaky legs and gathered the photographs into a neat stack. And after tucking them into the envelope they'd come in, she put them back into Drew's jacket pocket and headed upstairs.

To pack.

"Good thing we brought the horse trailer along," Drew said, closing the gate behind the filly.

Troy walked toward the front of the pickup, shaking his

head. "Got me a bad feelin'," he said. "Gabby loved that horse. She's gonna know right off this one ain't Molly."

Drew's brow furrowed and his lips thinned as he said, "Then it's up to us to convince her it *is* Molly. She thinks the horse ran off, that she's been running wild. Makes sense the critter wouldn't behave like her old self, after a couple of months with the mustangs."

Troy only continued shaking his head.

"Besides, you know as well as I do what the doctors said. We have to keep—"

"Yeah, well, that's all a whoppin' heap of medical malarkey, if you ask me. Makes no sense, pretending that one lie piled on top of another is gonna help her get better."

Troy was right, and Drew said so. "But we have to give it a go, for now, at least."

"Yeah, well," the foreman repeated, "by then it might be too late. Gabby might feel she can't believe anything we tell her, once she finds out about all the lies, and head right on back to her apartment in Livingston."

The thought chilled Drew worse than if he'd been standing in the meat freezer at the stockyards. Troy was right; Gabrielle might just get so *mad* when she found out how many ways he'd duped her, that she'd leave again, this time for good.

Buying time, that's what he'd been doing. And if the Almighty had heard any one of the thousand prayers he'd said in the past year, the payoff would be worth it. Things might be rocky for a bit, but only for a bit. Because how many times had he read in the Good Book that faith as small as a mustard seed could move mountains.

Not a bad comparison, Drew thought, grinning bitterly, because Gabrielle could be as immovable as any mountain, once she dug in her heels.

But he had to believe things would right themselves. A

small hope, admittedly, but he clung to it like a dying man clings to a life preserver.

What choice did he have?

She wouldn't have answered the doorbell if it hadn't kept ringing with such insistence. "All right," she called, running down the stairs. "Hold your horses, I'm coming."

"'Hold your horses,'" Doc Parker teased, stuffing his cell phone into his medical bag. "Great line for a rancher's wife." He snapped the bag shut, as Gabrielle stepped back to let him in. "What took you so long to answer the door? I was about to dial 9-1-1."

"I was…upstairs," she said carefully. "But I have a better question—what're you doing all the way out here?"

He plunked the medical bag on the foyer table. "Came to check on you. What else?"

"I'm fine," she said, closing the door.

Parker turned to face her. "How 'bout you let me be the judge of—" Clamping his lips together, he frowned. "'Fine,' my foot!" he growled, looking her in the eye.

He opened his bag. "What's been going on around here?" he demanded, shining a thin beam of light into her eyes. She let him, because she couldn't help but wonder if *remembering* had done her any lasting damage.

"Well?"

"Deep subject," she joked.

Narrowing his eyes, he gave her a sideways glance. "Stow it, Gabrielle. Now out with it. What's up?"

"Nothing."

"Now, why am I having trouble believing that?" Gently, he pressed his fingertips into her temples. "Does that hurt?"

She shook her head. "No."

He palpated the rest of her head, saying, "How about that?"

"I told you, I'm fine," she said again.

"'Fine,' my big flat foot!"

"How about a cup of coffee?" She walked toward the kitchen, hoping the invitation would change the subject.

"Gave the vile stuff up years ago."

She poured him a glass of lemonade instead, then gestured for him to sit at the table.

"Now, why don't you tell me what's got your face looking like you've just gone nine rounds with Mike Tyson."

She knew how Drew felt about sharing their business with outsiders. And lately, she'd come to agree with him, so she said nothing.

Parker must have read her silence to mean Drew had upset her, because he scowled and shook his head. "I'm gonna give that bullheaded husband of yours a good swift kick in the bee-hind," he said. "I told him a dozen times if I told him once—'Beg, borrow, lie, steal, cheat if it takes that to keep Gabrielle calm.'"

"But you said yourself on the telephone that I'm not in any danger, that I'd probably be back to my old self in a week or two."

He flushed a bit, bobbed his white-haired head and took another sip of the lemonade. "Well, of course I'd tell you that. You're the *patient,* for the luvva Pete." He shook a beefy finger. "But Drew—Drew knew the whole story. I made it clear as glass what could happen if—"

"He's been treating me like *I'm* made of glass," she admitted sullenly.

He tugged at the cuffs of his starched white shirt. "Well, that's good. But why the red eyes, then? Why the puffy face?"

She bit her lip to keep it from trembling and held her

breath to control the urge to cry. "My memory is back, Doc," she announced. "I know about the separation, and I know what caused it."

Whistling through his teeth, he leaned back. "Well, now, that does change things, doesn't it."

Not trusting herself to speak, Gabrielle only nodded. The pictures she'd found in Drew's pocket were nothing compared to the ones in her mind—the ones of Molly...and the rifle.

"He's been miserable without you, Gabrielle. And I happen to know for a fact that he hasn't so much as looked at another woman in all this time. I asked him about it once, and he said—"

"I don't care," she snapped. "Drew and I are legally separated. If he wants to start up a new relationship—" The image of it flashed through her mind, and she stiffened. "He's a free agent now," she added.

Parker lifted his chin a notch. "So you're saying it won't bother you to read about his engagement in the paper."

Engagement? She remembered more than the things that had driven her away; she remembered the days and nights they'd spent since the concussion, too. *Engagement?* The very idea stung like a hard slap to the face.

"I'm an old man, so humor me, will you?"

She blinked back hot tears and nodded. "What could it hurt?" she asked around a sob.

He took her hands in his and leaned forward, nearly upsetting his lemonade. And, like a doting mother, Gabrielle slid it farther away from his fidgeting fingers.

"My wife and I had just celebrated forty-two years of marriage when she passed away. That was almost ten years ago, but let me tell you, young lady, I loved that old gal with everything in me, and not a day goes by that I don't miss her like crazy." He gave her hand a gentle squeeze.

"You think we didn't fight?" Thunderous laughter filled the sunny kitchen. "Why, we'd go round and round so long and hard that sometimes we'd end up hoarse from all the shouting, especially in the early days."

She knew what he was thinking—that after a few months together, how could either she *or* Drew honestly say they'd made a serious effort to salvage their marriage? Why wouldn't he think it, when she'd asked herself the same question, over and over?

"It took time, getting used to one another." He shrugged. "Just because we'd both come from the same small town, went to the same schools, attended the same church didn't mean we had a lot in common."

"Sounds to me like you did."

"That's what we told each other, too, before the wedding." The old doctor chuckled. "But her mama liked to open presents on Christmas Eve, and mine made us wait 'til after church Christmas morning. My daddy didn't see anything wrong with a few beers and some poker on a Saturday night, but hers thought it was a terrible sin. She loved fish, and I hate it..."

When he sighed and sat back, an expression softened his aging features, a look caused, Gabrielle supposed, by reliving warm, sweet moments with his wife.

"We fought about when we'd start our family, if the children would call me 'sir' and her 'ma'am,' or 'dad' and 'mom.' We battled over everything, from whether I should use pepper and Tabasco on my scrambled eggs to whether or not she ought to have her ears pierced.

"And then one day she up and says to me, 'Robert, I'm sick of all this fussing and fighting, and here's what we're going to do about it. We're going to have ourselves half a dozen children, starting right now.'

"Well, I failed to see what on earth *that* would do to

help matters, and I told her so. And do you know what she said?'' he asked, grinning.

Gabrielle shook her head.

''She said, 'People don't fight when babies are around, because, well, loud noises scare them. So if we always have a baby in the house, at least we'll be *quieter* when we argue.'''

Parker threw back his head and laughed out loud at the memory. ''Now I ask you, what man in his right mind could disagree with logic like that!''

It was a lovely story, so she wouldn't spoil the doctor's good mood by telling him that she and Drew were about as likely to have a meeting of the minds as were a coyote and a fawn!

Hunter and prey—a fairly bleak view of things. She'd been hard on Drew that night, she reminded herself, so which was *she?*

Parker stood and shoved his chair under the table. ''Promise me something?''

''If I can.''

''Don't do anything rash. Give yourself time—a couple of weeks, maybe, to sort through all this.'' He aimed a professorial finger at her. ''See if, despite it all, you can remember why you married Drew in the first place. If that doesn't give you a good reason to try and work things out, *then* you can pack up and move out.''

It was good advice, but...

''So you'll sleep on it?''

Gabrielle honestly didn't know if she had the patience, the courage or the fortitude. But she nodded in agreement, because somewhere deep inside her, hope still sparked.

She walked him to the door, thanked him for the visit...and the advice.

''I'll make a deal with you,'' he said, winking.

"What kind of deal?"

"Take my suggestion, and I won't send you a bill."

Laughing quietly, she said, "G'bye, Doc. Have a good day, and drive safely."

After closing the door behind him, Gabrielle realized she had a lot of thinking to do.

Chapter Eight

〜

"What're you doin'?" Troy asked, when Drew stopped the truck.

"Well, we can't bring the horse to the ranch looking like that."

The ranch hand removed his hat and scratched his head. "Like what? She's a beauty. You said so yourself."

Getting out of the truck, Drew nodded. "And that's the problem. She looks a mite *too* good."

Troy leaned against the passenger door, one boot crossed over the other and arms folded over his chest, shaking his head, while Drew led the Molly look-alike through the muck and mud of the riverbed. He hid his face behind one hand as his boss whipped out a pocket comb and back-brushed the horse's mane. And when the younger man searched the bank for thistles and burrs to weave into her tail, Troy groaned. "I hope you don't expect *me* to clean up that mess," he said, laughing.

Drew laughed, too. "It'll be my pleasure, gussying her up for Gabrielle."

When they were on their way again, Troy's mood grew serious. "I sure do hope this works."

"Has to," Drew said. "Molly was the reason Gabrielle left me. I have to stall her memory of that as long as I can, so I have more time to prove I've changed."

Nodding, Troy said, "All I know is, you must have a powerful hankerin' for that li'l gal."

He could think of several other ways to put it, but didn't they all mean the same thing? Drew loved Gabrielle more than anyone—anything—in his life.

"She tell you about the set-to between her and Emily?"

"Started to," Drew answered. "But then I had to rush her to the hospital." He shot Troy a look that said *Talk.*

"Seems my darlin' wife knocked the bean pot over. You're one of her favorite people, and Gabrielle isn't— least not since she walked out on you."

Drew shot him a withering look.

"Relax, I said she knocked over the bean pot, not that she spilled the beans. Leastways, not all of 'em." He shrugged. "Way I figure it, Emily sorta adopted you, seeing as we have no young'uns of our own. Anybody hurts you, hurts her."

Drew nodded. "Guess you could say there's a soft spot in my heart for old Em, too." But she'd riled Gabrielle; whatever Emily had said was partly responsible for the collapse. "If there wasn't," he tacked on, "I'd have read her the riot act by now for upsetting Gabrielle."

"Reckon I'd feel the same way, somebody riled my woman that bad."

"What's done is done," Drew said. And shooting Troy a warning glance, he added, "We'll just have to see it isn't done again."

They pulled into the drive and headed straight for the barn. Drew's plan was to get the fake Molly into a stall before going to the house to fetch Gabrielle. He'd let her get an eyeful of the horse, all filthy from weeks of running with the mustangs, then send her back inside while he cleaned the animal up.

Troy agreed to unhitch the trailer while Drew put the filly in the barn. He wasn't looking forward to telling yet another lie, but with any luck at all, it'd be the last one he'd have to tell for a while. *And Lord,* he prayed, *when this is over, I'll never tell another in my whole life!*

He was walking up the flagstone path leading from the barn to the back porch when something caught his attention. His heart started pounding. Cougar tracks, he realized, squatting to examine the prints more closely. And recent ones, too, from the look of things.

A creepy-crawly *Something is watching me* feeling shimmied up his spine, prickled at the base of his skull. He'd had the sensation before, more times than he cared to remember, out there on the trail. Once, on a cattle drive, the chilling wave had pulsed over him, making him tense and wary. It saved his life that night, for if it hadn't coaxed him out of his bedroll right when it did, he might not have gotten the whiff of damp grizzly fur in time to save the horses and the men who were rounding them up for the winter.

Standing, he glanced cautiously around. Cougars didn't much care what time of day it was; if they wanted a meal, they took one, wherever and whenever they could find it. The cat that had left these tracks could very well be perched on a tree bough right now, watching, waiting for the right moment to pounce.

The hairs on the back of his neck bristled and his mouth went dry. Immediately, his mind went to work, searching for an escape route in the event the cougar was indeed close by.

It was more than a hundred yards back to the barn, fifty to the door. If Gabrielle had locked it, he'd be a midday meal for the cat, for sure.

A few ranchers in the area, having lost livestock and pets, and some even a relative, had developed raw hatred for the stealthy creatures. The Good Book said it was a sin to hate the dumb beast. Drew, knowing cougars acted out of pure, primal instinct, laid no blame at their feet. But he'd seen firsthand the kind of savagery the cats were capable of. Respect aside, *this* cat had violated an unspoken code, coming this close to his house…to his wife.

Living on the border of the wilderness, a man had to learn early to keep his priorities in order. Had to hone his own instincts to a keen edge. Anything else was tempting fate, pure and simple. A certain degree of acceptance of the often cruel laws of nature was required, too; if one of the cows or horses bearing the Walking C brand wandered into the cat's territory, well, it was just survival of the fittest.

By the same token, if a bear or a cat decided to take a shortcut across the ranch, maybe helping himself to a meal of horse or cow along the way, it was risking certain death. Because no self-respecting rancher could allow a predator to develop a territorial sense of control. Not on his land.

It had been years since he'd needed to keep the rifle, loaded and ready to fire, in the corner near the front door. But the tracks were proof that it was time. And much as he hated to frighten her, especially in her fragile physical state, Drew knew he'd have to warn Gabrielle to be careful any time she decided to go outside. If he didn't, she was as vulnerable as a teacup in a bull pasture.

Drew took a few cautious steps toward the porch before something else in the dirt beside the path stopped him.

Footprints, likely size five, were scattered here and there, amid paw prints of almost the same length.

While he'd been gone, Gabrielle had come out here for some reason—to check for those confounded dark-eyed Suzies, no doubt—and had walked back and forth on the very soil where the cougar had trod!

He could almost picture the thing, pacing back and forth on a high branch, licking its coal-black lips, tongue wrapping around three-inch fangs as it waited for the right moment to attack.

The steely fingers of fear wrapped around Drew, and heart pounding, he covered the ground between the walk and the porch in a few long strides.

Flinging open the door and slamming it behind him, he stood there for a moment, trying to catch his breath. If he let Gabrielle see him this way—panting, sweating, trembling at the thought of her being carried off by a hungry cougar—no telling what reaction she might have.

Slumping against the wall, he hung his head. *Dear God in heaven,* he prayed, eyes closed and jaw clenched, *please keep her safe.* Mopping perspiration from his brow with a gloved hand, he took a deep breath and stared at the ceiling.

Somewhere up there, beyond the roof of the ranch house, beyond the clouds in the blue Montana sky, a heaven existed. Paradise, where the leopard lay with the kid, and man never raised an angry hand toward his own kind.

Outside, a dangerous cunning cat lurked in the shadows.

Inside, no darkness, and nothing that could harm them.

He glanced around the kitchen, and saw that Gabrielle had scrubbed the stainless steel sink until it gleamed, polished the stove so that it shimmered.

A sense of peace drifted over him, warming and soothing him like the featherlight quilt she'd draped him with in the predawn hours this morning.

How she'd guessed he was cold, he didn't know. But then, how had she been able to tell when his head hurt? When his shoulders ached from mending fences or baling hay? How had she figured out which were his favorite foods, without him having told her?

Love, he realized, was what made her observant.

Drew remembered what she'd said over breakfast, about his not being suited to a policeman's life. And she was right. For every ten things she'd noticed about him—and acted upon—on his behalf—he might have filed away *one* thing about her.

If he'd had a normal childhood, raised in a home with a mother present, would he have learned to look for the things that mattered? Or was his self-centeredness simply part of his character?

Whatever he had been, what he was now didn't matter. What he'd become, that's what mattered. Mattered very much.

Because Gabrielle deserved Paradise.

And by all that's holy, he vowed, *she's gonna get it.*

Gabrielle sat on the edge of the mattress, one hand resting on her open suitcase, the other absently stroking the tufted quilt that covered their bed.

She'd been at the window when Drew's truck rolled into the drive. At the first sight of the horse carrier, she knew what it meant. Racing around to the back of the house to peer out the guest room window, she watched Troy drive away, trailer in tow, while Drew led a horse into the barn.

If she didn't know better, Gabrielle would have said it was Molly out there, covered with grit and grime. But of course that couldn't be, because Drew had killed Molly, she thought, teetering between anger and guilt.

She hadn't had as much time to think as she would have liked, but Gabrielle had figured out a thing or two.

Like the wedding rings. The only way he could have gotten them was through Mrs. Blake. Only one way to find out.

She dialed the landlady's number. She had time for one quick call while Drew stabled the horse. After a few moments of friendly conversation, and a few more assuring Mrs. Blake she was on the mend, Gabrielle asked about Drew's visit.

"Yes, dear. He was here."

"And you gave him the key? You let him into my apartment?"

"He told me you'd had a bad fall, that a concussion and amnesia were part of the bargain." The older woman paused. "Are you saying he misled me? That those things aren't true?"

Oh, he'd told more than his share of lies since the accident, but that hadn't been one of them. "No," Gabrielle answered, "I'm not saying that."

She heard the landlady cluck her tongue. "Well, he seemed quite rational and sane to me."

And when had she said anything to indicate she believed he *wasn't?* Gabrielle wondered. But then, in all fairness, she supposed, when a woman runs away from home and sets up a new life in another town, what else can folks assume, except that she'd run from a horrible, perhaps even a violent past?

The thought made her feel terrible, because for all his faults, Drew had never been anything but gentle with her. If her behavior made people think otherwise, she had a lot of fence-mending of her own to do.

"He's very handsome," Mrs. Blake said. And laughing

girlishly, she added, "Why, if I were fifty years younger, I might just tell him so myself!"

Immediately, the anger was back, hot and bright as ever. Mrs. Blake would be welcome to him, Gabrielle almost said, because he was free as a bird—flying high on having gotten away with lie upon lie.

"So tell me, Gabrielle, did you get your rings back?"

"He told you that's why he wanted inside the apartment?" *You mean to say he didn't concoct some wild story about space invaders,* she fumed, *and doctors' orders?*

"Yes. He doesn't say much, does he? But then, why should he, when what he says has such impact?"

"I don't understand."

"Gabrielle..." The landlady sighed impatiently. "Despite your differences, surely you know how much he loves you. Why, I'd wager he loves you more than his own life."

Doc Parker had said pretty much the same thing earlier. "Drew said that? He told you that he—"

"Well," the woman interrupted, "let's just say that I've learned to read people fairly accurately. And believe you me, from what I saw, that boy is hopelessly mad about you."

She thought of the days they'd spent together since her fall. Every moment had been warm and wonderful and loving, she admitted to herself.

"So tell me, is it safe to say you won't be coming back?"

She hadn't had time to think about it. "I-I'm not sure."

"Don't worry. You're paid up through the end of the month. And it's a nice space, especially since you fixed it up, so I'm sure I won't have a bit of trouble renting it right away."

Gabrielle pictured her apartment, all sunny and airy, with bright-colored furnishings, with things right where she wanted them. She didn't know if she wanted to give that up. "Thanks, Mrs. Blake. Soon as I know what I'm doing, I'll give you a call."

"That'll be fine, dear. Now, will you listen to some friendly advice?"

"I can do that much, I suppose."

"Keep in mind as you try to decide what you're going to do that your choices will affect the rest of your life, and your husband's."

And if she were pregnant, an innocent child's, too. "Thanks. I'll remember that," she said, and hung up.

Gabrielle had read somewhere that it took eight to ten days to know whether or not conception has taken place. She might as well stay, at least until she knew for sure. What could it hurt?

Drew's boot heels chugged up the wooden stairs, and she grabbed the suitcase. He came into the room just as she'd finished shoving it under the bed.

"Hey," he said, smiling. "What're you doing, searching for dust bunnies?"

On her feet now, she faced him. "I didn't know you were going into town," she said. "When you left here this morning, I thought it was to help Troy with some problem in the barn."

She couldn't help but notice the way his pupils constricted, and his cheeks glowed blush-red.

"I, ah, I thought Billy would tell you where we'd gone."

Another lie? she wondered. "Billy didn't tell me." She crossed both arms over her chest. "So where did you go, you and Troy and the horse trailer?"

Smiling crookedly, he approached, put both hands on her shoulders. Gabrielle resisted the urge to slap them away, remembering how her dad used to say that if you gave a man enough rope, he might just hang himself with it.

"Troy got a call this morning, about..." He licked his lips. "About your horse. So we went to pick her up."

"Molly, you mean?"

He didn't answer, she noted. Instead, Drew glanced out the window. "She's in the barn. But before I take you down there, I have something important to tell you."

The truth for a change? she wondered.

"When I was coming up the back walk just now, I saw cougar tracks near the walk."

"A cougar so close to the house?" She bit her lower lip. "That's not normal, is it?"

He drew her into a hug...and she let him.

"It's been a long, dry summer," he said into her hair, "and the mule deer and elk herds—"

"It's moving in on the livestock, isn't it?"

"I've been through this before," Drew said, his voice full of assurances. "We'll set some traps, and if we manage to catch it, we'll ship it to a zoo back east." He kissed the top of her head. "But just to be on the safe side, I've put my rifle near the front door. The safety's on, but it's loaded. So be careful, okay?"

She nodded, wondering how it could feel so incredibly good, so comforting to be standing here absorbing his strength now, when only moments ago she'd been preparing to leave him.

Drew stood back, held her at arm's length. "So," he began, smiling, "you want to head on over to the barn now?"

She smiled, thinking it just might be interesting to see how he'd cover his tracks *this* time.

"I love it when you do that," he said.

"Do what?" she asked self-consciously.

"Grin, like you're enjoying your own private joke."

She looked into his face, at the patrician nose and well-arched dark brows, at a powerful jaw and sun-kissed cheeks, and lips that were full and well-rounded.

Gabrielle laughed inwardly, admitting that Mrs. Blake hadn't stretched the truth. He *was* a handsome man, particularly when he smiled that way. The landlady and the doctor had both stressed that Drew loved her. Strangely, neither had asked how she felt about Drew.

Was it written on her face? Did it glow from her eyes or resonate in her voice? Somehow, they'd known she loved him with every pulse of her heart. Why else would neither of them have mentioned it?

"What?" he interrupted her thoughts. "Do I have spinach on my teeth or something?"

She'd been staring, and Drew had caught her at it. "No crime against a wife looking at her husband, far as I know."

"You're such a nut," he said, laughing and hugging her tighter.

"Which is—"

"—only one of the reasons you love me like you do," they said together.

Okay. All right, so she loved the big lug. That didn't mean much, all things considered. She decided, standing in the warmth of his embrace, to give him the benefit of the doubt. This time, anyway. He'd been trying hard to make her happy these past few days, and deserved a little credit for that.

"Good grief," Gabrielle said, patting Fake Molly's nose, "you're filthy! What have you been up to, girl?"

It pleased Drew that Gabrielle was happy to see the horse. It almost made it worth the money and deception it had cost to bring her here. *Almost,* he added, *but not quite.* Drew remembered something his third grade Sunday school teacher had said, about lies being like ugly splotches that darken your spirit, one by dishonest one. If she'd been right, he was well on his way to a coal-black soul.

Gabrielle plucked a burr from the filly's matted mane. "Wherever did you find her?"

Drew put his hands in his pockets. "Out near Bozeman Pass." That much, at least, was true. "She was running with a wild herd, having a grand old time." Also true, he thought. He'd more or less been keeping track, and by his guess, this "protect Gabby from the truth" situation had forced him to tell about a dozen lies.

"Bozeman Pass, eh? Well, little girl," she said to the horse, "you've had yourself quite an adventure, haven't you."

"Soon as you've finished getting reacquainted, I'll clean her up. Then maybe tomorrow the two of us can take Molly and Triumph out for a—"

"This isn't Molly," she said.

Drew's mouth went dry and his hands grew damp at the terseness of her tone. He'd inspected nearly a hundred horses, looking for one with a white diamond on her forehead, one that resembled Molly. This one could have been her twin. "What do you mean?"

Gabrielle shrugged nonchalantly. "She's beautiful— well, I imagine she will be when she isn't a muddy mess— but she isn't Molly." She moved the horse's mane aside. "*My* horse had a tiny white patch, right here," she said, pointing, "and another there," she added, moving the bangs aside. "If I'd bought her as a foal, I would have named her Freckles." Facing Drew, she propped a fist on one hip and smiled. "As it was, she already had a name when I found her."

He had the strangest feeling she was trying to send him a message of some kind. For the life of him, Drew wasn't reading that message any better than he'd have been able to decipher those Indian drumbeats she'd referred to the other night.

Caught like a gnat in a spider's web, he shuffled from one booted foot to the other. "I, ah, just didn't want to upset you," he said, and logged another truth in his mental ledger. "I would have told you, once you got a clean bill of health from the docs."

Her piercing gray gaze unnerved him. He tried to read the meaning of the intense scrutiny, but had no more luck than he'd had with her encoded words just now.

"Well," she said, dusting her palms on the seat of her jeans, "you go ahead and clean the poor thing up. If she's anything like Molly, she hates being dirty."

In the double doorway, she paused, turned. "Supper will be ready by the time you're finished, so you might want to change your clothes before you come to the table."

It looked like Gabrielle, but it sure didn't sound like her. The icy timbre of her normally honeyed voice gave him the feeling that something terrible was about to happen. Her smile, too, seemed oddly out of place, like something reserved for strangers and lingering houseguests.

Drew shivered involuntarily as he took hold of Fake Molly's bridle. "I should be done in—"

"—hour, hour and a half, from the looks of things," she finished for him. She started out the door, then hesitated. "That cougar," Gabrielle began, "you don't think it's out there now, do you?"

He didn't want to frighten her unnecessarily, but neither did he want her feeling overly secure. To Gabrielle, that was as good as written permission to be reckless. "I doubt it," he said, choosing his words carefully, "but it wouldn't hurt to keep an eye peeled."

"See you in a while, then," she said, nodding.

It was a long way from the barn to the house—a hundred yards, minimum. He knew, because he'd laid the flagstone walk with his own two hands. "Gabby," he blurted, "wait."

She'd only gone about twenty feet. "What?" she asked without stopping.

"Nothing," he said, catching up and falling into step beside her. "It'd make me feel better, is all, if you let me walk you to the porch."

Sending him a mysterious grin, she lay one hand atop the other on her chest and said, "My hero!"

He felt, rather than heard, the biting sarcasm in the remark. But since nothing had happened to cause it, Drew chalked it up to his guilty conscience. Served him right, he thought, for stacking lies like logs for the woodstove. Both could start a mean fire, he reasoned. He knew how to handle the heat of the stove. Gabrielle's ire was something else again.

"Don't overdo it, now," he said, holding the door for her. "We don't want to make another trip to the emergency room."

"Right back atcha, big guy." She gave him a light, playful punch on the arm. But her expression grew solemn when she added, "It'll be getting dark by the time you're finished. You be careful crossing the yard, you hear?"

It looked like she meant it. At least, she sounded sincere. Impulsively, he tugged her to him and wrapped his arms around her. Overcome with sudden emotion, he kissed her. "I love you," Drew said, giving her a gentle shake. "I mean it."

Blinking, she licked her lips, still blush-pink from his kiss. "I...I love you, too." She stepped into the kitchen and pulled the screen door shut behind her. "The sooner you get started, the sooner you'll be finished."

He nodded, wishing he'd never gone to that farm, wishing he'd never muddied Fake Molly. Because there was nothing he wanted more at that moment than simply to hold his beautiful wife.

Gabrielle set the table with the everyday dishes, but put cloth napkins instead of paper ones beneath the silverware. The plan was to have a pleasant supper. And instead of a sweet dessert, she'd have it out with Drew. Best diet plan she'd heard of, bar none, she thought, grinning dully.

She hoped for Fake Molly's sake that he hadn't layered on too much river muck. On the other hand, it wasn't as though he hadn't earned the hard work. How long had it taken, she wondered, and how much effort had he expended trying to disguise his latest lie?

Disappointment, she decided, was harder to cope with than outright anger.

Gabrielle went upstairs to unpack the suitcase. There would be plenty of time to repack it later, if things didn't turn out well after supper. For now, she'd take Doc Parker's advice: no decision, at least not yet. Besides, most of her things were at the apartment already.

She remembered that morning, in the closet, when she'd asked him about the shelves. Without understanding the reason, she'd been so stunned at his answer that she'd forgotten to ask the other question on her mind. *Where are all my clothes?*

The jeans and T-shirts she'd been wearing since the accident were all things that Drew had bought when she'd accompanied him on business trips to Livingston, Bozeman, Billings and Butte. The night she'd left, Gabrielle hadn't wanted to take them, for each item represented another incident in which Drew's opinion outweighed hers.

She didn't care for polo shirts, yet there were an even

dozen hanging in the closet. Those boot-leg, hip-hugging jeans that had become so popular? Gabrielle thought they looked silly, yet four pairs sat on the shelves he'd built her. The pointy toes of cowboy boots made it easy to quickly slide one's foot into a stirrup; their slanted heels guaranteed a secure fit. Snazzy as they looked, Gabrielle had never been able to find a pair that didn't pinch her toes. But she had brown ones and black ones, and a pair that were two-tone gray.

Over and over, Gabrielle had told him that while she appreciated the gifts, she'd gone into town to be with him, not to shop. She didn't want things, she'd insisted, she only wanted *him*.

"I know, I know," he'd said, "and I love you for it."

But if he had really believed that, why did he buy the gifts, anyway? Gabrielle wondered now.

Did he see her as the type who endured the long trips simply because there'd be a present in it for her? she'd asked him. If he believed *that,* what kind of life partner did he see her as!

He'd flushed and stammered in his usual cowboy way, but he hadn't given her a straight answer. And she'd read that to mean he didn't see her as a partner *at all.*

The memory lay heavy on her shoulders, adding to her gloom. It also made her decide—as long as she was upstairs, anyway—to put clean sheets on the guest room bed. Because even if she chose to stay for a while, she couldn't sleep with a man she didn't trust.

And how could she trust Drew, after learning about all the deliberate lies he'd told?

As she made up the bed, her heart and her head went to war. Amazingly, her heart fired the first shot:

According to Doc, he only told the lies to protect you.

And her brain rallied with *He's a smart guy—if he'd*

wanted to badly enough, Drew would have found a way to protect you and tell the truth.

But Gabby, came her heart's next volley, *he's only human. And you'd been gone nearly a year. He was probably afraid the truth would only drive you away again!*

Nonsense, her brain sent back, *he knew where you were. If he wanted you back that badly, why didn't he ever come after you?*

Her heart skipped a beat. *All right. So maybe he's guilty of false male pride. It's not a hanging offense.*

He's guilty of more than that! He's a control freak, and a know-it-all, and he—

I won't let you talk that way about him, insisted her heart. *He's a good and decent man, doing the best he can with what God gave him.*

God?

Gabrielle might have given Him a total of thirty minutes' thought in twenty-seven years. *Twenty-eight,* she corrected, reminding herself of the time she'd lost.

Well, it wasn't entirely true that she hadn't thought of God in all that time. Gabrielle had called upon Him when she was small, and vulnerable, and naive enough to believe He might answer. Dozens of times, she'd begged Him to give her father a job he could settle into, permanently. But her dad continued to pick up and leave when things at his latest job got rough. Even after her mother died, he couldn't seem to find satisfaction in any one place.

So when the last of her prayers went unanswered, Gabrielle's faith died. Because what was faith with nothing to bolster it? God might have thrown her a bone, at least once in a while, just to keep her believing.

Despite Drew's devoutness, she hadn't seen any evidence of God's presence in his life, either. Why, his past had been many times more traumatic than hers. Surprisingly, he never let go of that incredible, unending faith—faith that his Lord would come through for him.

That had always been a mystery to her, and she'd never been shy about admitting it. A few weeks before she left, she'd accused him of being naive, believing in a being who allowed two little boys to grow up without a mother, who let one of them die in a fiery car crash even before he'd graduated from high school. "If He's so mighty and loving, why does He allow us to suffer like that?" she'd demanded.

"It isn't *God* who causes pain and suffering," he'd explained in his calm, quiet way. "We do that to ourselves, by being impatient or disobedient—by doubting."

"All right, then, if He doesn't cause it, why does He *allow* it? Doesn't He feel some responsibility to protect His followers?"

"He's not doing such a bad job, all things considered."

That was nonsense, and she told him so. "You're an orphan, and so am I. Explain *that*."

He looked at her, long and hard, saying with the dark intensity of his gaze, *He gave us one another.* Out loud, he'd said, "Much as I regret what happened to your family and mine, I wouldn't change a thing if it meant you wouldn't be part of my life."

Even in the heat of the argument, she'd had to admit how much she loved him. How could a woman *not* love a man with a mind like that?

The strange thing was, Gabrielle acknowledged now, that even during the darkest, bleakest times, Drew turned to God, and no matter what the outcome, *thanked* Him.

Was the book he'd been reading still on his nightstand? Gabrielle left the guest room to find out. In moments, she was holding it in her hands.

Last time she'd picked it up, she'd wondered what troubles had inspired him to search for answers in a self-help paperback. This time, it dawned on her that he wouldn't have needed it at all—unless something had shaken his faith.

His mother's abandonment hadn't accomplished that. Nor had the deaths of his brother and father, merely two years apart. He's suffered crop damage and odd diseases that killed his cattle. Lost half a herd of quarter horses to a bitterly cold winter. None of that had shifted his heavenly allegiance.

She put the book back where she'd found it as the stark reality of it dawned: he'd pinned his hopes and dreams on her, setting aside suspicions and fears about a woman's ability to remain loyal. It had been a big risk, one that could cost him more than the price of a lost herd.

Then she'd left him—this man who'd always seemed to have all the answers, who'd always appeared so sure of himself, so certain that his way was the right way. And her leaving had forced him to seek solace, answers, *reasons* in something other than his precious Bible!

Could he truly love her that much? So much that the thought of life without her had brought him to his knees?

Yes, he could, and the proof was everywhere.

Gabrielle went downstairs into the kitchen and finished setting the table, humbled by the knowledge that she was so very, so completely *loved.*

She loved him, too. More now than ever, despite the reasons that sent her packing, despite the recent lies.

But was it enough?

Would love alone get them through tonight, and these next uncertain days?

Gabrielle sat at the table and folded her hands. Then, closing her eyes, she whispered, "Lord, help me. Help *us.*"

Chapter Nine

"**I**'ve figured a few things out," Gabrielle said, closing the dishwasher.

Drew stood beside her at the sink, drying the pot she'd cooked the chicken in. "Y-you've what?" he asked, nearly dropping it.

That look on his face told her he believed she intended to follow up her comment with *I'm leaving*. And why wouldn't he think that, when she'd barely said ten words to him all through supper? She had every right to demand explanations, but saw no point in doing it unkindly.

And there was no reason to leap into it. "It's chilly tonight," she said. "Why don't you start a fire, while I make us some hot chocolate." She swallowed. "I think we need to clear the air about a few things."

Drew shelved the pot, and, nodding silently, left the room. She felt helpless and sad and a little bit guilty, because in spite of everything, she loved him.

But did she love him enough to stay?

If she knew the answer to that, the upcoming discussion wouldn't be necessary.

She'd already spooned cocoa mix into their mugs and was about to add steaming hot water, when something on the other side of the window caught her attention. Had one of the horses gotten out of the corral? The thought put a frown on her face. If what she'd seen was a horse, the next few hours would be spent chasing it down and repairing the gate. Groaning inwardly, Gabrielle shook her head. She couldn't very well expect Drew to feel like talking after all that.

The darkness outside made the windowpanes seem like shiny black mirrors, reflecting the bright interior of the kitchen. Gabrielle switched off the light to get a better look.

Her breath caught in her throat.

There, not twenty feet from the back porch, was a cougar.

Cautiously, she stepped back from the sink, never taking her eyes from the cat. She'd heard a few reports on the local radio station about dogs and cats and chickens disappearing from ranchers' yards. In one report, the newscaster had speculated that the woman who'd disappeared while jogging mountain trails wasn't lost at all...

"Drew," she called in a hoarse whisper. "Drew, come here."

A quick glance at the door told her it wasn't locked. Why that was important, she didn't know. Cougars were intelligent creatures, but Gabrielle hadn't heard any reports that they'd figured out how to turn doorknobs.

She could hear the low tones of the TV weatherman, warning of possible light snowfall tonight. "Drew!" she said, a bit louder this time.

The sound of his boot heels seemed like hammer blows as he crossed the floor.

"What're you doing, standing in here in the dark?"

In place of an answer, Gabrielle stared straight ahead and pointed.

He followed her gaze, then whispered something unintelligible under his breath.

"Did you set the traps?"

Drew nodded. "Yeah. Two of 'em. One near the barn, the other beside the house. Maybe that's where he's headed. I baited them with raw chicken."

Drew went to the back door, and the sound of the deadbolt clicked into place echoed in the darkened room. Gabrielle gave a sigh of relief.

Too soon—for Drew was on his way to the living room. To get his rifle, no doubt, she realized as fear rippled through her. "Drew, don't go out there alone," she said, running after him.

He stood in the foyer, grim-faced, double-checking the weapon's ammo. "I'll have help," he said resolutely.

"Who?" she snapped. "Smith & Wesson?"

Drew looked up and released the gun's safety at the same time.

"I'm calling the rangers' station," she said, when he turned the doorknob.

"I don't need the rangers. I've handled things like this before. Besides, it'll take 'em hours to get here." He turned to leave.

Gabrielle rushed forward, grabbed his elbow. She'd never been more terrified in her life. But she had to tread carefully; Drew had no patience for histrionics. Neither did she, for that matter. At least, she didn't used to.

Gabrielle took a calming breath. "Please don't go out there."

His voice was hard-edged when he said, "I don't have any choice. The horses are sitting ducks out there in that corral."

But if Drew went out there, *he'd* be a sitting duck!

"Stay inside," he told her. "I mean it."

He hadn't needed the qualifier; his no-nonsense attitude and stern expression made it clear he'd been serious.

"I'll be fine," Drew said, softening his tone. And grinning slightly, he added, "I'm an old hand at this, remember?"

At the moment, nothing mattered except keeping him inside, where it was safe. She took no comfort from his words. What difference did it make that he'd done this before? What if this animal was an old hand at it, too?

Dear God, she prayed, *tell me what to do.*

It came to her in an instant. *Trust. Have faith. Believe.*

"Go on, then. Do what you have to." She sent him a feeble smile. "But keep in mind that your cocoa is getting colder by the minute."

Laughing softly, Drew gave her a quick hug and a light kiss. "Y'little nut."

"Be careful?"

Winking, he said, "Promise."

And with that, he was gone.

Immediately, she whirled around and dialed the rangers' station. The dispatcher assured her the rangers would be there as soon as possible to cage—or kill—the cougar. After hanging up, she remembered how she used to think she'd been born in the wrong time period, that life would have been better, easier for her, if she'd come along during pioneer days.

You wouldn't have lasted a week on the trail, she admitted, ashamed at the terror still surging through her veins. At the first sight of a bear or a wild cat, she would've died of fright, right on the—

A gunshot rang out, followed by a blood-curdling, ear-piercing yowl that startled her so badly she nearly bit her own tongue. Within seconds, another shot echoed across the yard.

There was an angry roar, then silence, deadly and still.

Running to the foyer, Gabrielle yanked open the front door, praying that she'd see Drew, triumphant hero, on his way into the house. On his way back to her.

In place of his heavy boot steps, Gabrielle heard nothing. The night birds had ceased calling; crickets had stopped chirping. Even the distant wail of the coyote had faded.

And then a menacing snarl cracked the quiet. She saw the cougar, streaking toward the woods like a beam of golden light, tail flicking behind like a thick velvet rope.

Stepping onto the porch, she leaned against the rail, looking left, right, straining her eyes for a sign of Drew. "Dear God," she whispered, "let him be all right."

As if in answer to her prayer, he rounded the corner.

Gabrielle closed her eyes and breathed, "Thank God."

Rifle barrel leaning on one shoulder, he grumbled, "Missed," and stomped up the steps and into the house. After resetting the safety, Drew leaned the gun in the corner. "I saw him run off toward the woods."

Gabrielle threw herself into his arms. "I know," she said, hugging him tightly. A sob of relief escaped her throat.

Drew returned the hug with equal ferocity, then stood back and stared at her.

Why was he standing there, smiling that way? she wondered.

She began to pace; maybe that would distract her—keep her from reacting to the warm light beaming from his dark eyes. The mere thought of what could have happened to him out there sent a shiver through her. And then what? she silently demanded. How would she have gone on without him?

"You'd cry a little, I reckon," he drawled, pulling her to him again, "and then you'd cuss my ornery hide for not listening to you in the first place." Kissing her forehead, he chuckled. "And by the way, I love you, too."

Until Drew's comment, Gabrielle hadn't realized she'd spoken her fears aloud.

"You think there's any chance the hot chocolate is still, ah, hot?"

Relief and joy and a tinge of annoyance stiffened her. "If it isn't," she said through clenched teeth, "I can always stick it in the microwave."

A myriad of emotions flickered in his eyes: confusion, hurt, guilt.

"Gab—" Drew shook his head. "It's okay, Gabrielle. *I'm* okay. I've dealt with these cats before, so it's no big—"

"Well, *I've* never dealt with one before, so to me it *is* a big deal. And I don't mind admitting, it's pretty scary having your husband out there, trying to catch one single-handedly."

He'd started to call her Gabby, she knew, then changed his mind and said the whole name instead. He'd been doing that a lot lately.

"Why don't you ever call me Gabby anymore?"

Drew's brows rose as his eyes opened wide, as if to say *What has that got to do with anything?*

"Because you don't like it," he said instead. "Believe it or not, even a mule-headed jerk like me can change—if he wants to." He held up his hands in mock self-defense. "I have miles to go, but I'm tryin', *Gabby*, I'm really tryin'."

Seconds ago, her relief at the sight of him, healthy and whole, had her thanking God, of all things. And just now...

She hung her head, embarrassed and confused by her

childish outburst. Yes, she'd told him once, early in their relationship, that she preferred "Gabrielle." But she'd grown to like "Gabby," particularly the way he said it, with that sexy cowboy drawl of his.

So why hadn't she told *him?*

There were so many feelings tumbling in her head that she wasn't sure which was to blame for her behavior.

Gabrielle knew—though she had no scientific support for it yet—that their baby-making attempts had been successful. Maybe the cause of her turmoil could be chalked up to hormones.

No, it's too soon, she realized. She'd read up on it, before the separation; with a blood test, it took seven to ten days to know for sure.

It dawned on her suddenly that despite the fact that Drew had told her not to, she'd phoned for the rangers. "I, uh, I called the rangers' station. They'll be here any minute."

She could see him struggling to bite back his anger as he checked his watch.

"That cat's long gone, so you've wasted your time and theirs." Then rolling up his cuffs, he headed for the kitchen. "While we're waiting for the uniformed heroes to arrive, what say I fix the hot chocolate? You can put your feet up and—"

"No," she interrupted, "I'll do it." Blocking his path, she faced him. "I'm sorry, Drew. I didn't mean to cause a scene." She ran a hand through her hair. "I know you've handled things like this before. Shot a cougar or two, for all I know." The image of Molly, dead on the barn floor flashed through her mind, and she blinked it away. "It's just that...thank God, I've never been around to witness it."

Wrapping her in his arms, Drew rested his chin atop her head. "I have a confession to make," he said softly.

Hands flat against his chest, she met his eyes, waiting.

"Shook me up, too. Always does." He cleared his throat. "Any man says otherwise is a liar. Or crazy."

"Or both."

She felt his muscles tighten beneath her palms.

"I'm sorry for scaring you," he said softly.

"Guess I'd better start getting used to it, hadn't I?"

One hand gripping each of her upper arms, he stared into her eyes; while a hopeful, loving gleam shone in his. Drew opened his mouth to speak, but changed his mind and clamped his lips together.

The moment was as taut as the thread of a spiderweb pulled to its limit. And in that moment, Gabrielle realized something: what they had had once was worth fighting for. If there was a God, she prayed, He'd better give her strength. Because something told her it wouldn't be an easily won battle.

Did the intensity of his gaze mean Drew was thinking the same thing?

She was about to ask him, when they were startled by pounding on the door.

Three uniformed rangers combed the yard, .9-mm hand guns at the ready as the beams of their flashlights crisscrossed the blackness like hyperactive strobes.

Side by side on the front porch, Drew and Gabrielle watched.

"Where do you suppose it went?" she whispered, her breath puffing softly into the chill night.

He knew the cat could be holed up anywhere—in the branches of an oak, beneath a canopy of pine boughs. Sliding an arm around her, Drew said, "All the ruckus those guys are making will likely drive it deep into the hills."

She nodded. "I read in yesterday's paper that because

of all the new development, their territory is getting smaller, and they're making their way into neighborhoods more and more often.''

Drew pulled her a little closer. A man didn't have to be a genius to know she was scared out of her shoes, he thought. If her white-knuckled hands gripping the railing didn't prove it, her shallow, rapid breaths surely did. ''Couple years back the paper ran a story like that,'' he said. ''Coyotes and cougars were coming down from Beartooth, helping themselves to pets and livestock…'' *And the occasional unattended toddler,* he added mentally. ''Turned out they got tired, real fast, of folks taking potshots at 'em.'' He shrugged. ''After a while, they went back where they belonged.''

Gabrielle leaned into him, whether seeking warmth or comfort, he didn't know. Didn't much care, either. She was *there,* and nothing else mattered.

A ranger ambled toward the porch, his flashlight's beam darting across the lawn in wide, golden arcs. ''You're lucky we were in the area,'' he told Gabrielle. ''Otherwise, could've taken us hours to get here.'' He focused on Drew. ''You were right. Doesn't look like we're gonna bag that cougar tonight,'' he said, one boot on the bottom step. ''But I think you're in the clear, for now, anyway.''

''Will you be back tomorrow?'' Gabrielle asked, reaching for Drew's hand.

The officer and Drew exchanged knowing glances. ''No, ma'am,'' he said politely. ''But don't you worry. Your husband has had plenty of experience with things like this. We left you a couple extra cages.'' He turned to Drew. ''Might be a good idea to get 'em set up bright and early. If you catch 'im, give us a holler. We'll come pick him up.''

Linking his fingers with Gabrielle's, Drew said, ''Well, thanks for your help.''

"That's what we get paid for." He turned off the flashlight, touched it to the brim of his hat, and smiled. "G'night, folks."

He and his partners climbed into the four-wheeler and drove away, their exhaust pipe leaving a ghostly gray cloud in their wake.

"Must be a conspiracy of some sort," Drew said, leading her inside.

"A conspiracy?"

He bolted the door and turned off the porch light. His back was to her when he said, "Have you ever seen two people get interrupted as many times as we've been tonight?"

Her heart lurched. She really wasn't in the mood for a showdown. Not after what they'd just survived.

Grinning, he rubbed his palms together and started down the hall. "I'm going to have that cup of cocoa before we hit the hay. And this time, *nothing* is gonna stop me."

Forcing a smile, she joined him in the kitchen. There's a time for everything, she told herself, and this didn't seem like the time for a confrontation. When faced with the possibility of losing him, she'd all but come apart at the seams. That told her something, loud and clear.

Suddenly, Doc Parker's advice made more sense than ever.

First thing the morning after the cougar incident, Drew was making a routine check of fences along the Walking C's north border when he noticed a dark mound in the middle of a pasture. He steered Chum in for a closer look, hoping it wasn't a muley. The ornery, hornless cows could cause more trouble than they were worth. But the defenseless critters kept to themselves, and being a bit of a loner himself, Drew felt protective of them.

Turned out to be a muley, all right—dead. And, if Drew read the signs right, taken down by a cougar. Chum, sensing the cat's scent, jerked back his head and whinnied. "Easy, boy," Drew soothed, "easy."

Despite his calm words, Drew shared the horse's agitation. Cougars usually avoided contact with humans; if this was the same cat that had been near the house, they were in a heap more trouble than he'd thought.

Something told him his hunch was on target.

Down on one knee, he held Chum's reins tight in one hand and inspected the cow with the other. The kill had been recent, as evidenced by the warm blood still oozing from the punctures in the animal's broken neck. He hoped the cow hadn't suffered much. For Drew, an animal's pain had always been the hardest part of ranching.

Surprise attacks were typical of the cougar, he remembered.

But he didn't believe hunger had motivated the attack. Not a morsel of meat was missing. Which could only mean one thing.

This cougar *liked* killing.

It happened sometimes, with no rhyme or reason that he could fathom—a fact that made it all the more unnerving.

Drew adjusted his Stetson and scanned the horizon. At times like these, with nothing for protection but a .50-caliber in his rifle holder, even a seasoned cowboy could feel a mite defenseless.

Ignoring the shiver snaking up his spine, he unsheathed his knife and began disemboweling the animal, ensuring the meat wouldn't turn rancid.

He hated to leave the muley, even for the time it would take to get to the Walking C, fetch the pickup, and return with the winch and hauling harness. But it had to be done, because he couldn't expect Chum to pull a half-ton animal. Not for several miles, anyway.

And even if his horse did have the brawn to drag a half ton of fresh meat for more than a few feet, doing so would make Drew potential prey.

Giving the skyline another cautionary glance, he climbed back into the saddle and *chk-chked* Chum into motion.

The feeling that he was being watched followed him as he rode Chum full-out back to the ranch.

He handed the grooming chores off to Billy the moment he arrived home. It took a few minutes to find and load the hauling harness into the truck bed, and to find Troy, too.

From the time Drew left the muley's carcass to the time he returned to the site of the kill, no more than twenty minutes had passed.

"Look-a there!" Troy shouted, as they rounded the bend leading to the pasture.

The cougar lifted its head. And eyes gleaming menacingly, he stared directly into Drew's eyes.

Indian legend has it that when man looks into the eyes of a wolf, the pair become soul mates of a sort. But looking into those glowing green-gold orbs, Drew felt nothing but quiet, unrelenting dread. Because it was as if the cat had sent a warning on that eerie, invisible cable that connected man to beast.

As if to punctuate the seriousness of its threat, the cougar cut loose with a piercing snarl that hung in the chill October air like icicles.

"You must've walked up on him right after he made the kill," Troy said, "and when you left to get the truck..."

Drew swallowed hard and tried to steady his breath. Troy was right, of course. Which explained the hair-raising feeling he'd had earlier that someone, some*thing*, was watching him.

Both men sat in the truck, Drew gripping the steering wheel like a lifeline, Troy's hands squeezing the dash. In the instant it took for Drew to slide his rifle from the gun rack, the cat was off and running, leaving behind nothing but a ghostly howl.

Cautiously, they got out of the truck and half ran, half walked toward the hornless cow. After securing the harness, Drew fixed the chain to the truck's winch and, with Troy behind the wheel, guided the limp muley into the truck bed.

Troy whistled. "Whew. That was a close one."

"Too close." Drew couldn't shake the feeling that the cougar had been trying to let him in on a secret of nature: *Don't let your guard down. It could mean your life.*

He floored the gas pedal, spitting pebbles and hard-packed dirt against the tree trunks and fence posts along the road.

Back at the ranch, Drew took his time setting the traps. This cat was more cunning than most, and Drew wasn't about to risk losing it again. After baiting the weights with the remains of the muley, he bagged its skin and head and buried it deep to cover its scent.

He slept fitfully that night, awakened by dreams of the cougar and its kill. And Gabrielle, days earlier, collapsing in the kitchen. Dreams of holding her in his arms, making love to her the way God intended married folks to do. And a nightmare—Gabrielle standing at the front door, suitcases around her feet, saying she was leaving and never coming back.

The next morning, he hoped the shower would revive him. That a hearty country breakfast would snap him to attention. But not even three mugs of strong black coffee helped.

It looked like it was just going to be one of those days, he told himself as he headed outside. And he'd had more than his share of experience with those during the first lonely months after Gabrielle left him.

Sometimes, he'd learned, hard work did the trick. First thing on the agenda this morning: check the traps he'd set last night.

But even before he reached the first steel cage, Drew knew something was wrong. Very wrong. Because while the beef was missing, the trap hadn't been sprung.

Saucer-size paw prints at the entrance of the cage proved it had been a male. A big one. His cat had returned, this time with an appetite.

One by one, Drew checked all four traps. The many-toed prints had padded around each. And all the traps had been entered…and emptied.

An eerie tingle prickled the back of his neck. Heart pounding, Drew scrutinized the area…and saw that the tailgate of the pickup was down.

The truck was old, and he pushed it hard, which was precisely why he babied it in every way he could. One way was to keep the tires inflated. Another was to make sure the tailgate stayed shut, so the hinges wouldn't rust from exposure to sun and wind, rain and snow. Despite Drew's attention to detail, the latch didn't always catch.

He ran toward the pickup, not caring that the Stetson had blown from his head. "Lord Almighty," he prayed aloud when he got there. The bags he'd stuffed the muley's hide and head into for the trip to the far end of the Walking C had leaked, and now, big bloody paw prints were all over the truck bed, as if the cat had aimed to stamp the property *his*.

Drew slammed the tailgate, hard. He'd head inside and

grab the rifle, and make a quick check of the perimeter of the house.

On his way, Drew realized he'd dropped his hat, and as he bent to pick it up, a noise in the barn stopped him.

Why hadn't he noticed before that the doors were open?

Pulse pounding, he clamped his teeth together so tightly that his jaw ached. Most of the horses were in the corral. But Triumph was in there, and so was Fake Molly.

Drew had made a point of closing and latching the barn's big double doors last night. Surely the cougar hadn't—

Her voice sailed toward him on a blast of cold air.

Gabrielle!

Had she lost her mind? What could she have been thinking, going alone into the barn and leaving the doors wide open—with a deadly cougar on the loose?

There was no time to go inside and get the gun. If the cougar was in there...

Running at full speed, Drew blew into the building as if propelled by a tornado. And what he saw stopped him as surely as if he'd run smack into a brick wall. There was Gabrielle, brushing Fake Molly, and from the looks of things, she'd already groomed Triumph, too.

"You're a beauty," she crooned softly. "I don't know where Drew found you, but I'm sure glad he did."

She wore a baggy, blue sweatshirt and snug blue jeans with her white sneakers. Scrubbed clean of makeup, and with her hair pulled back in a ponytail, she looked like a fresh-faced teenager.

Drew hung his head as relief surged through him. He could scold her later for putting herself in jeopardy.

Right now, all he wanted to do was look at her...and thank the Good Lord for bringing her back into his life.

A week later, Drew still didn't have a clue what was causing Gabrielle's peculiar behavior, but he had a pretty strong inkling. In all likelihood, she'd somehow puzzled things out and had worked up a head of steam over discovering he'd kept a few things from her. It wasn't like her to keep anything to herself, especially something like that. Reflexive and spontaneous, she'd normally blurt out whatever she learned the moment she stumbled upon it. The fact that she'd decided to sit on the information gave him an uneasy feeling that even the cougar hadn't elicited.

He tried blaming her reticence on all she'd been through during the past few weeks. Several times, he even considered calling Parker or Adams. But fortunately, the neurologist would be running another battery of tests in a few days, "for insurance," Adams had said.

In all honesty, Drew thought, grinning to himself, he much preferred the way Gabrielle had used the word.

Yawning, he wondered if he'd ever get a good night's sleep again. It sure would help if he could catch that cat. He'd been up since dawn. Had been every day since first spotting the cougar's tracks. Even if he weren't a married man, Drew stood to lose a lot if the animal wasn't stopped. The livestock alone was worth upwards of a hundred dollars a head, and he had every cent he'd earned tied up in them.

But he *was* a married man now, with a fragile wife to look out for. And if all her "insurance" talk had paid off, he reminded himself, maybe there was a baby on the way, to boot.

All the more reason to hope the results of Gabrielle's tests would be the same as before: the fall had caused no significant or permanent damage.

Regardless of what the technicians and their x-rays said, the minute he knew for sure that Gabrielle was all right, Drew intended to get things out in the open. Because he couldn't live this way any longer…not knowing if she was staying or leaving, if she loved him, if she was carrying his baby.

They hadn't exchanged a cross word since the night she'd spotted the cougar out back. Drew had sensed there had been plenty she'd *wanted* to tell him, but every time Gabrielle opened her mouth to say it, she snapped it shut faster than if a swarm of bees hovered near her lips.

After the rangers had left, she'd made them both a cup of hot chocolate, and they'd sat at the kitchen table, sipping it in the dim glow of the stove hood light. He'd told her about the times when other cougars—and bears, and coyotes, and once, a white wolf—had strayed onto Walking C property. One or two of them had forced him to use the rifle, he'd admitted. The rest, thankfully, had been captured and sent to zoos across the country, or scared off.

There had been tears in her eyes when Gabrielle said, "It's so sad that their wilderness is dying. It isn't their fault that they wander onto land owned by ranchers and farmers, because once upon a time, it was *all* theirs."

Who but Gabrielle could see the critters' side of things? he asked himself. One of the reasons her mind-set touched him was that he'd always felt the same way. Drew hated what was happening to Montana as much as she did. "But progress comes with a hefty price tag," he'd said.

When Gabrielle had suggested ham and eggs this morning, Drew had passed. "I'll have a bite later," he'd said before heading to the barn. "There's a board loose in the loft. Better get it fixed before someone trips and lands headfirst in a stall."

She had laundry to do, anyway, Gabrielle countered, her voice chilly. "Just let me know when you're ready to eat, and I'll fix breakfast."

Quite a contrast from the way she'd cuddled up beside

him in bed the night of the cougar's visit. Though it was warm and toasty in their room, she'd snuggled up tight, falling asleep with her head on his shoulder. Drew hadn't had the heart to wake her, even when pins and needles roused him two hours later.

She must have sensed his discomfort, for Gabrielle wriggled her tiny body until she found a new spot to cozy up. And they'd spent the remainder of the night that way— Gabrielle's delicate hands wrapped around his biceps like a silken armband.

All right, Drew thought, pulling up the warped loft floorboard and tossing it aside. He'd made two trips up here this morning. One to bring his tools, and one to haul the wood. He reached for the replacement board and tape measure, wishing it were as easy to solve the riddle of what was wrong with Gabrielle as it was to replace the board. Because wouldn't it be nice to know that twenty-four inches of two-by-six planking and a couple of ten-penny nails would fix everything.

If he thought it would do any good, Drew would ask her. But she'd been on her best "company" behavior since moving into the guest room. Polite and helpful, she was always mindful to respect his privacy.

And he respected hers by giving her the space to tell him *why* she'd made the move.

Too mindful, if you ask me, he grouched silently, banging the first nail into place. Much as he'd always hated their arguments, he would have preferred a knock-'em-down, drag-'em-out fight to this restrained courtesy.

Now, as he drove the last nail into place, he nodded resolutely. *Choose your battles well* hadn't become an age-old proverb because it was bad advice. Next time an opportunity presented itself, no matter how insignificant it seemed, he intended to seize it.

The board went into place easily. He could only hope it would be as easy to live with the aftermath—if the show-down sent her packing.

Chapter Ten

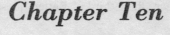

The moment she found out Troy was headed into town, Gabrielle asked, "Mind if I hitch a ride?"

If he minded, it didn't show.

"Meet you out front in five minutes," he'd said, grinning.

Much as she'd enjoy "catching up" with the weathered old cowboy, that wasn't the main purpose of the trip.

Gabrielle needed a pregnancy test kit.

All the signs and symptoms were there—occasional light-headedness, upset stomach, cravings for hot fudge sundaes and buttered popcorn, and mood swings. Incredible mood swings! This, more than anything, prompted Gabrielle to seek answers. Was her erratic behavior psychological or biological? She had to know, because she and Drew couldn't go on this way much longer.

"Dear Drew," she wrote in a note. "Going to town with Troy. Shouldn't be long. There's a ham sandwich in the fridge if you get hungry." And she signed it, simply, "Gabrielle."

Troy honked the horn, and Gabrielle propped the note

against the salt and pepper shakers. Shrugging into her jacket, she grabbed her purse and headed outside.

"How're you this morning?" she asked, climbing into the truck.

Troy winked. "Can't complain," he said. Shifting into first gear, he chortled. "Well, that ain't exactly true. I *could* complain, but what would be the point?" He slid the stick into second gear, then third. "Better question is, how're *you?*"

"Wonderful," she fibbed, staring straight ahead. "Did Drew tell you? My memory is back, and the doctors have given me a clean bill of health."

He nodded. "Glad to hear it."

"So tell me, what's the latest on the cougar?"

Troy looked over at her, an expression of puzzlement adding to the creases in his sun-bronzed face. "Drew didn't tell you?"

"Tell me what?"

Shaking his head, he focused on the highway. "I declare—you young'uns."

Gabrielle didn't need to ask what he meant. Troy had known her husband most of his life and had also noticed the strain in Drew's face. She felt partly responsible for that tension.

But only partly.

The concussion, the amnesia, the cougar were all good reasons to forestall any confrontation with him. She'd recuperated from the aftereffects of the accident, so when the cougar incident was finally put to rest...

"That wily feline got into every cage, managed to steal the meat without springing the trapdoor shut." He whistled.

"That's one smart cat, I'll say that much."

"Come to think of it, Drew did mention something about that."

Gabrielle had been grooming the horse Drew had tried to pass off as Molly, when Drew had come into the barn. Stubbornness gave her the willpower to pretend she hadn't noticed him. After a pause of no more than a heartbeat, she'd gone back to brushing the animal.

In her peripheral vision, she'd seen the look on his face—a look that reminded her of a moment, a week or so earlier, when something roused her from sleep. She'd opened her eyes to find him staring.

It had struck her as odd that he'd seemed so sad and forlorn—maybe even a little bit afraid. She'd chalked it up to worry over what had happened when she fell from Triumph's saddle.

"...but Drew fixed those springs," Troy said, breaking into her thoughts, "so we oughta get that cat the next time."

She nodded as if she'd been paying attention. Drew had said something about having to adjust the tension in the springs controlling the drop-down doors on the traps. "I hope so," Gabrielle said.

She hadn't been near the barn when Troy and Drew brought in the muley. Gory as the sight had probably been, Gabrielle wished she'd gotten an eyeful. Because the real picture couldn't have been as grisly as the pictures in her mind—pictures that, ever since, had flashed in her head like blinding lightning strikes. The cougar, head low and ears back, putting one silent paw down in front of the other as it moved closer, closer to Drew...and Drew, down on one knee, so focused on fixing the traps that he never sensed what lurked behind him....

Gabrielle shivered and bit back an involuntary gasp.

"Cold?" Troy asked.

Arms wrapped around herself, she shook her head.

"Maybe you're comin' down with something. Emily tells me the schools in Livingston are havin' a time with some new flu bug." Troy turned on the radio, fiddled with the dials until he found a clear station. "You goin' into town to see Doc Parker?"

Again, she shook her head.

He hummed a bar or two of the country tune wafting from the speakers. "You are lookin' better than I've seen you since that fall," he said. And whistling, he added, "But I have to admit, you had us scared there for a while."

Us? she thought. He must have been referring to himself and Drew. Because the foreman certainly couldn't be referring to his wife.

"Speaking of Emily, how is she?"

Troy chuckled. "Don't recall mentioning her, but she's fine. Ornery as ever."

Ornery was a mild word compared to the one Gabrielle would choose to describe the woman.

"She told me what went on at the house the other day."

Gabrielle looked at Troy, wondering what sort of spin Emily had put on things.

One hand let go of the steering wheel, and he held it up as if taking a pledge. He opened his mouth, then snapped it shut and gripped the wheel again, thumb drumming the black imitation leather in time to the music.

"I never really made an effort to get to know her." Gabrielle shrugged one shoulder. "Easy to see why she thinks the worst of me."

"I'm the first to admit, Em takes some gettin' used to." Shaking his head, Troy smiled. "But once that woman takes a liking to a person, she's loyal for life." He chuckled. "Got this idea in her pun'kin head that Drew had it rough as a boy. He could rob a bank, I tell you, and she'd figure a way to excuse him for it!"

Gabrielle smiled. "Hard to hold a grudge against anyone who feels that way about him."

"Hard not to feel that way about him."

Many times, when she'd come back from riding Triumph, Troy had invented some excuse or another to keep her company while she groomed the horse. He could go on for hours about the once-wild and untamed West of his youth, but terms of endearment didn't come easily to this man. And that made his plain words anything *but* plain.

He wasn't the type to ask probing questions, so she told him what it seemed he wanted to hear: "I love him, too."

The wide brim of his hat shaded the upper half of his face, but not enough to keep Gabrielle from seeing the intensity of his gaze.

"Drew claims to feel the same way about you." Eyes on the road again, he added, "I sure as shootin' don't make a habit of pokin' my nose into other people's business..." He met her eyes again, and in a fatherly tone, said, "But the pair of you could-a fooled me."

Troy pulled into a parking lot beside Swifty's Hardware and shut off the motor. Staring straight ahead, he said, "I was there the day he was born, so I know better'n most that Drew can be even ornerier than my Emily."

He thumbed his hat to the back of his head. "There's a verse in the Bible goes something like 'Greater love hath no man than that he lay down his life for a friend.'" Troy opened the driver's door and put one boot on the pavement. "Drew's the only man I ever met makes me believe it's possible."

With both feet on the ground and his back to her, he

made a move as if to slam the door. "He's good people. So whatever he did... Well, I'm sure it wasn't on purpose."

Not knowing what to say, Gabrielle said nothing.

"Meet you back here in an hour," he said, closing the door.

He pocketed the truck key and returned a good-natured greeting from a man across the street before disappearing inside the hardware store.

A few minutes later, wandering the aisles of the pharmacy, Gabrielle replayed the things Troy had said. She couldn't dispute a word of it, and so she didn't even try. Pregnancy test kit in hand, she said a silent prayer: *Lord, help me do the right thing.*

"What're your plans for the rest of the day?" Drew asked.

Gabrielle pictured the brightly colored box she'd stowed under the bathroom vanity. According to the directions, the results were most accurate when the test was taken first thing upon waking. And oh, did she want it to be morning.

The best way to make time pass quickly, she reasoned, was to keep busy.

Very busy.

Gabrielle stepped out of the hall closet. "I thought I'd do a little organizing, you know, in case I decide to go back to work after the doctor gives me the final go-ahead."

She read his tight-lipped expression to mean he wanted a say in that decision. But the slight bulge of his jaw muscle told her he'd decided to keep his opinions to himself. Maybe he *can* change, she thought, remembering what he'd said after the cougar's visit. One thing was certain: he really was *trying.*

If that was true, she owed him equal effort.

In the past, she would have dug in her heels and refused

to tell him what she was thinking. "Maybe we can talk about it after supper," she suggested, "because if it turns out I'm going to have a baby, I'm not sure I want to work."

A bright smile relaxed his features.

But it wouldn't be fair to mislead him, so she quickly added, "I don't know if I'll want to work *full time,* anyway."

Drew nodded, but the smile evaporated. "In other words, there's nothing to discuss," he said in low, even tones. "You'll do what you want, as usual."

A spark of anger came to life inside her at what sounded like sarcasm. He'd said something similar the night she left. "Go ahead," she'd snapped then, "admit it. You can't control me one hundred percent of the time, so you *want* me to leave."

Now, he stood there blinking, shaking his head, looking hurt and betrayed, as he ran both hands through his hair. His usually smooth voice wavered. "I wish I could make you understand." He winced, took a step closer. "I just want you to be happy, Gabrielle. So whatever you want, that's what I want. Honest."

She read his face, and saw the purity of his intentions written there. It wasn't his fault that she'd learned to defend herself early in life. Always "the new kid," it was either that or become the target of every schoolyard bully. *You don't need your fists to win a battle* had been her father's advice. *Stay calm. Watch and listen. And when you find your enemy's weak spot, attack that.*

Drew's weak spot, she'd realized fairly quickly in their relationship, was feeling that if he didn't remain in full control, he'd lose *all* control. To him, life was like a bronco ride; without a tight grip on the reins, it would throw you, trample you into dust.

If that's the way he was, if he really couldn't help himself, why was she so filled with anger?

She thought about that for a moment, and realized she *wasn't* angry. Because it didn't take a genius to figure things out.

As a boy, Drew had felt helpless to keep his mother from leaving; had felt he had even less power over how the desertion affected his father. Drew had told Gabrielle how he'd broken his hand, days after his mother's departure. "I was just so mad that I hadn't been able to think of a way to stop her," Drew admitted, "that I punched a steel filing cabinet in Dad's office."

Gabrielle sighed as guilt wrapped around her like a cold, damp blanket. She'd seen how vulnerable Drew had been, and when push came to shove, she'd used it...to win.

She took a deep breath, then faced him. He hadn't been completely on the up-and-up with her, but then, she hadn't been totally honest with him, either.

"Was there something you wanted me to do when you asked what I had planned for the rest of the day?"

"Oh. That." Drew nodded. "I was just—" He cleared his throat. "I just thought maybe we could drive into Bozeman, walk around a few car dealerships, let you pick out something you'd like."

Again he ran a hand through his hair—something he only did when he was nervous, she knew. Drew was making the grand gesture, admitting without words that he was sorry for foisting the compact on her.

"Speaking of cars," she said, "what *really* happened to that little red car?" Gabrielle smiled a bit when she said it, so he'd know the question hadn't been rooted in sarcasm or reprisal.

"I, ah, I sold it to a dealer in Livingston."

Giving a full-out grin now, she asked, "Did you get a good price?"

He met her eyes and, sending her a half smile, shook his head. "Hardly. Took a two-thousand-dollar loss.... But that's what I get," he said, flushing slightly. "Small price to pay, when you think about it, for not treating you like a full partner."

Gabrielle wanted to throw her arms around him, tell him she understood what motivated his authoritative behavior, admit that she loved him for being willing to change—for her.

So why couldn't she? What kept her rooted to the spot as though someone had nailed her sneakers to the floor?

He was working hard to please her. Once, she would have viewed this, too, as a weakness, a vulnerability to be stored in her memory bank and used as ammunition down the road, when he was getting the best of her in a disagreement.

That might have been a good tactic for handling ruffians on the playground, but Drew wasn't the enemy.

Didn't she owe it to him to meet him halfway? To prove she wouldn't take advantage, ever again? She'd accumulated quite a list of "wrongs" he'd committed. Lucky for her, Drew wasn't the list-keeping type.

She glanced at the grandfather clock in the front hall. "It's almost lunchtime," she pointed out, shoving a box into the closet and kicking the door shut.

It was a risk, she knew, giving him this chance to get back in control. But the things Doc Parker, and Troy, and even Emily had said niggled. Gabrielle felt she owed it to herself, to Drew, to the baby she might be carrying, to at least give it a try. "Let me make us something to eat, and then I'll get cleaned up, and we can go to town."

"No."

It stunned her, hearing the finality of his word, seeing the resoluteness on his face. Shocked her, and hurt her, too. *This is too much like the early days,* was her dark thought, *when you'd give him an inch and he'd take a mile.*

He took another step closer, wrapped a tendril of her hair around his forefinger. "Put on something pretty. We'll have lunch in a nice restaurant, maybe catch a matinee before we see what kind of car you'd like to drive home in."

Her relief at realizing she hadn't been mistaken about his attempts to change rekindled the urge to wrap her arms around him.

And this time, Gabrielle didn't resist.

That hug was the first real contact they'd had in more than a week. Oh, there had been the occasional touch—his hand brushing hers as they both went for the doorknob at the same time. But nothing intentional. Unless they counted their good-night kisses. Though the way their taut lips came together for a fraction of a second could hardly be called a kiss.

Gabrielle thought about that embrace as she showered, then changed into her white turtleneck and denim jumper, and pulled the wild mass of curls back from her face.

It had been a long time since she'd read a romance novel, but Gabrielle felt a lot like one of the heroines. Because while she didn't giggle out loud, she *wanted* to, and though she was sure Drew couldn't actually hear the fluttering of her heart, it certainly seemed possible.

In the pickup, on the way to town, she pressed her palm to the bench seat, steadying herself as the truck bumped along over the potholed ramp leading to the Interstate.

Drew reached across the seat and wrapped her hand in his. "You look real pretty today," he said without taking his eyes from the road. "Did I tell you that?"

She'd *wanted* to look pretty for him, and had put more than a little effort into it. "Only half a dozen times."

Drew chuckled, gave her hand an affectionate squeeze.

They rode in silence for several miles, her hand in his, before Drew said, "You were thinking of a used four-wheeler before—" He cleared his throat. "You still want something with four-wheel drive?"

"Makes sense, considering we live miles from anywhere. It'll be nice for you, too, having a backup vehicle, don't you think?"

She watched his Adam's apple bob up and down, heard his slow intake of air. "I reckon it's logical, all right."

He'd always been a fastidious bookkeeper, and his desk was littered with ledgers that tracked everything from the household bills to the ranch hands' salaries. Something told her he was keeping track of her every reference to their future together, too, and Gabrielle warned herself not to be so free with her comments. Just because things between them now were fine was no guarantee it would continue this way.

His quiet chuckling interrupted her thoughts.

"What's so funny?"

"I was just sitting here wondering what color car you'd get."

Gabrielle waited, wondering what he found comical about *that*.

"I'll go out on a limb here and say—" he gave her hand another squeeze "—it ain't a-gonna be red!"

Rolling her eyes, Gabrielle slid her hand from beneath his, gave him a playful shove. "Oh I don't know." She did her best to emulate his Montana drawl. "I reckon it'll stand out right nice against the snow. Because if I should get rear-ended, I wouldn't want the other driver to say, 'But Officer, I didn't see her!'"

She hadn't heard him laugh in a long time, and the sound of it was as welcome as those first warming rains after a biting-cold winter.

"Do me a favor?" Drew said. "Come over here and sit close to me." He released her hand, then made a half-circle of his arm and waited for her to fill it.

Unbuckling her shoulder harness, she scooted across the bench. It felt so good, so secure, having his strong arm around her shoulders that if Drew hadn't reminded her, she wouldn't have remembered to secure the center seat belt across her thighs.

It seemed the most natural thing in the world, leaning her head on his shoulder. Felt more natural still when he pressed a light kiss to the top of her head.

Gabrielle wondered when it would be best to tell Drew that she'd bought the pregnancy test kit.

Not over their delicious lunch in the quaint Italian restaurant. Not during the lulls of the movie he'd asked her to choose. Not while they walked up and down the colorful aisles of shiny new cars at the dealership. And certainly not as they sat in the stiff-backed chairs in the salesman's tiny cubicle.

Right up until she was about to sign her name on the bottom line, Gabrielle was torn. Take this generous gift for what he'd said it was—a practical addition to their assets—or refuse it out of fear that it would come to represent one more way he'd taken control of her.

But if control was what he wanted, would he have put the title in her name? If he aimed to hold the gift over her head later, would he have paid for it, cash on the spot?

It was a good solid car with a reputation for safety—an important element, she thought, should the pregnancy test confirm what she already knew. Besides, whether or not she decided to go back to work, she'd need a car to run household errands...provided she decided to make a go of their marriage.

Who are you kidding? she asked herself, as the salesman handed her a ballpoint pen. *You decided that when you emptied your suitcase and stuffed it in the attic.*

So it was official. Gabrielle was now the proud owner of a pearl-white sport utility vehicle.

They'd driven about ten miles when she remembered the way Drew had insisted that she lead their two-car caravan back to the ranch. "In case something goes wrong," he'd said. "Happens sometimes with new cars."

How would you know? she'd silently asked. It had been decades since he'd driven anything new.

Which gave her an idea that put a mischievous grin on her face. Gabrielle turned on the blinker, signaled a right turn, and braked until the car came to a halt on the gravel shoulder.

"What is it?" he asked when he reached her car. "Is it overheating?" He stuck his head partway in the window. "One of the warning lights come on?"

"There's nothing wrong," she said, "except that you're in my way."

Straightening, he said, "What?"

She got out of the car and pointed. "You drive it the rest of the way home." With a deliberately silly giggle and a dainty wave of her hand, she patted back a fake yawn and sighed. "I'm bored with it already."

Drew studied her face for a moment before breaking into a smile. It hurt more than she cared to admit that, even for a second, he'd had to stop and think about whether she was serious.

"All right," he said, "but I still want you to take the lead."

Nodding, Gabrielle headed for the pickup. "Think you can keep up with me?" she tossed over her shoulder.

He laughed. "Well, we'll see, won't we?"

Almost as an afterthought, he caught up with her. He pressed a palm to each of her cheeks, his expression somber, his voice stern. "Do me another favor?"

"Sure. What?"

"I know you like to drive fast, but go the speed limit, okay?"

"I'll think about it," she teased.

But he didn't smile. "I'm serious, Gabby. I don't know what I'd do if anything happened—"

She couldn't be sure, because of the fading light and the Stetson's shadow, but Gabrielle could have sworn she saw the beginnings of tears misting his eyes.

"—to that truck of mine," he finished on a ragged sigh.

He'd never been one for sweet talk, but then, she'd never wanted a poet. Even as a teenager, she'd sensed that pretty rhymes and fancy words were, as often as not, cheap and meaningless. A solid, dependable man who'd do the right thing, even when it cost him—that was the armor *her* dream knight would wear.

"Don't you worry," she countered, tidying his shirt collar. "I'll take very good care of your...*truck.*"

She could tell by the warm light in his eyes that Drew knew she understood exactly what he'd meant. In place of a thank-you, he kissed her, right there beside the highway, where God and nature and every passerby could see them.

"See you at home," he echoed, heading back to the car.

Home.

Gabrielle liked the sound of that.

They sat side by side on the couch that night, sipping hot chocolate and watching reruns of sixties sitcoms on TV.

Try as he might, Drew couldn't seem to relax. If his mind wasn't wrapped around catching the bloodthirsty cougar, it fixed on Gabrielle's erratic behavior.

He didn't much like admitting it, but the truth was, he missed those first days when she'd forgotten about the separation. And a little of him wished she'd never gotten her memory back.

All right, he acknowledged, *a whole lot of you wishes it.*

He tried to look on the bright side. If they wound up hashing things out, and she decided to stay, those old issues would fade into the past like any bad memory ought to.

But how were they supposed to hash things out if the *time* never seemed right to start up the discussion?

Drew remembered how, when he was a boy, a classmate had found a box turtle on the playground. The kid had turned the critter upside down, and if his knee-slapping, hooting-hollering laughter was any indicator, he enjoyed watching its small claw feet paddling at the air in a futile attempt to turn itself over.

When the bully's attention turned to a big black beetle, Drew picked the turtle up and carried it to the edge of the stream that ran behind the school. Gently, he set it down—right side up—feeling like a coward for waiting so long to do the right thing.

Now, he felt a lot like that turtle, struggling to stay on his feet in a world turned upside down. And the only person who had the power to right things sat beside him, munching popcorn from the glass bowl in her lap.

For all its untamed beauty, life on the Walking C could be cruel. The muley's fate was proof of that. Living on the edge of the wilderness had taught Drew not to waste time, or words, because who could say when God might decide that time was up?

He'd squandered enough time, treading warily around

the subject of their future together. So he sat on the edge of the couch, elbows on his knees, and asked straight-out the question he'd been putting off for days.

"What are your plans, Gabrielle?"

She froze, mid-chew, and looked at him. "Plans?" Gabrielle put the bowl of popcorn on the coffee table and picked up the remote. She turned off the TV, then sat beside him on the edge of the sofa. "About our future together, you mean?"

Her voice, whisper soft, trembled slightly, and he couldn't help but wonder what had caused it. *Please God,* he prayed, *don't let it be because she's about to say good-bye.*

He nodded. "If you're not ready to talk about it, well, I'll try to be patient." Clasping and unclasping his hands, he added, "It's—It'd just be nice to know where I stand, is all."

She licked her lips, pressed a palm to her stomach, and heaved a sigh. "It isn't that I'm not ready to talk about it," she began. "It's just that I—" Another sigh—longer, deeper this time.

Drew turned and faced her, gently gripped her forearms. "I know I messed up big time, that I have a lot to make up for. But I'm workin' on it. Honest I am." He gave her a little shake. "All I ask is that you meet me halfway."

Picking absently at her cuticles, Gabrielle stared blankly at the floor.

"Sorry," he said, releasing her. "I forgot."

Her head snapped up. "Forgot what?"

He smiled, though his heart wasn't in it. "That you never do anything halfway. It's one of the reasons I went crazy over you." Drew shrugged. "Can't have it both ways, now can I?"

She pinched the bridge of her nose between thumb and

forefinger. "I don't get it. Both ways?" She met his eyes, waiting for him to explain.

"Never mind," he said, frowning at the blank TV screen. "Doesn't matter." He got to his feet. "Didn't mean to rush you. That was selfish of me, especially after all you've just been through."

He couldn't help but notice that she still held one palm against her stomach. It fluttered there for a moment before she held it out to him. "Thank you."

Wrapping her hand in his own, he echoed, "'Thank you'? For what?"

Smiling, she rested her cheek against his knuckles. "Oh, just...just for being you."

Then she stood, too, picked up the popcorn bowl and their half-empty cocoa mugs, and walked toward the kitchen. "You sleepy?"

Overwhelming sadness wrapped around him, making it hard to breathe. "Yeah. But I need to check the cougar traps and lock up before I go upstairs."

She whirled around so fast that several kernels of popcorn spilled from the bowl. "Check the traps? Now?"

There was an edginess in her voice, a high-strung tension that told him she still cared enough to be concerned for his safety.

"Can't that wait 'til morning," she added, "when *you* have the advantage?"

"Might be too late then. That cat..." Telling her that the animal was an anomaly of nature, cunning and cruel enough to kill for the sheer pleasure of it, would only scare her. And Drew saw no point in that.

"All right," he said instead. "I'll wait 'til morning." When he was certain she'd fallen asleep, *then* he'd go out and check the traps.

She breathed a sigh of relief. And sending him a look

he hoped meant *I love you,* she nodded, then hurried up the hall and disappeared into the kitchen.

Woodenly, he made his nightly rounds, checking every window lock, double-bolting every door. There was a time when such precautions would not have been necessary, not way out here in the foothills. But these were different times...

Standing in the now darkened living room, he peered out at the moonlit yard. Wind, soughing through the trees, caused branches to bounce lightly, casting eerie, ever-changing shadows on the night-black earth.

The corral fence glowed silvery white, and the pale manes of the palominos shimmered softly. Dew twinkled from every blade of grass, the leaf of each tree, reminding him of the tiny white lights that decorated the Bozeman town square at Christmastime.

A sense of calm settled over him as he gazed at these oh-so-familiar sights, listening to the sounds of Gabrielle's tidying waft in from the kitchen. *You're gettin' soft, Cunningham,* he thought, grinning, *but Lord, it is a beautiful sight.*

On the heels of his prayer, a ghostly gray cloud slid in front of the moon, blocking all but the memory of its pearlescent beams.

And in the distance, as if answering the call of the gloom, the high-pitched shriek of the cougar.

The ferocious cry echoed in Drew's ears, thundered in his rib cage. He snapped the blind shut with a quick, hard pull of the drapery cord.

"Drew, did you hear that?"

Gabrielle, huddled in the doorway, twisted a terry-cloth kitchen towel in her hands.

He tried sounding casual, unconcerned. "Yeah. But don't worry." She was wide-eyed and pale as a bedsheet;

one thing she didn't need was another trip to the emergency room. "Sounded way off to me."

"Then what were you looking at out there?"

"I was just standing there thinking how pretty everything is in the moonlight," he said, smiling self-consciously.

"Weatherman says we could get a dusting of snow tonight."

He could tell she was putting on a brave front for him. "That's what he's been saying every night for a week."

Hanging the towel over one shoulder, Gabrielle said, "Do me a favor?"

Her voice sounded small and timid and very far away. "Sure."

Gabrielle held out her arms. "Hold me?"

Drew went to her, wrapped her in a warm embrace.

"Promise me you won't go out there?"

In place of an answer, he kissed her.

Just then, a clap of thunder shook the house, rattled the windows, followed by an explosive bolt of lightning that cut the electricity with a single quiet *pop*.

Gabrielle pulled back a bit, rested her cheek on his chest. "Wow," she teased, laughing into his shirt, "that was some kiss."

But before he could respond, the paralyzing *gnar* of the wild cat knifed through the gloom.

Chapter Eleven

Later that night, the memory of the cougar's menacing growl echoed in Drew's mind. The cat wasn't nearly as far off as Drew had led Gabrielle to believe. He hadn't told her about all the other cougar kills he'd found; if he had, he wouldn't be sneaking out of bed now. Instead, he'd be going out there boldly.

There had been a mare, an old bull, a cow and a barnyard cat, all exhibiting the cougar's trademark broken neck.

Given his druthers, Drew would prefer to capture the cougar, ship it off to a zoo somewhere. Not the happiest life for a critter who'd lived wild and free, but better than the alternative.

Much as he hated that alternative, Drew knew this—he'd do whatever he had to do to protect the ranch.

The glowing red numerals of the alarm clock said 11:45. Gabrielle had been asleep nearly thirty minutes. Long enough, he hoped, to double-check the animals and be back before she knew he'd been gone.

After locking up, he'd taken off his boots and left them at the bottom of the stairs. His jeans and shirt, he'd hung on the winged backrest of the chaise longue beside their bed. Grabbing his clothes, he padded down the hardwood steps on white-socked feet.

It was as he sat at the bottom of the stairs, pulling on his boots, that he heard it again—hateful and hollow and closer still this time. Perhaps no more than a few hundred yards from the house.

He pictured its phosphorescent amber eyes, glaring up from the muley carcass with a malevolence like none he'd seen before. And it wasn't likely he'd see anything like it again in his lifetime, he thought, shrugging into his jacket.

Making as little noise as possible, Drew crossed the foyer and grabbed the rifle. Earlier, he'd slid in two rounds of ammunition, but just to be safe, he depressed the lever, checked the chamber. Assured of the load, Drew nodded.

He wasn't looking forward to opening the door. Didn't relish walking across the porch and down the flagstone walk, either. But the livestock, penned in by fencing and stalls, were easy pickin's for the cougar's unbridled maliciousness. The very things that under normal circumstances protected them, now made them defenseless.

He had no choice but to go out there and see to their safety.

And so, one hand on the doorknob, Drew pressed the rifle's stock tight to his side, its barrel resting in his free palm, trigger finger at the ready, thumb on the hammer. Slowly, deliberately, he swung open the door, wincing at the quiet squeal of its hinges.

He was about to step onto the porch, when the bright beam of a flashlight illuminated the foyer.

"Drew!"

The sound of her soft voice might as well have been the blast of an air horn. Drew lurched with alarm, knocking a vase from the foyer table. It hit the wood-planked floor with a stentorian crash.

Simultaneously, he heard her sharp intake of air—

And the cougar's angry snarl.

The cat had been close. Real close. If Gabrielle hadn't interfered, he could have bagged it, put an end to the senseless, violent killings.

"You promised you wouldn't go out there," she said, making her way down the stairs.

"No. I didn't."

She thought about that a minute. "Semantics," she snapped, aiming the flashlight beam at the broken shards of glass on the floor. "You knew how I'd take it. You deliberately misled me."

All right, so maybe he had. But it was for her good as well as the animals'. Drew was struck by a mental image of her tiny boot prints there in the dirt beside the walk, mixed in with the cougar's paw prints. He shrugged off the cold chill that slithered up his spine. "I have responsibilities to the livestock, Gabrielle. They're easy prey for that killer. If I don't look out for—"

"And who will look out for *you?*" she demanded.

Frustrated, infuriated, exhausted, he squatted and started picking up fragments of the broken vase. As he collected them, one atop the other in his open palm, he began, "I have my—"

"Yes. I know." Her voice was icy with sarcasm. "Mr. Smith & Mr. Wesson there will protect you," she said, pointing at the rifle.

Gabrielle plopped onto the bottom step and stood the flashlight on its end beside her, its beam creating a bright golden bull's-eye on the ceiling. Holding her head in her hands, she took a deep breath and forced herself to calm down.

She had no explanation for the way she'd come awake with a start. But the moment she'd opened her eyes and seen that Drew wasn't there, she knew where she'd find him.

Of course he owed it to the animals to protect and care for them. She certainly didn't want to see even one more animal sacrificed to the cougar. And yes, she understood that the creatures were his livelihood. But what if her suspicions were correct, and she was carrying his child? It wouldn't be fair to the baby *or* her if the consequences of his actions meant they'd be without him.

The thought seemed to freeze the blood in her veins. "Leave that mess," she told him. "I'll clean it up in the morning. I'm tired," she added, meaning it. "If I go up to bed now, can I trust you to stay inside, where you'll be safe?"

Gabrielle wanted to trust him, because, God help her, she loved him. More than was smart or healthy, but she loved him.

Drew stood, and for what felt like ten minutes, stared at her, silent and brooding. If she'd been asked to define the slump-shouldered look, she would have said he was as broken as that vase.

He leaned the rifle in the corner and closed the door. The bolt slid into place with a loud, echoing finality. Then he sat beside her on the stairs. "I wish I could help you with this." Drew extended his hands, palms up, a gesture of helplessness that told her he was referring to the cracks in their relationship, not the glass-strewn floor.

And it nearly broke her heart, because Gabrielle wished the same thing.

He shook his head. "But trust is like faith, Gabrielle," he said. "Either you have it or you don't."

He breathed a weary sigh. "I know you're tired. You've

been through a lot these past few days. So let me just say this—and then we can go up to bed.''

Drew closed her hand in his. "I know it's hard to believe, because I'm not very good with words. But I'd never do anything to hurt you.''

She looked into his eyes, dark and warm and overflowing with love—for *her*. Gabrielle nodded. "I know,'' she whispered. "At least…not on purpose.''

Drew looked quickly away, as if to keep her from seeing that she had hurt him with her tactless comment. *Never let 'em see you sweat,* he'd told her once.

Maybe one of these days, she told him with her eyes, *you'll trust me enough to let me see you sweat.*

"See you in the morning,'' she said, pressing her palm to his stubbled cheek.

As she climbed the stairs, she hoped she had what it took to be around when—*if*—that day came, for her sake as well as his. Because if she didn't, Gabrielle was going to need strength. More than she'd ever needed before.

Where would she find it?

God echoed quietly in her head. *Turn to God.*

There were tears in her eyes when she turned out the light. And as she slid between the crisp, line-dried sheets, Gabrielle prayed.

Drew slept on the living room sofa that night, unable— *or unwilling?* he asked himself—to take all the blame for their argument.

Had it been an argument? Neither of them had raised their voices. Neither had spoken an angry word. What's a man to call it, then, he wondered, tucking his arms under his head. A discussion?

Poking out his lip, Drew nodded to himself. Made sense to him. He'd said his piece, and she'd said—

No. That wasn't entirely true. He hadn't said a *fraction* of what had gone through his head when she showed up and ended any chance he might have had of stopping the cougar.

Before going up to bed, Gabrielle had said she was tired. She'd looked and sounded it. That had been the only reason he'd kept his mouth shut.

Because he was tired, too. Tired of apologizing for being who and what he was. Tired of saying "I'm trying," when all he was guilty of was fulfilling his duties and obligations—some chosen, others inherited, a few thrust upon him by nature. Tired of being made to feel like a criminal for doing nothing more than trying to protect her.

She claimed to want equal treatment.

His mother had said that, too, with every bit as much conviction as Gabrielle. And his father, believing his wife when she assured him she could stand up under the sometimes burdensome weight of it, had given her equal treatment.

And look where that got the lot of them, Drew thought wryly.

Gabrielle was nothing like his mother. Not in the ways that mattered. He'd come to realize that, more and more, as the days without her turned to weeks, and the weeks became months.

It hadn't been easy admitting that, because in doing so, he had to wonder if maybe he'd inherited some of his mother's "quitter" genes, some of the same self-centeredness and greed and immaturity that had led her to believe she could have anything she wanted, any time she wanted it.

Not if he could help it. Long ago, he'd resolved to roll his acorn as far from his mother's tree as he could.

What he wanted was simple. Gabrielle, here, loving him

as much as he loved her, without questioning his motives. If that wasn't selfish and self-centered, he sure didn't know what it *was.*

He decided it was best never to give those traits, if indeed his mother had handed them down to him, the time or the space to develop.

And so he'd kept a tight rein on himself, working from dawn 'til dusk and sometimes beyond. It was his insurance against becoming like his mother, who wasn't only willing, but able, to take her happiness at the expense of others— without so much as a backward glance.

He couldn't hide from the ugly fact that Gabrielle was like his mother in one way: she'd walked out on him after dumping a bucket load of accusations at his feet, and hadn't looked back. If he'd known ahead of time that the acidic thoughts had been in her head, maybe he could have made some adjustments, tried to calm her fears.

Drew hadn't understood Gabrielle before she left, and he had frequently admitted it. Having grown up in a men-only home, he didn't have a clue what made women tick. Sometimes, it seemed to him that he was walking through a minefield.

Bottom line, Gabrielle had left. And if it hadn't been for the fall and its resulting amnesia, she wouldn't have come back.

Could he get beyond *that?*

Could he learn to trust that she wouldn't stalk off again, next time things got rough? Because it *would* get rough; time and life had taught him that much. Much as he wanted her to stay, relieved as he was to have her in his life again, it was unsettling not knowing if, or when, she'd head for high ground—alone.

Something struck him just then.

Folks didn't head for high ground unless they were afraid of drowning.

He flopped back against the armrest, disgusted, disappointed, dismayed. Because he *would* have altered course— if Gabrielle had been up front with him early on, when he could have done something about his behavior.

The way he had been up front about hunting down the cat?

Gabrielle could be mule-headed, but she'd never been impractical or unrealistic. If he'd been honest about all the killings the cougar had been responsible for...if she'd known about the pregnant barnyard cat and the aged bull and the young heifer...maybe she'd have understood why he felt the need to put a stop to it, once and for all.

He'd never know, because he hadn't given her a chance.

It dawned on him. *This* was what Gabrielle had meant that night, when she'd started her list of accusations with *Why won't you let me help you?* At the time, he'd taken it to mean she wanted to pound nails and stack hay bales and haul logs, right alongside him. Much as he appreciated the sentiment, he couldn't very well risk her getting hurt—tiny as she was—working like a man.

So why didn't you just say that? he asked himself, instead of reciting a list of No's that ended up sounding to her like rejections. That's what had inspired her to start keeping a *You Don't Want Me in Your Life* list.

And he'd unwittingly handed her the pen.

He felt awful. Dull-witted. Guilty. Angry. He'd put her through all that, for what? Pride? The Bible had plenty to say on the subject, and if he'd taken any of it to heart, maybe he could have spared them both a long, lonely, miserable year.

A chill rolled over him, and he turned onto his side, tucking the afghan tighter under his chin. What was he doing there, freezing on the narrow couch, when he could be warm as sunshine, snuggled beside his beautiful wife?

Standing, Drew removed his boots and headed up the stairs, feeling a little pleased with himself and a whole lot proud that he'd figured a few things out on his own.

When he told Gabrielle about his new mind-set, what choice would she have but to trust him?

Gabrielle opened the pregnancy test kit and followed its instructions to the letter. When the first pink dot appeared, signaling the test was working, her heart began to beat faster. Dry-mouthed and damp-palmed, she sat on the edge of the tub and stared at the stick that rested on the vanity.

She checked her watch. Just a little longer, she thought as anticipation increased her pulse rate even farther.

Would it be a healthy pregnancy? A quick labor? An easy delivery? Would she be a good mother, even when the baby's cries roused her from a deep sleep?

Gabrielle sighed, staring at the still-white stick. She hoped so.

She pictured a helpless being with tiny fingers and dimpled feet, rosy cheeks and hungry pink lips. A needy, defenseless bundle that would fit easily, naturally into the crook of her arm. The scents of baby powder and baby soap and baby lotion would cling to velvety skin.

Would the baby have Drew's warm brown eyes and thick wavy hair? She'd never had a chance to meet his family, but he'd shown her photographs. Would the child have Drew's lean-muscled build? His father's burly shoulders? His grandfather's broad jaw? She hoped so, for they were strong, handsome traits.

Grinning, she quickly added, *But only if it's a boy, of course.*

She glanced at the watch again. Why couldn't time pass

this slowly when things were going well between her and Drew?

That question raised other, scarier ones. Did she *want* the second pink dot to appear?

Gabrielle looked at the test stick, and realized it made no difference what she wanted, because the answer was there, plain as day.

Heart hammering, her eyes filled with hot tears, and she buried her face in her hands.

She allowed herself that moment of helpless, emotional silliness, then pitched the kit and its telltale results into the wicker basket beside the vanity.

After splashing cold water on her face, she combed her hair, knowing it was time to find Drew and tell him the news.

Gabrielle met the eyes of the woman in the mirror, the woman wearing the false and shaky *Be brave* smile.

"Well," she said to herself, "what are you waiting for...*mommy?*"

She headed downstairs, hope for the future growing within her—

"G'mornin'," he said, looking up from the newspaper. "I made coffee. You want a cup?"

"Not just yet," she said. "What about breakfast? Have you eaten?"

Nodding, he told her he'd fried himself an egg sandwich. "You want me to whip one up for you?"

"No." She tried smiling. "But thanks."

Gabrielle had a sinking feeling that if Troy hadn't come knocking at that particular moment, the confrontation she and Drew had been putting off for days would have taken place, here and now.

The rest of the morning, she moved as if in a daze, unable to believe a child lived inside her—evidence of her love for Drew and his love for her.

At least, it had seemed like love the night they were celebrating their supposed two-month anniversary.

She remembered how she'd fixed lasagna. Set the table with the good dishes, used the best tablecloth. After the trip into town to see Doc Parker, they'd eaten supper, and she'd talked Drew into going upstairs.

And he'd protested. Strongly, she recalled, at least at first.

As she put away the last of the breakfast dishes, Gabrielle realized two things. One, Drew had tried to keep her at arm's length because he believed saying yes to her "proposal"—in his mind—was tantamount to using her, to taking advantage of her weakened physical and emotional condition. And two, he'd given in because despite their many months apart, he still loved her.

She had no regrets, even now.

Careful what you ask for, she reminded herself yet again.

She'd wanted a baby more than just about anything, except Drew's love. And unless the pregnancy test kit had given a false result, she'd gotten *exactly* what she'd asked for.

Lately, she'd been giving a lot of thought to everything Drew had told her about his Lord and Savior. Maybe there was something to all this Christian stuff, after all. Maybe with enough faith, with belief that's strong, people could have what they asked for.

She'd check out Drew's battered old Bible, as soon as she made a few calls. To the bank, for one. Because baby or not, her job right now was to work on her marriage. To Mrs. Blake, for another. The sunny apartment wasn't as solid a home for the child as the Walking C.

She'd just started dialing the first number, when a soft

knock on the back door interrupted her, and she went to answer it.

It had all the earmarks of a good-neighbor visit. Emily stood on the porch, a plastic-wrapped, deep-dish pie balanced on one palm, the fingers of her free hand wrapped around the handles of her oversize black purse.

Tentatively, Gabrielle opened the door.

"Came to give this to Drew," Emily said, hoisting the dessert an inch or two.

"He left for town a few minutes ago."

"I know. Troy's with him." She clucked her tongue. "The pie is for Drew," Emily repeated, "but I have something for you, too."

"For me?" Gabrielle couldn't guess what it might be. *More insults? Accusations?* She opened the door wider, hoping she wasn't making a terrible mistake. "There's some coffee left from breakfast. Can I pour you a cup?"

Emily deposited the pie on the counter, then helped herself to a mug and filled it with coffee.

"It's cherry pie," Emily stated, sitting at the table. "Drew's favorite."

Was it Gabrielle's imagination, or had she heard *A good wife would know that* in Emily's voice?

"I see you've tidied up the cupboards. Well, good for you."

And the closets and the drawers, too, Gabrielle considered saying. But she didn't. She didn't feel she owed this mean-tempered woman any explanations. Not about what she'd accomplished around here since her memory came back, and certainly not about why she'd left Drew.

"I owe you an apology," Emily said.

Gabrielle's eyes widened. She hadn't known what to expect when she'd seen Emily standing there on the porch, but it sure hadn't been this.

"I judged you. Right or wrong, it isn't the way to be. "Specially if you're a Christian, which I like to think I am."

Her steely blue gaze met Gabrielle's head-on. It looked to Gabrielle as if it had been a long, long time since those hard eyes had smiled, and she wondered about that.

"I've been thinking on some of the things I said when I was over here the other day." Emily's brow crinkled. She ran her finger round and round the rim of her mug. "It was my fault you got so riled up. So I'm sorry. 'Cause that was the reason you ended up in the hospital."

She sighed. Then she looked up, straight into Gabrielle's eyes. "I never meant you to come to any harm, even if you did break my Drew's heart."

Her Drew?

"'Judge not lest ye be judged,' the Good Book says. I poked my nose in where it ought not to have been, and..." Emily lifted the mug as if to take a sip, and put it back down again. "Guess I'm lucky you didn't snap it clean off. My nose, that is."

The frosty glare had warmed considerably, and Gabrielle smiled.

"Troy and me, we had us a baby—long, long time ago." She plopped her heavy purse on the table, popped the latch and withdrew a yellowing photograph. As she handed it across the table, her eyes took on a hazy, far-off look.

Gabrielle's first response to the picture was to wonder why anyone would take a snapshot of a *grave,* of all things, even if it was lovely—as tombstones go—what with its guardian angels flanking the four corners. "'Anthony Edward Carter,'" she read aloud. "'Only a moment in our lives, a moment that changed us forever.'"

She looked at Emily and remembered what Troy had said on the way into town that day. *"Never had us any young'uns. Guess Emily just sort of adopted Drew as her own."*

"They call it Sudden Infant Death Syndrome these days," Emily said. "Back then, they just said 'Dead.'"

"I'm so sorry," Gabrielle said. As she handed the photo back, she lay a hand against her stomach. "So very sorry." And she meant it, more than Emily could ever know.

"Funny how a thing like that can keep right on hurting, even forty-odd years later." Emily shook her head. "Today would have been his forty-second birthday."

Clearing her throat, Emily sat up straighter and tucked the snapshot into her handbag. "I always get a little blue this time of year. That's no excuse for the way I behaved, but…"

Gabrielle lay a hand over Emily's. "No harm, no foul," she said, smiling. "Drew has told me about all the things you've done for him over the years. And I can see that you took good care of him while I was off tending to my tantrum. I appreciate that even more, now that I've come to my senses."

Emily stood, poured what was left of her coffee down the drain, then rinsed her mug and put it upside down in the sink. "Well, I'd best be getting home. It's nearly nine and Troy will be back before you know it. I promised I'd—"

A wild snarl that seemed to come from somewhere near the barn interrupted her.

"Dear God in heaven," Emily prayed aloud, a hand over her heart.

Gabrielle raced to the window and searched the yard. An hour or so ago, she'd walked Fake Molly, Triumph and several of the other horses out into the corral for some exercise. Something Drew had said echoed in her mind. *They're sitting ducks out there.*

If anything happened to them, Gabrielle would never forgive herself. She'd barely managed to cope with the fact that Molly's death had been her fault. If one horse's untimely death could torture her this long, what would *eight* deaths do?

She understood now Drew's powerful drive to protect these defenseless animals against the cougar.

She ran into the foyer and grabbed the rifle. One of the first things Drew had done after they returned from their honeymoon was teach her how to shoot. "You'll probably never need to put any of the lessons to use," he'd said, "but out here, it's important that you know how to handle a firearm."

"I'm such a terrible shot!" she'd complained, missing another of the bottles and cans he'd lined up on the fence.

"You'll get better with practice."

And she had.

"You're not going out there alone, are you?" Emily asked, eyes wide when she saw the rifle.

"I won't be alone." Gabrielle opened the door and stepped onto the porch. Pulling back the hammer, she said, "I'll have Mr. Smith & Wesson along for protection."

She scanned the barnyard, the corral, the drive. No sign of the cat.

She was about to breathe a sigh of relief when something—intuition?—made her look to the right—

And directly at the cougar, ears flattened and shoulders hunched as it crouched low, working its way slowly, slowly toward the corral.

She took a deep breath and held it to steady herself, then raised the rifle and lined up the cat in her sights. *Never take aim at any living thing,* Drew had taught her, *unless it's in self-defense.*

If she'd caught the cat mid-attack, Gabrielle might have

been able to shoot it. Instead, she aimed the gun toward the sky and pulled the trigger.

The explosive sound reverberated, and had the intended effect. The cat leaped into the air, all four paws scrabbling for a foothold, then hit the ground running full speed and disappeared into the dense green of the pine grove.

Trembling, Gabrielle clicked the safety into place as the acrid scent of smoke and gunpowder stung her nostrils.

Mind reeling, she made a quick mental To Do list: put the weapon back in the foyer, where it belonged. Take the horses to the barn and bolt the door. Pray that Drew would get back real soon, because she had no earthly idea what to do next.

The moment she jerked the screen door, Gabrielle spotted Emily sprawled on the kitchen floor. Gabrielle leaned the rifle against the wall and got down on her hands and knees.

"Emily," she said softly, gently brushing perspiration-dampened bangs from the woman's forehead, "what happened?"

An arthritic finger pointing at her chest, Emily gasped for air. "H-h-h…"

Heart attack.

Years ago, she'd taken a CPR course at the local community college. Now, as she dialed 9-1-1 on the portable phone, Gabrielle wondered if she'd remember any of the information, now that she needed it.

She spoke in a strong, sure voice. "Emily, I know this is a silly thing to say under the circumstances, but you just relax. Everything's gonna be okay, you hear?"

Nodding, Emily sent her a pained, crooked smile.

Maybe she'd had a heart attack before, Gabrielle thought, dumping the contents of Emily's gigantic purse onto the floor. Tubes of lipstick, ballpoint pens, mini-packs of facial tissue scattered every which way. Gabrielle spotted a brown vial and grabbed it, as the 9-1-1 dispatcher came on the line.

"This is Gabrielle Cunningham," she said, hoping he could understand her rapid-fire speech, "at the Walking C Ranch out on Highway 540. We have a woman here who's had a heart attack."

She put a minuscule nitroglycerine tablet under Emily's tongue, then flapped open her wallet. "Her name is Emily Carter," she told the dispatcher. "She's sixty-two years old, five-five and a hundred and eighty pounds. I've just given her a nitro tablet, but it doesn't seem to be doing any good."

Just then, Emily's upper body lifted from the floor in a painful spasm. "She's passed out. I'm going to try CPR," she said, dropping the phone.

She heard the tinny, distant voice of the dispatcher ebbing from the mouthpiece. "I'll be right here if you need me. Could be fifteen, twenty minutes 'til the ambo gets there. Think you can keep up the CPR long?"

"Don't have much choice, now do I?" she ground out.

After depressing Emily's chest a few times, she grabbed the phone. "Tell the paramedics we're around back, in the kitchen. The door's open." Without waiting for his reply, she dropped the receiver again. With that, she began mouth-to-mouth.

Gabrielle kept it up for the next twenty minutes. And she didn't think she'd ever heard a more beautiful sound than the ear-piercing blare of the siren.

Stepping aside so the EMTs could do their work, she slumped against the far wall and watched in awestruck silence. *Please God,* she prayed, *let Emily be all right.*

Drew and Troy rushed into the room as the paramedics

were strapping Emily to the gurney. Gabrielle snapped immediately to attention and filled Troy in on the details.

Reality didn't hit her until the boxy red-and-white vehicle screamed down the drive. She'd stuffed her nerve-twitching hands in her jeans pockets while the EMTs worked on Emily, and now the tremors began wracking the rest of her.

Drew closed the back door. "What's the rifle doing in here?" he asked.

She combed her fingers through her bangs, brushing them back from her forehead, and held them there. "The cougar was about to pounce on the horses. Emily and I were talking when we heard it." Gabrielle pointed to the counter. "She brought you a pie."

She watched as Drew checked the weapon's safety, then leaned its barrel against the doorjamb.

"You shot the cat?"

"No." She didn't tell him about firing at the clouds. "I missed."

"But the shot scared it off."

She shrugged. "Thankfully." A long, shuddering sigh exited her lungs. "I came back inside and found Em—"

Her gaze fixed on the spot where Emily had fallen. The woman's makeup, comb, a ring of keys were still strewn about the room. "She might need these. Will you drive me to the hospital?" Gabrielle got down on her knees and began gathering them up, one by one, and putting them back into the purse. "The way I'm shaking, I don't trust myself to drive."

Drew brought her to her feet and hugged her tight. "Let's get the horses stabled, in case that cat decides to come back. Then we'll head over to the hospital." He pressed a lingering kiss to her forehead. "My wife, the hero," he said.

Gabrielle leaned against him, absorbing his warmth, his strength. "Hero?" She laughed quietly. "You wouldn't say that if you'd been here ten minutes ago. I was a basket case!"

"That's not what the EMT said."

She looked up at him. "Which EMT?"

"The guy in charge. He told me as the others were loading Emily into the ambulance that if you hadn't been here, if you hadn't known CPR…"

Thoughts of what might have happened flitted through her mind, and she shuddered. Burying her face in Drew's shirt, she held her breath and chanted mentally *I will not cry. I will not cry!*

It all spilled out, then—the reason for Emily's visit, the cougar, her belief that if the cat had attacked, it would have been her fault for putting the horses in jeopardy in the first place. "I didn't even have the courage to aim at it, Drew. I fired into the sky!"

"You did your job, which was to protect the animals." He kissed her again. "Couldn't have done better myself."

He took her coat from the wall peg. "Now, let's get busy, 'cause who knows when Emily might need one of those tubes of lipstick."

Numbly, she followed him out the door.

It took all of ten minutes to get the horses secured in their stalls, and as soon as the barn doors were latched, Drew took her hand. "Ready?"

"Ready." And dashing inside, she grabbed Emily's purse.

Drew made small talk all the way into town, to distract her from thoughts of the traumatic morning, she supposed. And when they arrived at the hospital, he urged her to go inside, while he parked the truck.

But the haunted, terrified look she'd seen on Troy's face

popped into her memory. Gabrielle believed she'd see that expression in her mind for a long, long time.

What if something as serious as a heart attack had happened to Drew? How would she have felt if—

"Gabby?"

Blinking, she realized he'd been sitting there waiting for her to get out of the truck. "If it's all the same to you, I'd rather wait so we can go inside together."

He sent her a lopsided grin and drove into the parking lot. "Okay," he said, nosing the pickup into an available slot, "but it's a long walk from here to the ER."

She had no idea why the pregnancy test result came to mind now, but it did. "The exercise will be good for me," she told him. "Especially now."

Holding hands, they walked toward the ER entrance. Drew looked down at her. "What do you mean, 'especially now'?"

Gabrielle shook her head, sorry that she hadn't kept a tighter rein on her mouth. This was neither the time nor the place to tell him about the baby.

They'd deliver Emily's purse, check on her condition, then head home. Maybe this evening, after a nice hot meal, she'd break the news. "Don't pay any attention to me," she said. "This has been quite a morning, so don't be surprised if I make even less sense than usual."

The ER doors whooshed open when they stepped onto the black mat. A nurse at the counter confirmed Emily was there. "But you can't go in. Only immediate family."

"Of course," Gabrielle said, holding out the big purse. "I only came to bring Mrs. Carter this."

She was about to hand it over when a green-suited doctor shoved through the swinging doors leading to the treatment rooms. "Is there a Gabrielle Cunningham out here?" he asked, looking around the waiting room.

"Right here." Gabrielle and Drew walked toward him.

"She's asking for you," the doctor said, holding the door open.

Chapter Twelve

"Emily is asking for *me*?" Gabrielle couldn't seem to make her legs work.

"Right this way," said the doctor, inviting her inside with a sweep of his arm.

Gabrielle started moving, and sent Drew a *Don't leave me alone* look. He took her hand, and together they entered the ER.

Despite the oxygen mask, the IV drip, the wires connecting Emily to various monitoring devices, the older woman's gaze followed the movements of every doctor, every nurse, every relative of other ER patients. When she focused on Gabrielle, she gave a faint smile, fingertips weakly patting the mattress.

Gabrielle responded immediately, standing beside the bed, one hand resting on Emily's wrist, the other brushing soft white waves from her forehead.

"They've pretty much stabilized her," Troy said. "And now that you're here…" He looked up at the steady *blip-blip* of the bright green line of the heart monitor screen. "Calm as can be," he said, smiling at Gabrielle. "Before you got here, she wouldn't settle down. Kept asking for you.''

Troy's eyes brimmed with unshed tears. Had he been thinking what Gabrielle was thinking? That Emily had been holding on to say goodbye?

In coming to see Gabrielle to apologize—something she'd seemed unaccustomed to doing—Emily had extended the hand of friendship. Had she done it for Drew? For Gabrielle? Or had her simple explanation been the nut of it: "'Judge not lest ye be judged'"? Gabrielle might have found out, if it hadn't been for the cougar.

If Emily didn't make it…

Gabrielle refused to believe in that possibility. "You're going to be fine," she said, patting Emily's shoulder. "Soon as you're up to it, I'm counting on you to teach me how to make Drew's favorite pie. If that loudmouthed cat hadn't interrupted, I'd have the recipe already.''

Grinning, Emily nodded her consent.

"Cat?" Troy said. "What cat?"

He must have been so preoccupied by the EMTs' activities that he hadn't heard her telling Drew about the cougar. In as few words as possible, she filled him in.

"Well," he said when she finished, "don't that just beat all.'' Running a hand through already-mussed, smoke-gray hair, he said, "You did all that, then went inside and found Em, and…"

Troy's brow furrowed and his lips formed a taut line as he struggled to regain his composure. He shook his head. "Drew, m'boy, if I hadn't left my hat in the ambulance, I'd take it off to you right now." He grinned at Gabrielle. "'Cause that's some woman you've got there.''

Emily squeezed Gabrielle's hand.

If the doctor hadn't come in just then, Gabrielle might have given in to her tears.

"Sorry, folks," he said. "I'm afraid you'll have to step outside. All but Mr. Carter, of course."

Drew and Gabrielle said their goodbyes, made Troy promise to phone them when he needed a ride home, and headed for the exit.

"He won't call," Drew said, as she climbed into the truck.

She waited until he slid behind the wheel to ask, "How do you know he won't?"

"Troy isn't gonna move from that spot. Not 'til he knows for sure Emily is going home, good as new." He paused, looked over at her. "I know I wouldn't, if it had been you."

Gabrielle's heart fluttered in response to his loving gaze. He'd already proven the truth of those words. When Dr. Adams had held her at the hospital overnight for observation, Drew had been within arm's reach every time she opened her eyes.

He merged the pickup into highway traffic. "What say we stop at the diner for—"

"No," she said, smiling, "let's just go home."

Drew returned the smile. "Okay, but if that cougar shows up again, it's my turn to handle things."

She was about to suggest he let the *rangers* handle things, when he said, "There's something I've been meaning to tell you about that cat." Pausing, Drew shook his head. "The muley wasn't the only animal he killed."

Gabrielle swallowed. "How many more?"

"Four, that I know of."

Heart knocking against her ribs, she said, "Where?"

"Too close for comfort."

Turning toward him, she asked, "Why didn't you tell me before now?"

He shrugged one shoulder. "Didn't want to worry you, what with all you've been—"

"Drew," she interrupted, "you can't keep shutting me out. I realize you do these things to protect me, and I appreciate the sentiment." Gabrielle unbuckled her seat belt, slid across the bench and lay her fingers upon his forearm. "I'm tougher than I look. I can handle the truth, you know."

Nodding, he said, "Yes, I know that now."

"You work so hard, Drew. I just want to help lighten your load a bit." She scooted closer. "I wasn't born on a ranch, but I know there's more to running one than throwing feed at the animals once a day." She stroked his arm. "I know I have a lot to learn, but I'm a quick study."

Smiling, he slung his arm around her shoulders. "You're something else, you know that?"

Gabrielle sat back, linked her fingers with his. "So tell me why we're trying to cage this cougar," she said. "Sounds to me like he's deranged. If he's allowed to continue mating—because who knows how many cubs he's fathered—he'll pass his killing gene on to his offspring. So wouldn't it just be better to put him out of his misery?"

"You don't have as much to learn as you think," he said after a moment of silence. "Most of our neighbors would have blown him away, no questions asked, first time they spotted him."

She heard disapproval in the hard edge to his voice. "But given a choice, you'd rather catch him than kill him."

Drew winced. "When you put it that way, I sound like some tree-hugger type." He sighed. "It's just, I've always believed killing an animal should be a last resort, not the first line of defense."

It had seemed strange that he'd missed the cougar that first night, because she'd seen what was left of paper targets after he finished with them; the bullet that hit outside the bull's-eye was the exception, not the rule. If he aimed at that cat and missed, it was because he'd *wanted* to.

Now Gabrielle understood the expression that had darkened his face when he said, "Sorry, Gabby, but I had to put Molly down." She remembered his slumped shoulders, his red-rimmed eyes, his stammering and stuttering. Drew had done what he'd believed he had to do, but he hadn't liked it.

If only she'd known then what she knew now.

"Can I ask you a question?"

He looked at her. "Sure."

"That night with Molly," she began in a soft voice, "did you know I wanted to be the one who—"

"I didn't want you going through that. It was hard enough for me, and I didn't love her the way you did."

She sighed and stared straight ahead. "I should have known."

"Known what?"

That you're a true hero, she thought, grinning inwardly. But to say something like that out loud would only make him blush and utter a denial. Better to *show* him, she decided.

"After supper," Gabrielle said, changing the subject. "I have something to tell you. It's a surprise."

Drew looked over at her. "Finding out you scared off a killer cat and saved a woman's life in one afternoon isn't surprise enough?"

When she didn't answer, his expression grew somber. "Tell me this, then, is it good news or...bad?"

She stared at the floor mat, traced the manufacturer's logo with the toe of her sneaker, remembering the dozens of times she'd asked him if they could start their family—

and the dozens of reasons he'd given why they shouldn't. *Good or bad?* "Guess it depends on your point of view."

Drew's fingers tightened around the steering wheel and his jaw muscles bulged.

Lord, she prayed, closing her eyes, *let him be as thrilled about this baby as I am.* Gabrielle realized then that for a woman who claimed to have no faith in God, she was sure talking to Him a lot lately.

The thought made her smile, made her feel stronger, more certain of the future than she'd felt in a long, long time.

Good thing, too.

Because if Drew *wasn't* happy about the baby, she'd need strength like she'd never needed it before.

Their throw-together meal cleaned the leftovers from the refrigerator: spaghetti, ham and green beans. "Not exactly gourmet," Gabrielle said, spooning it onto plates as Drew filled the water glasses, "but it beats throwing away perfectly good food."

She was rambling, and knew it, but seemed powerless to stop herself. She blamed the close call with the cougar. Emily's heart attack. Knowing about the baby and having no idea how Drew would react to impending fatherhood. She babbled about mundane chores, errands to be run, a bill that had come in the morning mail.

If he saw her nervousness, Drew never mentioned it, and Gabrielle thanked God for his patience.

Over their dessert of canned peaches, he said, "So this big surprise..."

He was smiling, she noticed, but not with his eyes.

"How long do you intend to torture me?"

Gabrielle hesitated.

Now even the smile was gone, and in its place there was

a worried frown. Drew tossed his napkin onto the table. "*Talk* to me, Gabrielle, because this hemming and hawing is driving me nuts."

Standing, he began to pace. "We've been putting this off—and I think you know exactly what I mean—waiting for the right time." Arms raised like a man being held up at gunpoint, he said, "Now, I know you've been through a lot since the accident, but the way things have been going, it doesn't look like there's going to *be* a right time. So why don't you just spit it out."

He stared into her eyes. "We'll deal with the fallout afterward."

She met his intense gaze with one of her own. "Drew..." Gabrielle searched for the right words. "I—" After several false starts, she sighed with frustration.

"You know what our marriage reminds me of?" he snapped. "It reminds me of that little horse out there in the barn, that's what. She *looks* like Molly, but she isn't." He paused.

Gabrielle immediately understood the comparison. To the casual observer, it looked as though she and Drew had a happy, stable marriage, but—

"I hunted four counties to find that filly," he continued, gesturing over his shoulder toward the barn, "hoping, praying it would keep you from remembering what I did to Molly."

He heaved a heavy, exhausted sigh and tried again. "If I believed Doc Ivers could've gotten here fast enough, I'd have hired him to do the job. But every minute that passed was another minute she suffered. So I did what had to be done.

"Never gave a thought to seeing how you felt about it, because nobody should have to watch the life drain out of an animal, especially not if you're the one who—"

He cleared his throat. "I didn't want you seeing that in your mind's eye for the rest of your life. I saw what it did to you, the way you blamed yourself for Molly's injury. If you had to put her down, well…"

It seemed to Gabrielle that Drew had bottled all this up for too long, that he needed to say these things.

And she needed to hear them.

"I almost came after you that night. *Almost.*"

He stood, feet shoulder-width apart, arms crossed over his broad chest, shaking his head. "But I was too ashamed. Couldn't face you." And in a soft, far-off voice, he said, "Didn't think you wanted to see me, anyway. I thought I'd lost you forever because of…that night—the night I shot Molly. And then, like an answer to a prayer, you came back. I didn't question the 'how' or the 'why' of it. I just *thanked God.*"

He sat down again, poked at his peaches with the bowl of his spoon. "I feel like a heel admitting this, even now, but if it meant having you in my life again…" Drew looked imploringly into her eyes. "If it meant you wouldn't leave, I didn't want you to get your memory back."

Gabrielle swallowed. She'd been beating herself up for a long time over what had happened to Molly, because if she was honest with herself, she'd known—even that night—that although Drew had pulled the trigger, *her* actions had killed the little filly. Unable to cope with the ugly fact, she'd run away from home.

Drew had said something about "time" a few minutes earlier. Well, now it was time. Time to start acting her age, to behave like someone's mommy, someone's life mate.

Time to 'fess up.

"I'm sorry, Drew."

"*You're* sorry?"

"I'm the one who threw in the towel. And if I hadn't

pitched a fit in the first place over, over..." She held her head in her hands. "I don't even remember over *what*." Straightening, she lifted her chin. "I just remember riding Molly hard and fast, way harder and faster than she was used to. If I hadn't been so busy thinking 'poor little me,' maybe I'd have seen that rotting log."

Gabrielle got a clear mental picture of the scene: Molly, whimpering and weak, big brown eyes wild with pain, trying to stand on the shattered bones of her front leg.

Twisting her wedding ring round and round on her finger, she whispered, "I knew the minute it happened she'd have to be put down. But I wasn't willing to take responsibility for my part in it, and—like a spoiled little brat—I took the easy way out."

She met his eyes, doing her best to keep the tears at bay.

"Gabby," he said, "don't."

Unable to meet his loving, forgiving gaze, she looked away. "Putting an end to her suffering was the right thing to do. I knew it then, I know it now."

When she looked back at him, Gabrielle saw his attention was elsewhere. She followed his gaze, touched the smooth, cool curve of his simple gold wedding band. "You never took it off, did you."

He didn't respond.

"Why?"

"Couldn't," he rasped.

She smiled softly. "Couldn't get it over your knuckle?"

He shook his head. "Something like that."

It had taken two to make this mess, and he'd already proven how far he'd go to clean it up—had proven he'd do it alone if he had to.

But he wouldn't have to, and she aimed to prove *that*. "I'm sorry, Drew," she said again. "You're solid as a rock, decent as they come. The way you've treated me since I got my memory back is proof that if I'd bothered to talk to you back then, *like a grown-up would have,* it would have made all the difference in the world. You would have understood, and—''

Tears choked off the rest of her words as Drew stood, pulled her to her feet.

''Ah, Gabby,'' he said, gathering her close. ''It wasn't your fault. It was *me*. Those first months after we were married, I prayed you'd be with me forever. And at the same time, I kept wondering if, the minute things got a little rough, you'd take off like—like my mother did.''

''But Drew, I *did* take off like your mother did.''

He hugged her tighter. ''There's a big difference,'' he said, his voice gruff and grating. ''You came back.''

''Do you think she'll ever come home, Drew?''

Shaking his head, he looked away and sighed. ''No.''

''But you wish she would, don't you?''

''Sure. I guess I've wished that pretty much every night since she left.''

Taking his face in his hands, she stood on tiptoe to say, ''Then that's what I wish, too.''

She watched as the muscles of his jaw relaxed, as a spark of happiness glowed in his eyes.

He gave a long, cleansing sigh. ''All I need is you, Gabby. Just you.'' Holding her just far enough away so he could see her face, he grinned. ''So the big surprise is, you're staying?''

Gabrielle nodded.

Tilting back his head, Drew laughed. ''And here I thought you were going to say, 'My bags are packed and I'm—'''

''You deserved an apology, Drew.'' She studied his face. ''Fact is, I should have given you that a long time ago.''

Nodding, she added, "Yes, I'm staying. But my staying isn't the surprise."

Drew looked into her eyes. Despite everything she'd said, she still read fear in his; he still wasn't sure of her, of their future.

She thought of all they'd said about time. It was high time she put an end to his fears.

"Drew, I found out this morning that we're going to—"

Outside, an angry snarl cut her off.

Immediately, Drew started for the foyer. "You know the drill," he said, grabbing the rifle.

Chewing a knuckle, Gabrielle nodded. This time, she decided, she'd behave like a true partner. "Okay," she said, "but first—" She threw her arms around him, kissed him soundly. "Be careful, you hear?"

If love could be gauged by degrees, she could have measured what poured from his eyes by the gallon.

"I will," he promised, smiling. "Now, stay inside."

As if on cue, the cat shrieked again, its chilling cry cutting the night like a machete.

Drew walked through the door, across the porch, and into the night. Gabrielle forced herself to turn from the image of him being gradually swallowed up by the dangerous murk of the darkness.

As she had done before, Gabrielle phoned the rangers' station. It wasn't that she didn't believe the ranger when he said help was on the way. Rather, it was that the Walking C was miles from civilization. If she waited for the rangers to arrive...

Maybe it was hormones making her feel as though something terrible was about to happen. Maybe it was knowing that a baby was on the way, and that she didn't want to raise it alone. Gabrielle knew this much: she couldn't stay inside and do nothing, while Drew was out there, alone. If there was some way to help him, she aimed to find it. But she wasn't a *complete* fool. Going outside unprotected was tantamount to suicide.

And so, unlocking the gun cabinet, she grabbed Drew's 30-30 from the rack, then ripped into a box of shells and slid seven into the chamber, put four more in her pocket.

"God helps those who help themselves," she said, stepping onto the porch. And glancing toward the inky, moonless sky, Gabrielle added, "At least, I sure hope He does."

He tried *not* to think about how beautiful the animal was—sleek and golden-gray, with intelligent, piercing green eyes. It would be a shame, putting an end to the majestic creature's life. But if he didn't, more cows and horses—and possibly humans—would meet grisly ends.

Drew heard a noise behind him and spun around, trigger finger at the ready.

He couldn't believe his eyes when he saw her, silhouetted against the brightly lit living room windows, stoop-shouldered and prowling around in the dark, rifle butt pressed against her hip, one hand gripping its barrel, the other hovering near the trigger.

What does she think she's doing? he wondered, clamping his teeth together.

But this was no time to get distracted. He had to find that cat before it found him, and put an end to this mess, once and for all.

He wanted to call out to Gabby, order her to get back inside, *now*. But the only thing that would accomplish would be to alert the cat to his whereabouts.

Something told him that although he was the one with the rifle, it was the cat that had *him* in its sights. Drew knew he had no choice but to stand stock-still and silent, and pray Gabrielle would spot him. Soon. Then, hopefully, she'd go back into the house—or at the very least come stand beside him.

Hearing her back there had startled him so badly that his heart was still pumping like an oil rig. It was a wonder, the way his nerves were jangling, that he hadn't squeezed off a round. Because what if he'd mistaken her for the cat?

The thought turned the marrow in his bones to ice. Heart drumming wildly, he held his breath, waiting, watching for the moment when she'd see him. She was facing this way. Surely any moment now—

A loud, metallic *clang* ricocheted through the cold, black air, scaring him so badly that he nearly bit his tongue. Instinct made him crouch, in case the noise had frightened Gabrielle, too, and she unintentionally took aim at *him*.

The moon slid out from behind a thick, dingy gray cloud, brightening the yard. Instantly, Drew could see that she'd kept her cool. Standing statue-still, she'd hoisted the rifle to cheek height. He could see her thumb, poking up like a stumpy antenna, poised above the hammer.

"Gabby!" he called, his voice a hoarse whisper.

Aiming the gun barrel skyward, she ran to him, and threw herself into his arms. "Oh, thank God, thank God, thank *God*," she chanted between kisses.

He should give her a piece of his mind for being out here in the first place. Should tell her he thought she'd lost her mind, coming into the dark with a killer cougar on the hunt. But she was safe in his arms now, and right or wrong, like it or not, it was exactly where he wanted her to be.

"Thank God you're all right," she repeated.

"Are you crazy, Gabby? What're you doing out here?"

"Yes, I suppose I am, just a little." She sent him a trembly little smile. "I couldn't just stay inside while you were out here, alone with that beast."

He could only shake his head.

"Do you think we caught it, finally?" she asked.

The snarling, shrieking howls of the cougar were answer enough.

"Guess all the commotion going on around here lately threw him off his game," Drew said. "We spooked him from the get-go, taking potshots at him one day, feeding him fresh beef the next, stomping around with flashlights like a bunch of clodhoppers."

Looking in the direction of the cage, she raised one eyebrow and smirked. Drew had a sinking suspicion he knew what that meant.

"Do you think it's safe to—"

"Forget it," he barked. "You're not goin' near that cat 'til the rangers get here." A knowing grin softened his features when he added, "You did call them, didn't you?"

"How'd you know?"

Wearing a lopsided grin, he only nodded.

Standing as near to him as a body could get to another, Gabrielle sighed. "They should be here any minute."

"Yeah."

"They'll have tranquilizers and stuff?"

"I reckon." Then, frowning past his smile, he said, "What were you *thinking* coming out here?"

"I was *thinking*," she repeated, mimicking his scolding tone, "that if you were going to die—" her brows drew together "—well, I sure don't want to live without you."

He drove a hand through his hair. "That's just plain crazy talk, Gabby," he growled. "You could have gotten yourself killed. If I had half a brain, I'd read you a piece of my mind, right here and now."

"And exactly what do you call what you're doing now?"

He could tell by the grin slanting her mouth that she didn't believe a word of his huffing and puffing. And the proof was the way her fingertips gently coaxed his lips into a kissable pout.

"I love you, too," she said, pressing her mouth to his.

When the kiss ended, Drew chuckled. "Life with you will be a lot of things, Gabrielle Cunningham, but boring ain't gonna be one of 'em."

She lifted her chin a notch, tilted her head flirtatiously. "I could say the same thing, *Daddy*."

Frowning, he tried to read her expression. But even with the silver-white moonlight spilling down from the heavens, he couldn't make head nor tail of that look on her face.

Wait a minute. Had she said...?

"D-daddy?" he repeated. A slow smile spread across his face. "*That's* your surprise?"

Nodding, Gabrielle said, "Well, are you?"

There she stood, long dark curls shimmering around her face like a halo, sexy-sweet smile curving up the corners of her full lips, big eyes flashing with life and love. He got a quick picture of her as she'd looked moments ago, prowling around in the dark with a loaded rifle in her dainty hands.

"Yeah," he said, grinning, "I guess 'surprised' is as good a word as any."

"I know it's a weird time to be starting a family." Gabrielle looked into the distance, where the still-snarling cougar strained against the bars of the big steel cage. A slight frown furrowed her brow.

Drew took her hand, led her to the porch, and relieved her of the rifle. Clicking the safeties in place, he lay both weapons on the wooden floorboards. And sitting on the top step, he pulled her into his lap.

With the tip of his forefinger, he lifted her chin, forcing her to meet his eyes. "Gabby, I may not be eligible for membership in Mensa anytime in the near future, but then,

I don't need to be a genius to know I'm the luckiest man alive.'' He placed a palm on each of her cheeks. ''I've made a lot of mistakes, and well, okay,'' he said, reading the warning in her eyes, ''so maybe you made a few, too.'' He pulled her closer. ''But we made it, sweetie. We *made* it!''

Her long, lush lashes fluttered and her lower lip quivered. ''Yeah,'' she whispered past a shaky smile. ''We did, didn't we.''

''I married the prettiest, sexiest, sweetest woman on God's green earth.'' Hugging her tighter still, he added, ''And after seeing the way you behaved with Emily today…''

Cupping her face in the palm of one hand, he kissed her. ''Something tells me if you put *half* the love into motherhood that you put into everything else…''

Tears welled in her eyes. Drew didn't know what had put them there, but it didn't make a whit of difference at that moment. Because amid the joy and relief and thankfulness, he saw the unmistakable look of *love*.

Gently, he kissed each tear away. ''I hope she looks exactly like her beautiful mother.''

Gabrielle bracketed his face with her hands. ''I was kind of hoping we'd have a boy first.''

''First? You mean, you want more than one kid?''

She nodded matter-of-factly. ''Well, sure. Four, six, maybe even eight!'' she said, giggling. ''But a boy first, so when we do have a girl, she'll always have a big brother to look out for her.'' Fingers over her lips, she snickered. ''And believe it or not, I want him to be exactly like his daddy.''

After all that had happened between them, he didn't understand, and said so.

''Because like they used to say in the old days, you're

true blue.'' She shrugged. ''Okay, so you have a couple of dings and dents in your armor.'' Wiggling her eyebrows, she added, ''I know how to use a hammer, *Daddy*.''

Daddy.

He'd been to the Maryland seashore once, at high tide on the eve of a hurricane. The feeling that washed over him as he acknowledged his soon-to-be fatherhood reminded him of those waves that pounded the beach, engulfing sand and shells and water-smoothed pebbles. Gabrielle was going to have a baby. *His* baby. And the realization washed away any fears and doubts he'd had about their future together.

''I want to go to church this Sunday, and every Sunday from now on.''

Brows raised, he said, ''You do?''

''I want to be a good wife to you, now more than ever,'' she said. ''I want to be a good mother, too.'' She took a long, deep breath. ''And I've finally realized if I'm going to succeed, I need help.''

''I'll be—''

Soft, loving laughter sighed from her lips. ''Oh, Drew, I know you'll help. Of *course* you'll help. Don't you see? It was your steadfastness that taught me that I need God's help, too.''

Every prayer he'd ever uttered, every wish and dream and hope came alive in that moment. If the blue-and-red strobes of the rangers' vehicle hadn't distracted him, Drew would have fallen to his knees, right then and there, and praised the Almighty.

But he had the rest of his life to give thanks, and God had *invented* patience.

''I love you, Drew.''

She didn't need to express it verbally; her feelings were

written on her face, poured from her eyes, showed in her smile. *But Lord,* he prayed, *it sure is good to hear.*

Everything in him wanted to say, *I love you, too.* Instead, a primordial growl of victory and gratification rumbled deep inside him as he pressed his lips to hers.

He heard the heavy footfalls, signaling the rangers' approach.

"Lookit the two of 'em," he heard one say.

Their boots crunched across the frosty lawn as they made their way toward the trapped cougar.

Gabrielle's lips were still pressed to Drew's when she whispered, "C'mon, Daddy, let's make sure they're nice and gentle with our little kitty-cat."

Drew's *Are you kidding?* expression inspired a merry giggle.

"What can I say?" she asked, shrugging daintily. "Pregnancy brings out the protectiveness in me."

Epilogue

Emily's knitting needles clacked along steadily amid the foursome's quiet chatter. "Haven't made one of these things in—"

"Decades," Troy interrupted. "And that's a real shame, too, 'cause you're right good at that—" he searched his memory for the correct term "—that needly stuff."

"Knitting, Troy," Gabrielle teased. "It's called knitting." And to Emily, she said, "It's going to be the most beautiful blanket any baby ever had."

The older woman blushed. "So long as you don't look too closely for dropped stitches."

Since Emily's release from the hospital weeks earlier, she and Troy had been spending Sunday afternoons with Drew and Gabrielle. "Adoptive parents and grandparents," they'd dubbed themselves.

"Have you two picked a name yet?"

Gabrielle sent Emily a *Play along with me* wink. "As a matter of fact, I have."

Drew looked up from the Sunday comics. "You have? That's news to me."

Nodding, Gabrielle said, "I'm going to call her Ditto."

"Ditto?" Drew repeated, scowling. "What kind of name is *that* for a young'un?" He paused. "Besides, I thought you wanted a boy first."

Gabrielle sat on the arm of his easy chair, patted its cushion. "Relax, Daddy, and I'll tell you how I arrived at such an unusual moniker."

"What's the matter?" he asked, laughing as he took a seat. "Is it so bad you don't think I can take it standing up?"

"Well, we can't very well keep calling her Fake Molly or The Molly Imposter, now can we? She'll end up with an inferiority complex!"

Shaking his head, Drew hid behind one hand and groaned. "You got me again," he admitted, grinning.

"Say," Troy said, pointing at an article in the paper. "Here's a story about that cat of ours."

He showed Emily the full-color photo of the cougar. Beneath, the caption read, "Recuperated Cougar to Be Released at Yellowstone."

Gabrielle slid an arm around Drew's neck. "My hero," she said. "If you'd done things the way everyone else does them, that poor animal would be dead and forgotten by now. Instead, he's going to live a long, healthy life, thanks to you."

Blushing, Drew frowned.

"Says here the cat had a .357 magnum shell lodged in its neck." Troy looked up from the paper. "Well, no wonder he was actin' like a crazy killer."

"I'd get a little testy, too," Emily put in, "if I had to go around with a bullet in my neck." She clucked her tongue disapprovingly. "What kind of person would do such a thing?"

Troy continued to relay information from the article.

"According to this, Doc Ivers cleaned up the wound and pumped the cougar full of antibiotics, and that cat calmed right down." He looked up again to add, "Folks have to keep in mind he's still a wild animal, but least now he's just a *normal* kind of mean."

"Well," Emily said, stuffing her project into her knitting bag, "get your hat, Troy, or we'll never make it home in time for 'Sixty Minutes.'"

Standing, the foreman jammed the Stetson on his head. "Thought I'd lost it for sure," he said to Drew. "Would've been a shame, too, since I've—"

"—had this hat goin' on thirty years, now," everyone said with him.

Grinning, Troy shook his head. "See if I leave it to any of *you* in my will!"

"Will," Gabrielle echoed. "Now *there's* a nice strong boy's name."

* * * * *

Dear Reader,

Not long ago, a friend's son married a lovely woman in a traditional ceremony. Side by side at the altar they recited the words that made them one, then marched down the aisle to greet friends and relatives gathered at the back of the church.

"Marriage is a partnership," cautioned his uncle. "It's both of you," her aunt advised, "giving one hundred percent, one hundred percent of the time."

"We'll try!" the bride and groom promised.

One year later, these two—who professed undying love before God and the congregation—decided to separate.

"It was *not* another woman," his mom insisted. "Well, it wasn't another man!" proclaimed her mother. What *had* come between them, then? Meddlesome in-laws? Money troubles? Her job...his? "Young folks give up too easily!" we, the confused, agreed.

Suddenly Reunited is the story of a young couple, once very much in love, who face the most important decision of their lives: Set aside petty, stubborn grievances, or lose all hope of ever finding their way back to one another's arms. Whether or not they succeed depends solely on their willingness to do as Jesus suggested: "Love one another as you love yourselves." Good advice. The best, in fact.

Oh, and my friend's son and his wife? They took Christ's words to heart and reunited...and just returned from a second honeymoon in Niagara Falls!

If you enjoyed *Suddenly Reunited,* drop me a note c/o Steeple Hill Books, 300 East 42nd Street, 6th Floor, New York NY 10017. (I love hearing from my readers and try to answer every letter personally!)

All my best,

Loree Lough

P.S. Be sure to look for my next Love Inspired novel (fifth in the SUDDENLY! series), *Suddenly Home.*